David Lowry

Life and Labors of the Late Rev. Robert Donnell

of Alabama, minister of the gospel in the Cumberland Presbyterian Church

David Lowry

Life and Labors of the Late Rev. Robert Donnell
of Alabama, minister of the gospel in the Cumberland Presbyterian Church

ISBN/EAN: 9783337260347

Printed in Europe, USA, Canada, Australia, Japan

Cover: Foto ©Raphael Reischuk / pixelio.de

More available books at **www.hansebooks.com**

LIFE AND LABORS

OF THE LATE

REV. ROBERT DONNELL,

OF ALABAMA,

Minister of the Gospel in the Cumberland Presbyterian Church.

BY DAVID LOWRY.

"In labors more abundant,"—
"A workman that needeth not be ashamed
rightly dividing the word of truth."

WITH

AN APPENDIX,

CONTAINING A SKETCH OF THE LIFE OF THE LATE

HUGH BONE, ESQ.,

OF KENTUCKY.

———

Alton, Illinois :
S. V. CROSSMAN, PRINTER, THIRD STREET.
1867.

INTRODUCTION.

A HISTORY of the early ministers of the Gospel, who struggled in the Cumberland Presbyterian church for an ecclesiastical existence, is daily becoming more and more an object of peculiar interest and inquiry. No incident, tending to illustrate character, or to show the sacrifices and difficulties they were obliged to endure, can fail to interest those, whether laymen or clergy, who are now laboring, or shall hereafter labor, to promote the prosperity of that church. A belief of this fact first suggested to the writer the propriety of making an effort while the subject of the following Memoir was on his death-bed, to collect, from his own lips, materials to preserve his memory. Accordingly, he was written to, to know if an effort, with that object in view, would be agreeable to him. An affirmative answer was immediately returned, through an amanuensis; and the late Rev. T. P. Calhoun, at my request, waited on him for several days, in short conversations, taking notes of incidents as they were presented. The thought had not then occurred, that the labor and responsibility of arranging those materials, and publishing a history of Mr. Donnell's life, would ever devolve on me;—to collect and preserve the materials, to be used as the church might direct, was the prime object. Before the interview closed, however, Mr. Donnell determined to commit to Mr. Calhoun's charge, all his papers, with the understanding that he should use them in that way which might seem best calculated to promote the interests of religion.

Shortly after the death of Mr. Donnell, Mr. Calhoun determined to move to Minnesota; and his unsettled state, while in Tennessee, prevented him from discharging the duties contemplated in the delivery of the papers. In the meantime, the writer was requested, by the son of the deceased, to aid Mr. Calhoun, in any labor he might undertake, to preserve the memory of his venerated father. We had scarcely commenced the responsible work, before Mr. Calhoun was called, by a mysterious Providence, to the eternal world; which left the whole affair in my hands.

On a minute examination of the materials that had been collected, together with those found among the papers turned over to Mr. Calhoun, I saw at once that they would not enable me to do justice to the character of the deceased, nor meet the expectations of the church. The facts derived from records made by himself, as well as those obtained from his own lips, by Mr. Calhoun, were important, but still modesty had led to the omission of many incidents, that ought to be embodied in the biography of one whose claims to posthumous regard are so clear and strong as Mr. Donnell's. Such incidents could only be expected from disinterested persons, who sat under his ministry,

I immediately opened a correspondence with many brethren, both among the clergy and laity, for the purpose of supplying the deficiency alluded to; and am happy to say, the call was not disregarded. The names of the contributors, appearing in the Memoir, will be a sufficient guaranty of the accuracy of the facts furnished.

In justice to myself, it is proper to say, that the additional labor, after the death of Mr. Calhoun, to supply the want of materials necessary, delayed the publication of the work; and about the time it was ready for the press, the unfortunate war, between the North and the South, broke out, which rendered further delay unavoidable.

Mr. Donnell maintained an extensive correspondence, through life; but it is to be regretted that so few copies of his letters are to be found among his papers. Much effort has been made to obtain the original letters, and not without some success; yet, it is believed, there are many others that might, with proper search, be procured. Some of the letters have not been given entire, in the Memoir. In cases where the separation of paragraphs produced too much abruptness, some liberty was taken with the language, in order to form a proper connection; and in other cases, also, where an alteration of phrases seemed advisable, it was made; but in no instance has the original meaning been changed. The same liberty was taken with the "Select Thoughts;" but the meaning of the writer was scrupulously preserved.

From the materials on hand, a much larger volume might have been prepared, with less labor of selection. But I preferred to limit the book to its present size, that its price would be such as to admit of its more extensive and useful circulation.

Should the cool and severe critic mark with his pencil any part of the work as wanting in literary taste and classical propriety, it is hoped that the noble character and useful life which it commemorates, will still be thought worthy of profound study, notwithstanding the imperfection of the history that records it; and that the humble labor bestowed upon the book, will contribute, in some degree, at least, to the edification and encouragement of many pious readers.

No apology is offered for the appendix, containing a brief sketch of the life of Hugh Bone, Esq. Mr. Donnell lived in his neighborhood when he first joined the "Council;" and Mr. Bone was among the first elders that took him by the hand, and encouraged him to enter the ministry. Would that the names of more of the elders who struggled with our church in her early history, could be preserved from oblivion, and their example handed down to posterity for imitation.

The facts embraced in the appendix, have been derived from a reliable source, and may be depended on as accurate.

May God attend the perusal of the history now submitted with His blessing; and may the piety and devotedness in the ministry of that good and great man, which it records, long be preserved in the church, is the prayer of

THE AUTHOR.

COUNCIL HILL, IOWA.

CONTENTS.

CHAPTER I.
FROM HIS BIRTH TO HIS CONVERSION.

CHAPTER II.
FROM HIS CONVERSION UNTIL LICENSED TO PREACH.

CHAPTER III.
FROM HIS ORDINATION TILL THE COMPILATION OF THE CONFESSION OF FAITH.

CHAPTER IV.
FROM HIS FIRST MARRIAGE TILL THE DEATH OF HIS WIFE.

CHAPTER V.
HIS LABORS IN NASHVILLE AND PENNSYLVANIA.

CHAPTER VI.

FROM HIS VISIT TO PENNSYLVANIA TO HIS SECOND MARRIAGE.

CHAPTER VII.

FROM HIS SECOND MARRIAGE TILL THE ESTABLISHMENT OF A CHURCH IN MEMPHIS, TENN.

CHAPTER VIII.

BECOMES PASTOR OF THE CHURCH AT LEBANON, TENN.

CHAPTER IX.

RESIGNS THE PASTORATE AT LEBANON, AND RETURNS TO ALABAMA.

CHAPTER X.

CORRESPONDENCE.

CHAPTER XI.

CORRESPONDENCE.—CONTINUED.

CHAPTER XII.

CORRESPONDENCE.—CONTINUED.

CHAPTER XIII.

CORRESPONDENCE.—CONTINUED.

CHAPTER XIV.

CORRESPONDENCE.—CONTINUED.

CHAPTER XV.

SELECT THOUGHTS.

CHAPTER XVI.

SELECT THOUGHTS.—CONTINUED.

CHAPTER XVII.

SELECT THOUGHTS.—CONTINUED.

CHAPTER XVIII.

SELECT THOUGHTS.—CONTINUED.

CHAPTER XIX.

REMINISCENCES AND GENERAL REFLECTIONS ON THE CHARACTER AND USEFULNESS OF MR. DONNELL.

CHAPTER XX.

REMINISCENCES AND REFLECTIONS.—CONTINUED.

LIFE AND LABORS

OF

REV. ROBERT DONNELL.

CHAPTER I.

FROM HIS BIRTH TO HIS CONVERSION.

Power of Example—Birth and Parentage—His Father in the Revolution—Anecdotes of the Revolution—David's Psalms in Metre—
Part taken by Presbyterian Ministers in the Revolution—Removal
of Mr. Donnell's Parents from North Carolina to Tennessee—His
Father drives the first Wagon from Sumner County, Tenn., to Lexington, Ky.—Death of his Father—Mr. Doak's Letter—Early Life of
Mr. Donnell—Excellent Traits of his Mother—His remarkable Dili-
gence in Reading the Bible—Last Interview with his Mother—His
Resolution to Pray—Attends the Ridge Camp-meeting—Prays alone
in the Woods—His Conversion—His Temperate Habits.

EXAMPLE is more instructive than the best rules of
the best moralists; it is the *practical* school of mankind speaking *in action*.

The Romans kept the likenesses of their patriots and
warriors hanging in their houses, that those who saw
them might be stimulated to imitate their noble deeds.
In this ancient custom, the church may learn a valuable lesson on the subject of religious biography—a lesson which she has been slow to learn, or, at least, slow
to practice—for many good and great men have been
permitted to die and be forgotten in their graves, whose
lives should have been placed on permanent record and

2—

widely circulated. It is much to be regretted, too, that persons whose memories *ought to be preserved*, are not more careful, while living, to prepare and arrange materials to be used in writing a biography. For the want of such materials, it often happens that surviving friends, whose feelings would prompt them to efforts to rescue the memory of the worthy dead from oblivion, are deterred from the undertaking.

With those who were acquainted with the late Rev. ROBERT DONNELL, or have ever heard of his extensive usefulness as a minister of the Gospel, there will be but one opinion respecting the obligation of his church to preserve some memorial of his character. He was no ordinary man; nor was he, in the providence of God, raised up for an ordinary purpose.

He was born in the spring of 1784, in Guilford county, North Carolina. The precise date of his birth is not known, as the family record was lost in the removal of the family, in 1791, to Tennessee. Owing to the difficulty of transportation across the mountains, most of the goods, including the family Bible, were sent in flatboats down the Tennessee river, and destroyed by hostile Indians at Nickajack. Robert's father, William Donnell, was a farmer; and in this vocation the son was principally employed till he professed religion, and turned his attention to the great work of the ministry; and even then, like the apostle of the Gentiles, he often "labored with his own hands" on a farm. While a mere child, he exhibited a strength of intellect which indicated elements of extraordinary power, and induced his friends to believe that he was destined to some important station in life.

His mother's maiden name was Bell. She was the daughter of Samuel Bell, the great grandfather of Hon. John Bell, of Tennessee. Samuel Bell was an elder in the Presbyterian church, and died on his knees, while praying in his family. His wife discovered that his voice faltered, and rose from her knees and went to him. He was barely able to speak, but said in broken accents, "Mollie, what is this; is it death?"—and immediately expired. Mr. Donnell's mother had five brothers: Samuel, Francis, James, Thomas and Robert. The Donnells and Bells formed a large connexion; and were much respected for their moral worth and standing as citizens, and were generally members of the Presbyterian church.

William Donnell, the father of Robert, was also an elder in that church; and while in North Carolina, his family enjoyed the ministry of the Rev. Dr. Caldwell, by whom all the children were baptized in infancy. He served his country in the war of the Revolution, and was engaged in the battle of Guilford Court-House when General Greene drove the invading army of Cornwallis from North Carolina. Indeed, most of the male members of Dr. Caldwell's congregation took part in the struggle of that eventful day; while the female members of his church, on the same day, united in prayer to Almighty God, on whose aid success in battle depends. Mr. Donnell's mother was, no doubt, in that praying band. The congregation of Dr. Caldwell had suffered greatly from the British troops previous to that battle. He himself, from the ardor of his patriotism, had become a conspicuous object of British hostility, and was obliged to conceal himself in the camp of General Greene—the price of two hundred pounds having been bid for his head by the British General. In the meantime, the invading troops were encamped on the Doctor's premises, and had driven his wife and children from their residence to the smoke-house for shelter, and insulted the mother in the most vulgar and ungentlemanly manner. Before leaving the encampment, the troops had burned every rail of fence on the farm, consumed all the provisions that could be found, and destroyed every living thing except one old goose. Even the Doctor's papers did not escape; nor was the family Bible spared.

This scene of desolation and distress was not confined to Dr. Caldwell's family, but spread throughout the bounds of his congregation. Indeed, wherever the British found David's Psalms in "*metre*," they regarded them as evidence that the owners were hostile to the King, and encouraged rebellion. This was true of the ministers of the Presbyterian church throughout the country, at the time of our revolutionary struggle. They preached the duty of resisting tyranny, and cheered their people in the midst of the conflict. Revs. Patrick Alison, in Baltimore, William Tennent in

Charleston, Geo. Duffield in Philadelphia, John Miller of Dover, and James Ward in Virginia, led the way in vindicating the cause of American freedom. Others served in the army as chaplains. Dr. McWhorter served in that capacity, in Knox's brigade, while it lay at White Plains, and often had General Washington among his hearers. James F. Armstrong joined a volunteer company, while a candidate for the ministry; and soon after his ordination, was appointed by Congress chaplain of the second brigade of the Maryland forces. Rev. John Blair Smith, teacher, and afterward President of Hamden Sidney College, served as captain of a company of students at the battle of the Cowpens. Rev. James Hall, of North Carolina, and subsequently pioneer missionary in the valley of the Mississippi, was captain of a company formed principally of his own congregation; and such was his reputation that he was offered the commission of Brigadier General.

These are but a few of those to whom honorable reference might be made, who freely risked their lives in their country's cause, when her liberties were in peril. It is more than probable, too, that valuable hints were received from the representative system of government in the Presbyterian church, in the organization of our civil government.

In their removal to Tennessee, Mr. Donnell's family endured great hardships, and were exposed to much danger from the Indians. The country lying between Knoxville and Nashville was an entire wilderness, and the safety of emigrants required them to travel in bodies under an escort of soldiers. A very serious alarm, on a certain night, was given in camp; and while Mr. Donnell's father shouldered his rifle, to aid in repelling the savages, his mother concealed the children. Packs were often dislodged by brush through which their horses passed, as roads were then unknown in that part of the country.

In the present age of steamboats and other facilities for traveling, it is comparatively an easy matter to remove to a new country to what it was when Mr. Donnell's family came to Tennessee; nor is there any analogy between the privations and inconveniences of new settlements *now*, and those experienced by emigrants to the West sixty years ago. It was then difficult to command, during the first year, the most scanty supply of the necessaries of life; but now the improved methods of transportation afford, in addition to the necessaries of life, many of the luxuries.

Mr. Donnell's father was the first man that drove a wagon from Sumner county, Tenn., to Lexington, Ky., whither he went to obtain salt for his own family and other emigrants. On coming to a stream that could not be forded, he took his wagon apart, and crossed in a canoe, swimming his horses.

The family obtained from the woods a substitute for tea and coffee, and made their sugar from the sap of the 'tree. Much of the clothing of boys, and even young men, in those days, was made of dressed deer-skins. Mr. Donnell's own rifle generally afforded an ample supply of this raw material of clothing; and with his own hands the skins were dressed. He is said to have had no superior, either in shooting at a mark, or in the successful pursuit of game.

The family spent the first year, after reaching Tennessee, in Captain Bell's fort, in Sumner county, near the place where Hendersonville now stands. Land had been bought in Wilson county, but hostile Indians were still infesting that portion of the country, and it was considered unsafe to occupy it. After the chastisement of the Cherokees, destruction of Nickajack, Longtown, &c.—service in which Mr. Donnell's eldest brother participated—the family crossed Cumberland river, and settled on the land previously bought, on Spring creek. This was in 1797.

The next year, young Robert had the misfortune to lose his father. He died of fever, in the fifty-first year of his age—leaving a widow and seven children—three sons and four daughters. Their names were: William, Samuel, Robert, Mary, Sally, Martha, and Jane. The father was a man of exemplary piety, and one of the first elders of the "Ridge" congregation. He was noted for his kindness to the poor and needy. The following incident, illustrating this trait of character, occurred the year before he died. William Donnelson, after riding several days, without success, in search of corn, to relieve the wants of his family, called on William Donnell, and made known his distress. "What have you to give for corn?" inquired Mr. Donnell. "Cash in hand, sir," was the reply. "Then," rejoined the other, "you can surely find it in the country. I have some corn to spare, but am keeping it for those who are unable to pay for it in money." After much persuasion, however, he consented to let Mr. Donnelson have three bushels. When the corn was measured, three dollars were laid on the table, being the current price at that time. Mr. Donnell took up one dollar, and pushed the other two back, saying, "One is all I will take."

The above incident has been furnished by the Rev. Samuel McSpedden, brother-in-law of Mr. Donnelson.

Robert, at the time of his father's death, was in the sixteenth year of his age; and his older brothers having married, the care of a widowed mother and two sisters devolved on him.

The following letter of Mr. John F. Doak, of Wilson county, Tenn., was written at my request, and contains information respecting the early history of Mr. Donnell, that no other pen could have furnished:

DEAR SIR:—I received your letter some two months since, requesting information relative to the early life of the late Rev. Robert Donnell.

I regret exceedingly that so few items pertaining to the early history of that good and great man are at my command; and there is no other person now living in this neighborhood that knew him in the days of his youth, except my sister, and her memory has become so impaired that she has no recollection of dates.

Mr. Donnell's family moved to this country the year before my father. Both families lived for a time on the north side of Cumberland river. My father, grandfather Foster, Alexander Foster, and Mr. Donnell's father, all bought land previous to their leaving North Carolina, on Spring creek, which was then a part of Sumner county. The tract purchased contained twelve hundred and eighty acres. None of the parties had seen the land; and to prevent difficulty in assigning to each one his portion, after personal examination, it was mutually agreed that the decision should be made before the families reached Tennessee. On seeing the land, each member of the company took possession of his own without a murmur, though the poorest part of the tract fell to the share of William Donnell.

I have been acquainted with Robert Donnell from my earliest recollection. He was quite a favorite with my father and mother, and was often in the family. His suavity of manner in his social intercourse, and industrious habits, early attracted the attention and admiration of the neighborhood generally. His expertness in the use of tools, was of great service to the community. Much inconvenience had been felt in the country for the want of a mill, and when the erection of one was commenced, Mr. Donnell, though but sixteen years old, and had never studied the trade, was the only person that could be found in the country to superintend the work. Indeed, he did most of the labor with his own hands. The mill proved to be a very good one, and lasted many years. The logs of the building were cedar, and some of them are still to be seen on the ground. I showed the place where the mill stood, not long ago, to Mr. Donnell's son.

The physical powers of Mr. Donnell were extraordinary. I knew him to split one thousand rails in a single day. The timber was cedar, it is true; but I am not aware that the number was ever equalled before or since. In the chase after the bear or deer, he was always foremost, and I never knew his superior in shooting at a mark.

3—

His profession of religion and determination to preach produced considerable excitement among his relatives and friends. In the common acceptation of the term, he was "uneducated;" and it was regarded as presumption in that day, in the Presbyterian church, to think of preaching without an education. Rev. Samuel Donnell, cousin of his father, was then teaching school in the neighborhood, and offered to educate him *gratis.* But Robert declined; took his Bible and went to work, saying it was too long to spend five or six years learning to preach, when there was such a pressing call for laborers in the vineyard of the Lord.

I recollect hearing my mother ask him, about the time he began to preach, if they—referring to himself and friends of the revival—had found a better and nearer way to heaven? He replied, that he had great respect for the Presbyterian church, and venerated the religion of the fathers; but that there were some things in the Westminster Confession of Faith that he could not believe. He then playfully asked her if, when she moved to Tennessee, they did not in crossing Spencer's hill, tie a tree to the hind part of the wagon, to hold it back and keep it steady? She said they did. Well, said he, I have no doubt the time will come when wagons will cross that hill without locking; so we must advance as light increases, and not merely hold to sentiments and usages because the fathers entertained them. In this good-humored way, he generally met opposition, so that everybody loved him, though differing with him in sentiments.

I regarded Mr. Donnell as one of the best men I ever knew, and his preaching and example have been of incalculable benefit to me.   JOHN F. DOAK.

Rev. D. LOWRY.

There is a great principle embodied in the above remark of Mr. Donnell to Mrs. Doak—"that we must advance as light increases." Enoch certainly understood the plan of salvation better than Adam; Isaiah better than Enoch; and John the Baptist better than either; while the least in the kingdom of Christ, *after his resurrection*, was greater than John the Baptist.

Pentecost was not the beginning of a new dispensation, but merely an increase of a degree of light previously enjoyed.

The reformation was not a new revelation from heaven, but the restoration of a degree of divine light in the church. In the days of Wesley, that light was increased; and in the days of Ewing and King, a still greater intensity of the Spirit was given in answer to extraordinary prayer.

It is the remark of Sir James Mackintosh, that all great men have had good mothers. It holds true in respect to the mother of Mr. Donnell. She was a woman of more than ordinary intellectual endowments, and her religious influence in her family was elevating, refining and spiritual. In the education of young Robert, she early familiarized his mind with the word of God. Before he was seven years old, he read, under her direction, the Bible through four times, besides committing to memory the shorter Catechism of the Presbyterian church. The Sabbath was a sacred day in the family, and so strictly kept that neither visiting nor worldly conversation was allowed. She never failed to pray in her family, morning and evening, when her husband was absent; and it was during one of these seasons of devotion that young Robert first felt the necessity of religion. He says: "My mother was, from my first recollection, attentive to the duty of family prayer in my father's absence; and her fervent supplications made an early impression on my mind of the importance of religion."

This excellent mother in Israel died on the seventh day of June, 1828, "in full assurance of hope." The following is the son's own account of his last interview with her: "About ten days before she died, I visited her, and found her mind calm, and in the full enjoyment of religion. When I approached her bed to bid her farewell, and to shake hands with her, as I believed for the last time, she requested me to kneel, and then offered up a short but fervent prayer for myself and wife, and all her children. At the close, she remarked, with much feeling, 'This will be our last meeting on earth.'" All her children, then living, were members of the church, and those that were dead had left satisfactory evidence that they had joined the church above. What a thought! *a whole family in heaven!*

It is an incident worthy of permanent record in the history of the late Rev. Thomas Calhoun, Sr., as well as Mr. Donnell, that both were early impressed on the subject of religion under the prayers of their mothers. Mr. Calhoun says: "My first impression of the necessity of religion was felt while mother was engaged at family prayer, in the absence of my father." Who can tell how much the church is indebted to the religious instruction and pious example of those mothers, for the two eminently useful ministers of the Gospel just named! The power of mothers in the church has ever been felt and acknowledged by the observing and thoughtful. "It is due to gratitude and to nature," said the late President Adams, "that I should acknowledge and avow that such as I have been, whatever it was, such as I am, whatever it is, and such as I hope to be in all futurity, must be ascribed, under Providence, to the precepts and example of my mother." Allusion might also be made, were it necessary, to such men as Bacon, Hall, Dwight, Edwards, and Newton, to prove the influence of mothers in moulding character. Those great men were all blessed with gifted and pious mothers. A few years ago, it was ascertained that of two hundred and thirty-four theological students, two hundred and four were the sons of religious mothers.

Mr. Donnell was not only the son of pious parents, but the descendant of a long succession of Scotch-Irish Presbyterians. In Ireland, there are three religious classes. One class descended from the ancient Irish, and are generally Roman Catholics. Another portion of the inhabitants descended from an English ancestry, and are mostly Episcopalians; while the Presbyterians of Ireland claim a Scotch ancestry. They came to *our* country at an early day; and have ever been distinguished for their love of civil and religious liberty. Political tyranny first drove them from Ireland. They took a prominent part in laying the foundation of our Government, and in giving type to church and state. They were strong believers in the

Abrahamic covenant, and never failed to dedicate their children to God, in the ordinance of baptism. This duty was generally attended to before the whole congregation; when tears of joy often appeared in the eyes of aged members of the church, as they beheld the descendants of a pious ancestry thus enjoying the privileges of "Abraham's seed;" and they would sometimes give vent to their feelings in an under tone, saying: "*The covenant, the blessed covenant, I will be a God to thee and to thy seed after thee.*" Infant baptism should *always* be administered, when at all convenient, in the house of God. It is too beautiful and impressive an ordinance to be done in a corner.

Mr. Donnell was early impressed on the subject of religion, by a dream. He imagined that the pastor of the congregation visited the family, and as "his custom was," catechised the children with unusual solemnity. Young Robert thought he took him by the hand, saying, with much feeling: "My son, you are a sinner, and must be converted." He awoke, and thought of the dream with seriousness for a time; but the impression passed away, as the effects of dreams generally do. The pastor, however, in a few days, *actually came*, and did almost literally as had been indicated by the dream. This so affected Robert, that when the preacher left, he retired for secret prayer; and while on his knees, resolved to pray regularly during life. Subsequently, however, he found himself growing indifferent, and in danger of neglecting the duty he had determined to perform ; and to guard against breaking his resolution, he wrote on a piece of paper, and carried it in his pocket, " *Remember Lot's wife.*"

The conversion of his brother William, and one of his sisters, added new strength to Mr. Donnell's anxiety on the subject of religion. Shortly after their profession, he attended a camp-meeting at the "Ridge," in Sumner county, Tenn., in the fall of 1800. Here he heard the Revs. Messrs. McGready, McGee, Hodge, Ewing and King preach. Many were converted during the meeting, and Mr. Donnell was often among the anxious, but obtained no relief. He felt glad, however, that there was a " way of salvation for others," though he might not be able to find it. His great difficulty was, he could not feel his sins as others seemed to feel theirs.

It was at this same meeting that the Rev. Thomas Calhoun first felt his abiding conviction, and resolved to seek religion. I have often heard him speak of the appearance of McGee and King, when he first arrived on the ground. They were praying for, and instructing mourners, and seemed to be absorbed in anxiety for their salvation. Little did those devoted ministers of Christ then know what an influence the labors of that meeting were about to throw upon the world through the instrumentality of Donnell and Calhoun. But " behold, how great a matter a little fire kindleth." Donnell and Calhoun labored each near half a century in the ministry, and with extraordinary success ; and their posthumous influence will not be developed till the day of judgment. Twenty young men were converted in the course of Mr. Calhoun's ministry, in *one* of his congregations—Big Spring—that subsequently became useful ministers of the Gospel; and I now have before me the names of sixty-one preachers, who were either converted or brought into the ministry through Mr. Donnell's instrumentality. Among this number were the lamented Bryan, Morgan, Moore, Alexander, Frazier, and others, all dear to the church.

But we left Mr. Donnell at the Ridge camp-meeting, complaining of the hardness of his heart. In this state of mind, he returned home from the meeting. On reaching home, he retired immediately to the woods to pray; but arose from his knees, still lamenting the hardness of his heart. While returning to the house, he began to think of Christ—directing his thoughts away from his heart—and became, in a moment, absorbed with the reflection that "Jesus Christ came into the world to save sinners." The inquiry at once arose, "Why not trust him as my Saviour?" While thus contemplating Christ as the saviour of the world, and endeavoring to trust him as *his* Redeemer, an indescribable peace and joy sprung up in his mind; and he then and there dated his conversion.

This account of his conversion—which occurred in the seventeenth year of his age—was given by himself, during his last sickness, to Rev. Thomas P. Calhoun, Jr.

Soon after Mr. Donnell professed religion, he resolved

to abandon the use of ardent spirits; not because he
had been intemperate, or feared that he should be, but
his principal reason was that he had a good constitution, and believed that drinking, even moderately,
might injure it. At any rate, he thought it would be
of no service, either to body or mind. After forming
the resolution, he made it known to his mother; and
they mutually agreed that no more intoxicating liquors
should be brought to the house. When the neighbors
heard of this determination, they said he could not get
his logs rolled, or corn husked, without whisky. Mr.
Donnell's reply was: "If my neighbors will not help
me, I can do without them"—a reply not dictated by
passion or conceit, but which displayed the manly self-
reliance of a superior spirit.

This determination, it will be remembered, was quite
in advance of the great temperance enterprise, as afterward introduced. The first regular temperance society
was formed in 1808, seven years after Mr. Donnell resolved on total abstinence. To carry out his purpose,
therefore, must have required much moral courage.
Public sentiment, both in and out of the church, and
also his pecuniary interest, were against that purpose.
Is it not more than probable that the temperate habits
adopted by him, at that early period of life, contributed
much in forming and sustaining that robustness of
physical constitution, which enabled him for so many
years to endure such labors as he performed in the
ministry? Preachers above all men should understand
and strictly observe the laws of health.

4—

CHAPTER II.

FROM HIS CONVERSION UNTIL LICENSED TO PREACH.

He joins the Presbyterian Church—His mind turned to the Ministry—
Commission of Kentucky Synod—The Revival Party—Camp-meeting near Murfreesborough—Spends a whole Night in Prayer—Joins
the "Council"—Encouraged to Exhort—Extent of his Circuit—Discouragements—Interview with Col. Provine—Cumberland Presbytery Organized—Licensed to Preach—Trial Sermon—Letter from
Mr. Ewing.

IN 1801, Mr. Donnell joined the Presbyterian church
on Spring creek, (in Wilson county, Tenn.,) of which
Rev. Samuel Donnell, cousin of Robert's father, was
pastor. Unfortunately, this preacher was strongly opposed to the great revival of religion which had just
commenced in the country, and did everything in his
power to keep it out of his congregation. But his
efforts were unavailing, for it soon spread among his
people. An unhappy division followed, and the revival
party formed a new church, called Bethesda. Though
no one, as yet, thought of a separation from the Presbyterian church, elements were, however, at work,
which finally led to that result.

Soon after joining the church, Mr. Donnell's mind
was turned to the great work of the ministry ; and he
commenced holding prayer-meetings and exhorting in
his immediate neighborhood. He saw, with regret,
the church throughout the country divided, and minis-

ters arrayed against each other; some for, and others opposed, to the revival of religion. But although he desired, in some active way, to help build up the "waste places of Zion," he could not see how it was possible for him ever to reach the ministry in the Presbyterian church. Without an education, and destitute of the means of procuring one—for he was compelled to labor with his own hands to support an aged mother and two sisters—the way seemed to be effectually barred against him. It occurred to him, however, to await the openings of Divine Providence, and in the meantime to do all the good he could in a private capacity.

After the illegal action of the "Commission of the Kentucky Synod," in 1805, forbidding the revival party of Cumberland Presbytery to officiate as ministers in the Presbyterian church, they determined to organize a "Council," and continue to preach and encourage the wonderful work of God, then in progress, as best they could—still hoping to obtain redress from the General Assembly. But they hoped in vain.

So soon as Mr. Donnell heard that a "Council" was constituted he resolved to place himself under its care, as a candidate for the ministry, and rise or fall with the revival party. This resolution was formed at a camp-meeting near Murfreesborough. The following is his own account of his final struggle of mind on the subject: "While the sacrament of the Lord's Supper was being administered, I looked over the large congregation, thought of the condition of sinners, scarcity

of preachers, the distracted state of the church, and
became so affected that I retired to the woods to pray,
and there remained all night.   The burden of my prayer
was, '*Lord, what wilt thou have me do?*'   I thought I
saw the path of duty plainly marked before me, and
resolved to pursue it."

He joined the Council in 1806.   Hodge, McAdow,
King and Ewing were the ordained preachers present.
Kirkpatrick, Porter, Bell, McClain and Farr were licen-
tiates under its care, and Calhoun, Harris and Chapman
were candidates—all of whom had been received by
Cumberland Presbytery, previous to its falling under
the unconstitutional violence of the "Commission of
the Kentucky Synod."   William Barrett, McLinn and
Bumpus joined the "Council" at the same meeting that
Mr. Donnell did, and with him were encouraged to exhort.   Mr. Donnell was directed to ride as an exhorter
over the country lying between the Cumberland and
Ohio rivers, extending as far as Burksville on the south,
and Louisville on the north.   It required three months
to go round his circuit.   God, in a very remarkable
manner, crowned his labors with success.   The kingdom of Satan trembled; the desolate and solitary places
of Zion bloomed like the rose, and he became the happy
instrument in turning many from darkness to light.
Trials and labors were patiently endured by him; wild
meat, without bread, often constituted his only repast;
while the rough floor of an humble cabin, with a blanket
to cover him, was his bed.   The following account of

a meeting, held by himself and the late Rev. William Barrett, before either of them was licensed to preach, will afford a faint idea of the condition of the country at that early day. He says: "The people grubbed up the cane to prepare a place for the congregation to assemble, and opened a road through the cane-brake to the ground. The pulpit was made of such materials as could be procured from the forest with a chopping-axe, with a pole in front as a hand-board." A powerful revival of religion followed as the fruit of this meeting; and one of the converts became a preacher of the Gospel.

But although Mr. Donnell took high rank in the pulpit, and extraordinary success attended his labors, obstacles sprung up from various quarters which severely tried his faith and moral courage. The established denominations of the country were arrayed against him. Elder Blackman, at a camp-meeting near where Huntsville now stands, debarred Cumberland Presbyterians from communion at the Lord's table. Bishop McKendree pronounced Cumberland Presbyterians to be in a state of disorder, having no church organization. The revival Mr. Donnell was laboring to promote, found but little encouragement among the Baptists of that day, and still less among the Presbyterians. The withdrawal, too, of Messrs. Hodge and McGready from the "Council," and return to the Presbyterian church, greatly increased his discouragements. Mr. McGee, also, his favorite preacher, for a time faltered.

Though identified in feeling with the revival party and "Council," still he hesitated about the propriety of organizing a new denomination of christians. His great difficulty was the want of a Confession of Faith, setting forth their system of doctrine. At one of Mr. Donnell's desponding moments, he visited old Col. Provine, brother of the late Rev. John Provine, and the interview produced a very happy effect. The old man said to him: "Your people will yet build up a great church, and I advise, should overtures ever be made by the old church for re-union, that they be rejected. You will do more good in a separate organization. I professed religion under the preaching of the Tennents. A schism in that day took place in the Presbyterian church. A revival and anti-revival party sprung up, and were arrayed against each other for many years. At length, the revival party yielded, and went back, and the revival ceased." This advice was given and statement made when Col. Provine was in his eighty-fourth year, and on his death-bed. A full account of the schism to which he alluded, and the causes leading to it, may be seen in Dr. Hodge's "Constitutional History of the Presbyterian Church;" also, in a work lately published, called the "Log College." The causes which led to that division, were somewhat similar to those which gave rise to the Cumberland Presbyterian church.

Mr. Donnell was always strongly opposed to an organic union with the old church, unless the Cumberland Presbyterian Confession of Faith could become the creed of both parties. The subject of uniting with the New School branch of the Presbyterian church, came up in our General Assembly, while in session at Lebanon, Ohio, some ten or fifteen years ago. Mr. Donnell gave it no countenance. His main argument against it was, that the creed of Cumberland Presbyterians was "*conservative*" in character, excluding the extremes or objectionable points of both Calvinism and Armenianism; that the success of the Gospel in the world required such a system of doctrine, and in order to preserve and hand it down to posterity, the identity of his church must be maintained.

When the news of the organization of Cumberland Presbytery reached Mr. Donnell, he was riding and exhorting in what was then Alabama Territory. In reference to his feelings when the intelligence arrived, he says: "If ever I was free from sectarian feeling, it was at that period. I often thought, 'For what am I laboring? I am connected with no constituted church, and know not that I ever shall be. For what, then, do I labor, if I cannot build up a church?' The reply was, 'For the glory of God, and the salvation of precious souls.' 'But what will become of the few so strongly united in the bonds of love?' This could only be solved by the Great Head of the Church, and of Him I often sought an answer; and am persuaded he did answer, some time before the Presbytery was constituted. I had become quite calm on the subject, under a firm belief that God would open a way for us. I was in this frame of mind when the news came, that Ewing, King and McAdow had met and organized. I felt truly thankful to God that he had thus opened a door of usefulness to a feeble handful, in spite of all the obstacles that had been thrown in their way."

Four years had now elapsed since Mr. Donnell had placed himself under the care of the "Council," during which he had spent most of his time in riding and exhorting. The "Council" had not deemed it proper to license or ordain any to preach, but merely encouraged those who seemed to be impressed on that subject to exhort.

It is impossible, at this day, to understand and appreciate the state of suspense that then prevailed. A faint view of it may be seen in the following extract of a letter, from the Rev. Finis Ewing to Rev. James B. Porter, written under date December 6, 1809:

"I feel determined to go into a constituted state, if I can get no more than one ordained preacher to join me. You may be startled at this. So was I when I first looked at the subject. But on a closer and more impartial examination of my aversion to such a measure, I was induced to believe that pride and tradition were the most formidable arguments against it. I therefore was induced to give up the point, for the following reasons —1st, because the necessities of the church demand it; 2d, because there is nothing in God's word forbidding it; 3d, because no reformed church in christendom, except the Presbyterian, requires absolutely, and under all circumstances, the number of three to ordain one; 4th, because even that church can depart from this rule, one of the members of Synod being in that predicament, J— B—. Therefore, for so doing, we could not feel, nor justly be, reproached from any quarter. I think, notwithstanding, the Presbyterian rule on this subject a good one, and I would not consent to depart from it only in case of extreme necessity. Whether we will be necessitated to do so, I cannot yet tell, for I have not yet heard from Messrs. McGee or McAdow.

"Brother Porter, if you will not think it discourteous, I will ask you a question, on which I wish you seriously to think :— Whether it would most wound your pride or your conscience to receive ordination from only two ministers?"*

Messrs. Ewing and King were then ready to act in the formation of a separate organization; but neither McAdow nor McGee had consented to co-operate. The former subsequently became convinced that it was his duty to accede to the wishes of Mr. Ewing; and at his own house, Cumberland Presbytery was, on the 4th of February, 1810, constituted. Mr. McGee did not join till the next fall.

It will be seen that Mr. Ewing, like Dr. Whately, was not a believer in apostolic succession. The latter "offered £1,000 to any priest, of any sect upon earth, who will prove, within twelve links, his personal succession from the Apostles." In reference to this proposition, Dr. Cummings remarks : "Now, since so many pretend to apostolic succession, it is a pity that they should not enrich themselves with such a reward, by producing their credentials, and showing that they sit in Peter's chair, and have a legitimate and regularly

---

* Ewing's Life and Times, p. 190.

5—

transmitted succession from him. Speak truth, and you sit on the right seat. Speak apostolic truth, and you give invincible evidence of apostolic succession. But the truth is, we can trace, historically, no such thing in modern times. It is the purest figment upon earth."

Tenacity for precedent has done much harm in the church. More importance has sometimes been attached to it than to the word of God. Wherever there is excessive attachment to *form* and *ceremony*, there is danger of laxity in morals. The truth is, no church on earth is "*ceremonially scriptural.*" All have usages not found in the Bible. Inflexibility, where vital principle is concerned, is commendable; but to dispute about a mere *custom*, that may or may not be observed without sin, is detestable.

Mr. Donnell was licensed to preach, at Big Spring, Wilson county, Tennessee, in 1811. Harris and Chapman were licensed at the same time. His trial sermon was from Romans v: 1. It is said to have been quite an ordinary discourse; so much so that Mr. Ewing remarked, that " it was a very little sermon for so large a man" — referring to his physical stature. The truth is, Mr. Donnell had given but little attention to its composition. He had, while riding his circuit, been exhorting in all the congregations before preachers and elders, and relied upon extemporaneous efforts to sustain him before the Presbytery, rather than his written discourse. No man placed a higher estimate on Mr. Donnell's talents, than Mr. Ewing; and an unbroken correspondence was kept up between them till the death of Mr. Ewing—indicating a very warm and mutual attachment. The following letter of Mr. Ewing will show the confidence and personal friendship existing between them :*

"MY BELOVED BROTHER DONNELL.—I am pleased with your very just and profitable reflections on the depression of our monied interests. Treasure in heaven will always keep us from being too much depressed under temporal loss, and too much elated with temporal prosperity.

"I design, this evening, to send on my resignation as postmaster, to take effect the last of March. I am led to this course on account of my anticipated removal in the spring. Yes, the die is cast. If God will, I expect assuredly to start with my family to Missouri. I trust I will not, in this act, resist or counteract the will of my Divine Master. Therefore, pray for me and mine. If God spares us, I hope we may meet at some Synods. In the meantime, write to me here before I leave, and then direct your letters to Boonville, Cooper county, Missouri Territory. For although I may not be postmaster in that country, I will always gladly pay postage on your letters. I feel that the greater distance will not decrease, but rather increase, my attachment."

This letter is dated February 4, 1820.

---

* Ewing's Life and Times, p. 264.

CHAPTER III.

MR. DONNELL was ordained in 1812, at the Three-forks of Duck river. Rev. William McGee preached the ordination sermon; and Rev. Thomas Calhoun presided, and gave the charge. The trial sermon, previous to the ordination, was from Romans I: 16—"*For I am not ashamed of the Gospel of Christ, for it is the power of God unto salvation to every one that believeth; to the Jew first, and also to the Greek.*"

To the duties of his sacred office he now devoted his whole time, except when obliged to labor "with his own hands," to supply temporal wants. The economical manner in which he divided his time between the pulpit and farm, seemed almost incredible. There is much complaint about the remuneration of preachers in *this* day, and perhaps not without cause. But times were a great deal worse when Mr. Donnell entered the ministry. The country was new. People were generally in limited circumstances; and perhaps *then*, as *now*, preferred a free gospel. In a conversation with the Rev. B. C. Chapman, Mr. Donnell, not long before his death, alluded to his early labors in the ministry. They were passing a certain field in Alabama, when he, pointing to it, said: "I cleared that field, and brought it under cultivation. It once belonged to me. When opening it, I often burned brush half the night, to get time to preach during the day." He also stated that, when a young man, he "frequently sat up all night at camp-meetings, exhorting, praying and singing; and that at the close of the meeting, his voice was as good as at the beginning."

Mr. Donnell held the first camp-meeting ever known in Alabama, and preached the first sermon ever heard in Huntsville. The camp ground was about one mile below where that city now stands; and out of the fruits of that meeting, the old Canaan congregation grew. He also held a meeting, at a very early day, where Mooresville is located. The inhabitants of the country were then called "squatters." Many professed religion, and afterward removed to Arkansas, and formed the nucleus of Cumberland Presbyterianism in that State. Mr. Donnell was among the first preachers who labored at Hazelgreen and Fayetteville. He also preached in the city of Nashville, as early as 1813; and the secular press of that place spoke in very high terms of him as an orator. Many large and flourishing congregations were planted by him—both in Alabama and Tennessee—and are now standing monuments of his usefulness; and many of them are worshiping in comfortable churches, built through his agency. Nashville, Huntsville, Memphis, and many other towns, can bear testimony to the truth of this statement. Wherever he preached, and judged it at all practicable, his policy was to urge the building of a house of worship. In the course of his ministry, he was the means of erecting twelve fine churches, in different parts of the country in which he labored. The following is something like the plan which he adopted: After preaching long enough at a place to secure the attention of the community, he would agitate the subject of building a house of worship. So soon as he could get the people to feel the necessity of it, he appointed a number of citizens to act as commissioners—making it their duty to appoint a building committee and treasurer. Next, he circulated a subscription paper, to raise funds to build the house; making the amounts subscribed payable to the treasurer, in installments. Every member of the congregation, and person in the community, were called on for aid, before the paper was sent abroad. When the amount subscribed was deemed sufficient, a contract was let by the building committee, and orders were drawn on the treasurer as payments became due. After many years' experience, he said he found this plan to be most successful.

Mr. Donnell, though a young man, was appointed on the committee that compiled the Confession of Faith of the Cumberland Presbyterian church. The following brief report on that subject, is found among his papers, in his own handwriting:

" Agreeably to an order of Synod, appointing a committee to prepare a Confession of Faith, in accordance with former avowed principles, we beg leave to report:

"That we all met, except Rev. William McGee; and although we never expect to form and arrange a creed that will be infallible, yet we think we have complied with the order of Synod. We have been careful not to depart from former sentiments as declared from our pulpits. The creed pleases your committee better than any now extant; and we beg leave to submit it for the examination of Synod.

(Signed,)   FINIS EWING,
        THOMAS CALHOUN,
        ROBERT DONNELL."

Whether the foregoing report was presented to the Synod, or the first draft of a more extended report that has not been preserved, there is no means of knowing.

In noting Mr. McGee's absence, it is presumed, reference is made to the "general meeting of the committee." It is known that, by special agreement, and for the sake of convenience in the prosecution of the work, Messrs. Ewing and Calhoun labored together, and McGee and Donnell formed the other branch of the committee. Mr. Calhoun met Mr. Ewing at his— Ewing's—own house. Where McGee and Donnell met, is not known to the writer. The understanding was, that the parties should take under consideration such portions of the Presbyterian Confession of Faith as were assigned to each; and then both branches of the committee meet together, to compare notes, &c.

The following brief sketch of the Synod that acted on the report of the committee, and adopted the Confession of Faith of the Cumberland Presbyterian church, is from E. Curry, Esq., who was present on the occasion:

"The Synod met at Sugg's Creek, Wilson county, Tenn., on the 5th of April, 1814. Rev. Samuel King was chosen Moderator; who, with modest step, advanced to the chair, and with a solemnity and dignity of countenance peculiar to himself, entered upon the duties of his station. Upon the right, sat Finis Ewing, with a keen eye, ready to scan everything that came before the Synod. Near him, sat Hugh Kirkpatrick, with a heavy brow, prepared to define hard words and sentences. On his right, sat James B. Porter, with a pleasing countenance, as though he was delighted that they were about to smite off the old shackles, and ratify a Confession of Faith congenial with their feelings. On the left of the Moderator sat Robert Donnell, writing resolutions to offer to Synod. Behind him, was David Foster, with a critic's eye to detect error. In this group, sat my favorite, Thomas Calhoun, who once spoke terror to my heart, and caused me to cry aloud for mercy. Just in front, sat Alexander Chapman, with a serene look and attentive ear, that he might be prepared to give a judicious vote. A little back, lay Samuel Donnell, brother of Robert, in an advanced stage of consumption, who seemed to be a kind of concordance, to whom all applied for scriptural proof. Further back in the house, William McGee was seen tossing to and fro, with deep thoughts and heavy groans, soon to be vented in a powerful speech. A little in front, sat William Bumpus, a man of ready wit and good judgment, and always had language to tell what he knew. In the corner of the aisle, stood William Barnett, about to deliver one of his thundering speeches, which made the walls of the church reverberate with his loud, shrill voice. Several more of the fathers of the church took part in the deliberations of that Synod.

" The closing scene was most heart-stirring. The Moderator poured forth a most powerful prayer, and it seemed that heaven and earth had come together. The fond recollection of that meeting is still fresh in my memory, and while I write, tears drop from my eyes."

This is the only record of the *appearance* of the members of that Synod known to be extant; and although written in haste for the columns of a newspaper—the " *Banner of Peace*"—it is deemed worthy of an insertion in this Memoir. Generations yet unborn will look upon even *the names* of those venerable men with interest.

CHAPTER IV.

FROM HIS FIRST MARRIAGE TILL THE DEATH OF HIS WIFE.

His Marriage—Enters into Covenant with God, and records a Solemn Prayer—First Death in the Family—His Reflections on the Bereavement—Illness and Death of Mrs. Donnell—Dedicates himself anew to the Cause of Christ.

On the 14th of March, 1818, Mr. Donnell was married to Miss Ann E. Smith, daughter of Col. James W. Smith, of Jackson county, Tenn. She was of highly respected and pious parents, of the Cumberland Presbyterian church, of which she herself was also a member. Col. Smith, who had emigrated from North Carolina at an early day, was a wealthy and intelligent farmer; and no gentleman in the State stood higher in public estimation for integrity of principle and moral worth.

The following prayer and covenant will indicate the state of mind with which Mr. Donnell entered upon that new and important relation:

"O, Lord! thou knowest the event that is before me. May I approach it under a deep sense of the responsibilities it involves, and may she who is to become my companion for life, prove a help-mate indeed—not only in the new domestic cares before me, but in the great work of the ministry. Thou knowest that many and pressing calls from various parts of the country to go and preach Thy word, are daily reaching me. May the spirit of preaching, heretofore felt, not only abide with me, but increase. Help me to feed the flock; take care of the lambs; bring back the wandering, and administer discipline in the church. May I become more and more useful in the service of Christ as I advance in years; and if spared till overtaken by old age, may the evening of life find me still 'abounding in the work of the Lord.'

"Should temporal prosperity be allotted me in my new position, may humility and a sense of dependence still dwell in my heart. If in Thine infinite wisdom and goodness, adversity shall seem best for me, may I not be discouraged, but remember that all things shall work together for good to those who love thee.

"And now, O Lord, I consecrate myself, my intended wife, my talents—whether one or five—my time, influence, all to thee. Wilt thou accept the offering? And now 'unto Him who is able to do exceeding abundantly above all that we ask or think, according to the power that worketh in us, unto Him be the glory in the church by Christ Jesus throughout all ages, world without end, Amen!' ROBERT DONNELL.

"*Ebenezer, March 13, 1818.*"

Col. Smith gave his daughter considerable property, which was gratefully received by Mr. Donnell; but he remained the same devoted minister of Jesus Christ that he had been previous to his marriage. Would that this could be said of all preachers, who obtain property by their wives! Too many, when riches increase, "set their hearts on them," and lose the spirit of preaching.

Mrs. Donnell became the mother of five children, four of whom died in infancy. The surviving son, James W. S. Donnell, of Athens, Alabama, is a gentleman of wealth,* influence, and much respectability. Those repeated bereavements in Mr. Donnell's family, were felt as heavy strokes of Divine Providence upon a fond parent's heart. The first death in the family occurred during a visit of Mrs. Donnell to her parents, and while the husband was attending a camp-meeting in Alabama. The following reflections were penned by him, shortly after intelligence of the affliction reached him :

"On the night my dear little Mary Ann Sidney Donnell died, I was one hundred and fifty miles from her, attending a camp-meeting at Canaan. I had heard of her sickness, but the last intelligence, previous to the news of her death, was that she was convalescent. On the night my child died, I dreamed of receiving distressing news from my family, and slept but little.

" Surely, children must be a part of a parent's life, for I feel that a part of my life—or, at least, of my enjoyment—was gone. At first, the news of the death of my own dear child produced some embarrassment of mind. I am a professed minister of Jesus Christ, and was trying to promote his cause ; had left my family in his care, and this was my plea at a throne of grace— ' that I was working for Christ, and on that account could not be with my afflicted family, like other men.' I trusted that he would keep what I had committed to him ; but Mary is dead. I turn, however, to the mourner's book, and there learn that God is her heavenly Father—a relation far above that of an earthly parent. I loved her dearly, but God loved her still more; and as I had to be often from home, laboring in his vineyard, He thought it best to take her to her heavenly home. Her mother loved her as a part of herself. But we had dedicated her to the church and to God, and He wanted her in the church above.

---

* The unfortunate war greatly reduced his property.

"Mary was born on the 8th of December, 1822, and baptized on the 3d of July ensuing, at Salem camp-meeting, Limestone county, Alabama, and taken to the church above on the 23d of September, 1823.

"Now, my dear wife, Mary cannot come to us, but we can go to her. Our loss is her gain. While I write these lines, and her little body lies at rest, and both her parents weeping, her happy spirit is with Jesus, who died for her, and is looking out for our arrival. O, Lord! conduct us and all the family safely to heaven.

"But oh, my dear wife, as little Mary is gone, yourself and dear little James feel dearer to me than ever. I desire to see you, and could I fly with the lightning's speed, would soon be with you, and mingle my tears with yours. But I am far from you, and mortal, and can travel but slowly.

"But for my appointments to preach, I would set out immediately to see my dear and afflicted wife. I have, however, given myself to the Lord, to serve in his vineyard, and am not at liberty, like men of the world, to leave my Master's work. Worldly business would not detain me here a moment. But I must stay and preach the funeral of others, while Mary's must be put off. My wife must weep alone while I am trying to comfort other bereaved mothers. But He who has called me to attend to others, will, I trust, attend to my family himself. In this I would feel honored. The great Physician sends me to others, and stays with my family himself. The servant sent to the family of others, while the Master remains with the servant's family. Besides all this, He will bestow a rich reward for my labors, but charge nothing for His.

"But, O Lord, I am but a man. Though I have long since given myself to Thee, and promised not to murmur at trials, and though I feel bound to bear all things, and by Thy grace can bear all things, yet I suffer lest others suffer through my neglect. When I think of my dear wife, who is dearer to me than my own life, and not so able as I am to bear affliction, be-

ing distressed by my absence, I am ready to ask, 'who is sufficient for these things?' O, Lord, may I not let the tear of
sympathy fall without distrusting Thy faithfulness.

"ROBERT DONNELL.

"*Hazelgreen, September 10, 1823.*"

The foregoing thoughts have been found among Mr.
Donnell's papers, and are probably the substance of a
communication sent his wife, on hearing of the death
of his child. They breathe the true spirit of a minister
of Jesus Christ in affliction, and manifest a willingness
to submit to sacrifice and self-denial in the service of
the church.

Mrs. Donnell's own health became seriously impaired
soon after her marriage, so that for years she scarcely
saw a well day, and was often confined to bed. This
greatly embarrassed her husband in leaving home to
preach the Gospel. He was, however, often absent,
planting and watering churches—particularly in the
milder seasons of the year. But such was his anxiety
about his afflicted wife, that he sometimes traveled all
night when returning home from a preaching tour.
The writer recollects receiving a letter from him, many
years ago, after returning from a General Assembly at
Princeton, Kentucky. He had traveled all night, and
got home just before sun-rise, finding Mrs. Donnell
very ill. He observed in his letter that he thought he
never would leave her again. This resolution, however, soon gave way to the pressing calls of what he
regarded as duty; and he was again in the service of
the church, many miles from his family.

But the sufferings of Mrs. Donnell were at length closed by death, which occurred in the fall of 1828. She left the world in peace, saying, as she departed, "O, Lord, into thy hands I commend my spirit." A short time before she expired, the afflicted husband recorded the following reflections:

"O, Lord! the partner of my joys and sorrows, with whom I was joined in matrimony on the 14th of March, 1818, and to whom, I trust, I was directed in answer to prayer, is now very weak in body, and not as comfortable, in view of death, as she desires;—wilt Thou prepare her for the change awaiting her, and let her feel the joys of religion ere she departs? Four lovely children have already been taken from us by repeated strokes of Thy providence. To these bereavements I have tried to bow with humble submission. Only one pledge of a dying wife's affection remains. Wilt Thou spare the life of dear little James, and enable me to raise him for Thee. May he in early life become a believer in Jesus Christ, and a useful member of the church.

"And now, O Lord, I again give up my unworthy self unto Thee. May I be a more faithful and useful minister of Jesus Christ than I have ever been. Save me from bringing reproach upon Thy cause in my new situation. If spared to old age, may the evening of life be calm, and may my sun set without a cloud.

"In the name of God the Father, Son and Holy Ghost, I now renew my covenant, and solemnly dedicate myself, and all I am and have, to the service of the church.

"O Lord, in Thy providence thou hast placed under my care a number of black people. For them I feel a deep interest. Help me, O my Master in heaven, to do for them what is right, and to give them what is right. O, hear the prayer of one who would feel himself to be 'less than the least of all saints,' and chief of sinners: yet, as he humbly trusts, Thy devoted servant.

"ROBERT DONNELL.

"*Bethesda, October 18, 1828.*"

Thus, after following to their graves four children, Mr. Donnell is separated by death from the partner of his youth, and companion of his bosom. His suffering under such affliction can only be appreciated by those who have been in a similar "furnace." True, the consolations of religion offer abundant relief amid such trials; but how difficult at such times, for even a minister of the Gospel, to claim them! "Behold, thou hast instructed many, and thou hast strengthened the weak hands. Thy words have upholden him that was falling, and thou hast strengthened the feeble knees. But now it is come upon thee, and thou faintest."— Job iv: 3, 4, 5.

CHAPTER V.

HIS LABORS IN NASHVILLE AND PENNSYLVANIA.

Organizes a Church in Nashville—The Article on Cumberland Presbyterianism in Buck's Theological Dictionary—Interesting Missionary Tour to Pennsylvania—Preaches in North Carolina, on his way—Letter from Leaksville — Dr. Burrow's Letter — Jealousy at the Presbyterian Camp-meeting—Great Revival in Pennsylvania.

In 1828, Mr. Donnell determined to establish a church in the city of Nashville. He had often preached there previous to that time, and was urged to organize a church, but had declined. In 1813, he preached in that city twice a month during the year, and at the close, aided by Messrs. Ewing and others, held a sacramental meeting. Mr. Craighead was then preaching in the town, and very hostile to the revival of religion prevailing in the country at that time, and numerous calls pressing Mr. Donnell to more inviting and promising fields of usefulness, he closed his labors in the city. He was, however, still recollected by many of the citizens of Nashville, and repeatedly urged to return. At length he began to preach at Mr. Cassellman's, five miles south of Nashville, where several persons from the city occasionally attended—partly for the pleasure of the ride, and partly to hear him sing—Mr. Donnell being a very fine singer. Among these were Mrs. Grundy McGavoc and Childers, and Col. Ewing. They

7—

soon became deeply interested with his preaching, as well as his singing; and Mrs. Childers professed religion. Her husband was an infidel, and when she first became convicted, he endeavored to remove her distress by worldly amusements; but she refused to be comforted, till she found it by believing in Jesus. The other persons, just named, soon professed religion also, and would doubtless have joined the Cumberland Presbyterian church, had one been organized; but although they united with other denominations, Mr. Donnell was highly esteemed by them as a preacher, and strongly pressed to preach in their city.

In the year as mentioned above, there seemed to be an extraordinary opening in Nashville for Cumberland Presbyterians. Members from the country had moved into the city. Dr. Jennings, pastor of the Presbyterian church, had just died, and his house of worship had burnt down. The Baptist church was torn to pieces, and their house of worship taken from them by the Campbellites. The Methodists had but a small membership, and religion throughout the city was at a low ebb. At this crisis, Mr. Donnell and Rev. James B. Porter commenced a protracted meeting in the Courthouse, employing a man to keep it in order; and took lodgings in one of the hotels. After the meeting commenced, however, and it became evident that a powerful revival of religion was pending, the preachers were pressed, from all quarters, to board in private families. Many were converted during the meeting; and at its

close, a Cumberland Presbyterian church was organized
in the Legislative hall. Soon after establishing the
church, "as his custom was," Mr. Donnell proposed
building a house of worship; and the edifice now occupied in Nashville by the First Cumberland Presbyterian church, is the result of his efforts. The congregation continued to prosper for a time, but untoward
circumstances arose—principally through the agency
of Rev. James Smith, who subsequently withdrew from
the Nashville Presbytery and joined the Presbyterian
church — which greatly retarded its progress, and at
one time threatened its destruction.

In 1831, the General Assembly, at Princeton, Kentucky, appointed Mr. Donnell, in connection with Revs.
Alexander Chapman, Burrow, Bryan and Morgan, to
visit Pennsylvania, as missionaries. This appointment
was made in compliance with pressing invitations from
that and other States of the East—invitations which
were suggested in part, doubtless, by the following
occurrence: Mr. Donnell, as early as 1815, on learning
that Mr. Woodward contemplated publishing "Buck's
Theological Dictionary," wrote to him to know if he
would admit a notice of Cumberland Presbyterians.
On receiving a favorable reply, he presented the subject to Synod—then the highest judicatory of the
church—and Mr. Ewing and himself were appointed
to write the article: which appears in the work alluded to, under letter "P." This article gave the first
notice of Cumberland Presbyterians in the East, and

excited much solicitude to become better acquainted with their doctrines.

Messrs. Donnell and Burrow traveled together, taking East Tennessee, Virginia and North Carolina in their route. The following communication, from Mr. Donnell, was made to the "*Religious and Literary Intelligencer*," while preaching in North Carolina:

"LEAKSVILLE, N. C., August 1, 1831.

"Brother Burrow and myself left Huntsville on the 27th of June last. We preached in most of the towns, and some of the country places, on our way to this State; but passed so hastily that we had but little opportunity of learning much of the state of religion, or doing much to aid the cause of Zion. We find, however, an open door in this State, and meet with much christian cordiality wherever we go, and find the field so large and white unto the harvest, and the cries of both saint and sinner so pressing for preaching, that we know not how to leave the country. At the request of many, most of whom were not members of any church, we appointed a camp-meeting near the high rock, Rockingham county, and had the privilege of preaching to a people who were willing to leave their comfortable homes, and encamp in the woods, to hear the Gospel. But it rained from Saturday until Tuesday morning, and we had no house or shelter to protect us except one log camp; and most of the people were compelled to leave the ground on Sabbath evening, so that the meeting closed on Monday. We preached during the occasion in our log camp, while many stood outside in the rain; and often the camp was surrounded by carriages, filled with people. One or two professed religion, and many left the meeting deeply convicted. We were urged to appoint another meeting, but could not, owing to engagements ahead. We agreed to stay a week longer, however, than was intended, in order to be at a camp-meeting with our old Presbyterian brethren.

"We have had several two-days' meetings in this country—one at Greensburgh, Guilford county. A good work had commenced there some two weeks before our arrival. We had from forty to fifty mourners, some of whom professed religion; and the good work, we learn, still goes on.

"In a few days we shall leave for Pennsylvania.

ROBERT DONNELL."

The following is an extract of a letter from the Rev. Reuben Burrow, D.D.:

"In the State of North Carolina, we had some special manifestations of Divine mercy, and many made a profession of religion. Twelve professed to find the Savior at our two-days' meeting at Greensburgh; and before the excitement abated, several hundred persons professed to be converted. We were compelled, however, by future engagements, to leave the place, in the midst of the revival. We preached at several other places as we traveled through the State, where prospects were very encouraging; and afterward we learned that revivals of religion followed."

Respecting the camp-meeting held by the Presbyterians, to which Mr. Donnell alludes, Dr. Burrow says:

"We attended at the solicitation of the elders of the congregation; but in the progress of the meeting, some of the preachers became jealous, and fearful that we might organize a church there, and treated us with neglect, which produced great excitement among the people generally. The Session met on Monday morning, and urged us to organize a church, and all promised to unite with us; but brother Donnell replied that we had come there to do good, and would not disturb their peace."

Messrs. Chapman, Bryan and Morgan took another route to Pennsylvania, and reached there in advance of Messrs. Donnell and Burrow. They commenced their labors in Washington county, by declaring the distinctive peculiarities of the church they represented. Having done this, they began to urge upon the consideration of the people the great and fundamental truths of the Gospel; and very soon indications appeared of what afterwards proved to be a wonderful revival of religion.

As Mr. Donnell's mission to Pennsylvania was connected with the introduction of Cumberland Presbyterianism into that country, and forms a prominent and important epoch in his history, it may not be out of place to dwell here with some particularity; and if I embrace some facts that more properly belong to church history, the reader's indulgence is claimed from the consideration that they have never yet appeared in print, and may hereafter serve as materials for the historian. In my remarks, I shall draw largely upon the pen of the late Rev. Jacob Lindley, D.D., who resided in Pennsylvania at the time of Mr. Donnell's visit. After describing the moral condition of the country, and expressing his belief that a revival of religion was at hand, he says:

" I heard that three preachers of the Cumberland Presbyterian church were in Washington, our county seat. I had heard of the Cumberland Presbyterian church in Kentucky, through the minutes of our General Assembly;* but the impressions made upon my mind were not favorable. Being well acquainted

---

* Dr. Lindley then belonged to the Presbyterian church, but subsequently joined the Cumberland Presbyterians, and became father-in-law of Mr. Donnell at his second marriage.

with the schismatics in the lower counties of Ohio—having been much with them in my first tour of preaching in that country—I associated them, in my mind, with Cumberland Presbyterians; which I soon discovered, however, was doing the latter much injustice. I also learned, what I did not know before, that the elders of a vacant congregation adjoining the one of which I was the pastor, had written to Kentucky, requesting Cumberland Presbyterian preachers to visit them. Therefore, I expected the clergymen just named, would preach in that congregation the next Sabbath. I at once began to dread that wild fanaticism that I had seen among the schismatics. I began, however, to search the records of the General Assembly, to see if I could find out any gross errors of which Cumberland Presbytery had been charged; and to learn if they had been ecclesiastically cut off from membership with the Presbyterian body. I searched these records with care, expecting to find something that would justify my standing aloof from the new preachers. In the records of 1824 or '25, I saw it stated by that Reverend body, that the members of the Cumberland Presbytery never had been deposed, and that the ordinances of the church administered by Cumberland ministers were to be regarded in the same light with ordinances administered by other evangelical churches not connected with the General Assembly of the United States. Finding this to be the true ecclesiastical standing of those Cumberland ministers, I felt myself bound, in christian charity, to extend to them the same fraternal hand, and to mingle with them in all the ordinances of God's house which I would with Congregationalists, Methodists, or any other evangelical denomination, just as the General Assembly had said.

"The first sermon I heard from them was delivered by the Rev. John Morgan. His text was James v: 16. The humility, fervor and unction that characterized the discourse, satisfied me that God was with him. I also heard the Revs. Messrs. Chapman and Bryan, and found them of the same spirit. But that I might know them thoroughly, and treat them as strangers ought to be treated, I invited them to make my house their home while they staid in the country. The more I became acquainted with them, the better I liked their christian spirit. They were from a warm revival country, and brought the revival spirit with them. There was nothing boisterous in their manner of preaching. The showers that descended from heaven under their administrations, were not hail-storms, but gentle, soft and refreshing. I was astonished at the adaptation of their preaching to the religious state of the country. They did not come with their carts loaded with shrubbery from the nurseries of theological disputants, to plant out in our soil. The seed which they sowed was simple unsophisticated truth, such as could be understood by all the school children of the country.

" Indications of a general awakening soon appeared, and all classes, both in and out of the church, attended to hear the new preachers. And a council was immediately called, consisting of the elders of my church, and the adjoining vacant congregation. The Cumberland brethren and I were present. The main object was, whether we should have a camp or protracted meeting. My personal feelings were in favor of a joint protracted meeting; but I was met by arguments that the general interest now existing extended into four congregations, and down to all the children of the Sabbath schools. The distance families would have to travel, and other inconveniences, would render a protracted meeting more difficult and less efficient, than for entire families, with their abundant provisions, to move into convenient tents. A camp-meeting was therefore agreed upon, and three men were chosen to select a site, and to lay out the encampment. A delightful grove, in a vacant congregation in Upper Ten-mile, was chosen. In a few days, an ample number of tents were erected, for the accommodation of all who might see fit to attend ; and the neighboring farmers, with provisions to feed them, were on the ground. For women who had no husbands or parents on the ground, a large tent was fitted up, and put in charge of a venerable mother in the church. Pastures were provided for horses, and one for milch cows, not more than fifty yards from the tents. Cows were driven five and six miles. A living spring gushing from the marble rock, clear as crystal, reminding us of the water of life, was near at hand.

"The preachers in attendance were the Revs. Messrs. Chapman, Morgan, Bryan and myself. The Rev. Dr. Dodd brought his family, but was called away some thirty-four miles, to see a patient, and did not get back till after the meeting closed. Religious services commenced on Thursday evening before the second Sabbath of September, with evident solemnity and profound order. Everything progressed with solemnity and increasing religious interest till Saturday. On Saturday evening, two venerable and strange preachers appeared, viz: Revs. Messrs. Donnell and Burrow. Morgan and the other brethren expressed great joy; but I told them that I regretted that they had come. Mr. Morgan asked me my reasons. I replied: It could hardly be expected that preachers, journeying on horseback a thousand miles, through a cold world, could immediately enter into the spirit of our present meeting; and that even one discordant note might shift the key, and change the present tone of religious feeling. Morgan said, in the language of the hunter: Never fear, these two old dogs will not cross the track. You will hear them open the moment they catch the scent, and before they reach the track, they will know which way the game has gone. They will never be off the track. Mr. Burrow was sick, and made but one attempt to preach during the meeting. Mr. Donnell did most of the preaching after he came, as those first on the ground were much fatigued."

An incident occurred at this meeting, which illustrates Mr. Donnell's knowledge of human nature, and his great skill in managing and controlling the evil passions of man. A company of rude fellows, on Sun-

8—

day night, under the influence of liquor, became noisy, and, though some distance off, very much disturbed the worship of God. A peace officer requested Mr. Donnell to go and try to quiet them—not having the courage to undertake it himself. Mr. Donnell immediately repaired to the place, and, taking off his hat, said to the company: "I am a stranger from the far West, where our means of intellectual and moral improvement are supposed to be inferior to yours. We, however, have camp-meetings there, and the people generally respect the worship of God. In coming to this old settled and intelligent country, I had hoped to find an example of outward regard, at least to religion, that would be worth reporting on my return to Alabama, to stimulate the people to higher degrees of politeness and good conduct at the house of God." Entire silence pervaded the crowd, and Mr. Donnell bowed and returned to the camp ground. The next day, many of those wicked men became mourners, and ere the meeting closed, professed religion.

But let us return and witness the close of the camp-meeting:

"At the rising sun," says Dr. Lindley, " Wednesday morning, at public prayer, after one or two prayers, a request was made for all those to come forward before the stand, who had found comfort in believing, since the meeting commenced, for the purpose of receiving counsel. Two hundred and twenty appeared. Such a transporting sight I had never before beheld, and I was very nigh losing the command of myself. The meeting closed on that day, leaving upward of one hundred anxious inquirers after the way of salvation.

"After breakfast, a council was called, consisting of the ruling elders of three congregations. The subject of consultation was the expediency of opening a door for the reception of members into the church. The five Cumberland preachers were present, but perfectly silent. The elders of the vacant congregation, who had written to them to visit them, informed the council that they had had a meeting by themselves, and decided to attach themselves to the Cumberland Presbyterian church, in their organized capacity, with such of the congregation as might see fit to go with them. They said their decision had been kept secret until now, for the sake of good order and common-sense propriety; that if they had, amid the great revival that had been going on, principally through the instrumentality of Cumberland preachers, proclaimed their church a Cumberland church, and opened a door for the reception of members, the converts, under the influence of religious sympathy, would have rushed with one accord into that church, and the feelings of many dear brethren would have been wounded. Here a pause in the council took place, and the Cumberland brethren had a short conference by themselves, and then called me, when Mr. Morgan said, a proposition had been thought of, if it met my approbation. He stated that, as my congregation was in a direct line, and half way between the vacant congregation (now Cumberland) and Dr. Dodd's congregation, he proposed to appoint a protracted meeting at my church four weeks hence, to meet on Thursday in the forenoon, and that the first business should be, while all were calm and free from excitement, to examine candidates for church membership; and that the three church sessions should be present to examine and enroll their several new members. It was further suggested that in four weeks, the converts would have time to know themselves, and to be known of others, and to receive the counsel of their parents, so that all might be harmony and kindness. The proposition pleased me, and was adopted, and published before the meeting broke up.

"What I have here stated is correct, and ought publicly to be known, for it reflects honor upon those five Cumberland preachers, and the Southern character and the liberal spirit of the Cumberland Presbyterian church.

"On Thursday, the day appointed for the protracted meeting, the sessions of the three congregations were in attendance. As they were all in one house, it was suggested that the sessions be constituted by one prayer, which was agreed to; and each session then proceeded to business. My congregation received one hundred new members; Dr. Dodd's, eighty; and the Cumberland church about the same. Each candidate was allowed to say for himself to which church he wished to be attached. The parents of most of the young people who had professed religion were present. The meeting then went on, and before it closed, about one hundred professed to be converted."

CHAPTER VI.

FROM HIS VISIT TO PENNSYLVANIA TO HIS SECOND MARRIAGE.

Mr. Morgan's Account of the Revival in Pennsylvania — Conduct of Presbyterians — Meeting at Athens, Ohio — Last Hours of Mr. Morgan — Mr. Donnell at Lebanon — Great Revival there — Mr. Golladay's Letter — Letter from Col. Topp — Mr. Donnell's second Marriage — His Covenant with God.

SOON after the camp-meeting at Ten-mile closed, Messrs. Donnell and Burrow set out for home, leaving the late Rev. John Morgan and Dr. Bryan in the country, to preach and organize churches. The following letter of Mr. Morgan, written to the *"Religious and Literary Intelligencer,"* will show the success of their labors up to the date of the letter:

"PRINCETON, KY., January 30, 1832.

"I arrived here on the 14th inst., on my way home from an Eastern mission. A brief narrative of my tour, perhaps, will be expected by the church. Accounts of our revival in Pennsylvania have already been published, up to the first of November last. I think about one hundred persons have professed religion since that time; making in all eight hundred since the revival began at our camp-meeting at Ten-mile.

"When I left Pennsylvania, the calls for preaching were multiplying, and the religious excitement among the people had increased and spread over a large portion of country; and in some places, whole families, and almost whole neighborhoods, had been embraced in the gracious work.

"Owing to a want of ministerial aid, we organized only five congregations: one in the town of Washington, Pennsylvania, consisting of fifty members; one twelve miles from town, in Washington county, of two hundred; one in the same county of twenty; one in the town of Wainsburgh, Green county, of forty; and another in the town of Jefferson, in the same county, of fifty-two. From the above, it is obvious that many of the converts joined other denominations, which was their privilege. The congregations formed were flourishing, and receiving accessions at almost every meeting. One great obstacle with the people was a fear of not getting a supply of preaching from our ministers. We, however, made such pledges as we thought we could redeem, by getting an additional supply of ministers from the West. There are several young men, subjects of the late revival, whose minds seemed to be impressed on the subject of preaching, one of whom I brought with me to this place.* He is to enter college next month, with a view to the ministry.

Our Presbyterian brethren in that country, with some few exceptions, did not receive us with that cordiality and christian friendship which they show us in the West. An act was passed by one of their Presbyteries, prohibiting us from preaching in their churches.

"We were written to from New York, soliciting preaching. Brother Bryan was to pay a visit to that country soon after I left; but would stay but a short time, having, in connection with brother Bird, agreed to supply congregations, already formed, with preaching.

"On my way to this country, I passed over a small portion of the State of Virginia; through several counties in Ohio, and so on to this State, by way of Maysville and Lexington; but owing to the extreme coldness of the weather, and delicacy of my health, I did not preach as often as I wished, though we had several meetings, some of which were more and others less interesting. One, however, in Athens, Ohio, I would remark on particularly, as it was unusually interesting. It was held in

---

* Mr. Morgan refers here to the late lamented Bidell.

the Presbyterian church, of which Rev. Mr. Spaulding is pastor, and who is much devoted to God and to the spiritual interests of his people. He did not wait to present a long catalogue of inquiries respecting the peculiarities of Cumberland Presbyterians, before he would ask me to preach in his church. His soul was wrestling in prayer with God for a revival of religion; and though he well knew we might differ in some non-essential points, he also knew that we agreed in all the essential ones; and, consequently, his actions, which spoke louder than words, said, 'Lord, send by whom thou wilt send, but let salvation come to my people.' Would to God all ministers had such a spirit. I remained with him eleven days, preached nine times in town and twice in the country. Mr. Spaulding and others preached occasionally. We had prayer-meetings every morning, before sun-rise, and inquiry meetings frequently. When I left, it was ascertained that thirty-five had professed religion, and about forty were still serious. Eight students of the college were among the converts, and a number more were inquiring for the way of salvation.

"The tone of religious feeling in Kentucky is very low, with a few exceptions. Elkton, and one or two other towns, have recently been visited with revivals of religion. So that, with all the encouraging circumstances and brightening prospects on the side of Zion, there is much to cause the christian to lament and pray. Wickedness abounds to an alarming extent, even where the Gospel is most faithfully preached; and many professors of religion are far below that elevated standard of practical piety revealed in the Word of God.

"I will add, in conclusion, that there is a very extensive field of usefulness open to ministers of our church in the Eastern States; and that more of our energies should be directed to that country than has hitherto been done. At least, as we have formed some churches, and by order of the Green River Synod expect to constitute a Presbytery, we ought, as soon as possible, to send on an additional supply of ministers.

JOHN MORGAN."

Mr. Morgan was converted and brought into the ministry under the preaching of Mr. Donnell, and stood very high in his estimation as a man of talents and piety. He was devoted to the interests of the church to which he belonged; and no preacher of his day labored more indefatigably to save souls, nor did any one surpass him in usefulness. His work was closed, however, by pulmonary affection, on the 17th of October, 1841, in the thirty-sixth year of his age, and fourteenth year of his ministry.

The following brief statement of his last moments, is from the pen of Rev. Milton Bird, D.D.:

"His protracted affliction he endured with patience and resignation. He had his right mind, was settled and calm to the last moment. I often heard him say that Christ had been precious to him, and altogether lovely when preaching salvation through his name. 'Now in affliction he is my comfort and consolation. O, there is nothing like communion with God. I know in whom I have believed. My trust is firm. I view the approach of death without fear. I feel myself to be a poor, unworthy sinner; but Christ is my only dependence. The plan of salvation is just such as man needs. O, how well adapted is the christian's hope to his condition. Nothing else can give comfort in affliction, and enable one to meet death without dismay.'

"He sometimes said, when he thought of the church and his rising family, he felt a desire to have health again, if it was the Lord's will. The third evening before his death, I called to see him. An aged minister, sitting at his bed-side, observed—'Brother Morgan, I suppose you remember our Synod is to meet to-morrow?' 'Yes,' said he, 'I remember it well; but I suppose I shall not meet with you any more till we meet in the General Assembly and Church of the First Born.' The apostle's language was then quoted : 'For me to live is Christ, and to die is gain.' 'Yes,' said he, 'that is the last text I ever preached from. Death is a very trying event—more than human nature could bear without the aid of religion. Leaving a rising family, is my greatest trial ; but the Lord gave them, and if He sees fit to call me away, He will take care of them.' I took my leave of him, and next morning started to Synod. On returning, the unwelcome intelligence was received that brother Morgan was no longer numbered with the living. His mind was composed to the last. He said, just before he expired, 'I am going, and hope the Lord will make short work of it,' and spoke no more."

Let us now return and accompany Mr. Donnell on his journey home from Pennsylvania. Nothing of special interest occurred till he reached Lebanon, Tennessee. There he found the Franklin Synod in session, at which an interesting revival of religion commenced, that added some of the most enterprising and wealthy citizens of the town to the church, who subsequently took the lead in establishing and building up Cumberland University—an institution which has prospered under an able faculty, until it is second to none in the great valley of the Mississippi. A law department has been added since its location, at which many of the most talented young lawyers have graduated, and already taken a high position in the affairs of State. A theological school has also been opened, where candidates for the ministry are being ably instructed, preparatory to their responsible vocation.*

---

* This chapter, and indeed the entire Memoir, was written before our unfortunate war commenced, which closed the operations of the
9—

Mr. Donnell preached frequently while Synod was in session, and his influence in the revival, and subsequent agency in building up the University, eternity alone can reveal. He was chairman of the committee that located the institution, and contributed largely of his means to endow it.

The revival continued long after the adjournment of Synod, with great power, and many were added to the church. The late Revs. Thomas Calhoun, Sr., and George Donnell, (cousin of the subject of this Memoir,) and other ministers yet living, labored day and night to promote it. It spread from Lebanon into the surrounding country, and many heads of families, and men of talents, were brought into the church.

The following letter from Mr. Golladay to Mr. Donnell, in reference to this revival, is deemed worthy of a place here:

"LEBANON, TENN., February 7, 1832.

"DEAR BROTHER:—Your letter, requesting an account of matters and things here since you left, has been received.

"The revival of religion that commenced while you were here at Synod, last fall, continued all winter, and there is still considerable interest manifested. The people attended church for many weeks, through all kinds of weather, both day and night, often remaining at our evening meetings till midnight.

"Many of our best citizens have been converted and joined

University; and during the progress of that bloody conflict, the fine edifice of the institution was reduced to ashes by Confederate soldiers. Laudable efforts, however, are being made, with fine prospects of success, to erect a new building; and the University has already commenced operations upon a limited scale, and it is hoped and believed that former prosperity will be fully realized at no distant day.

our church; and it is said others expect to join soon. Four weeks ago, at our meeting, there was quite a number of mourners.

"What a change in the state of things! For fourteen years I almost stood alone for Cumberlandism at Lebanon; no house of worship except the Court-house. I put it in order, and rang the bell, when brother Calhoun and others preached. But we are suffering now for want of stated preaching. The ministers who labored in the revival have returned to their respective charges, and our pulpit is only occasionally occupied. Brother George Donnell, who was expected to preach for us, is afflicted with sore eyes, and fears are entertained that he will have to give up preaching.

"May the Lord bless you, and direct you to visit Lebanon again.   ISAAC GOLLADY.

"REV. R. DONNELL."

Often has the writer heard Mr. Calhoun speak of Mr. Golladay—particularly of his attention to him when he first commenced preaching at Lebanon. Though not a professor of religion at that time, he never failed to ring the Court-house bell, and to have the house in order. He and Mr. Calhoun were strongly united by ties of friendship, till separated by death. Mr. Golladay was constant in his attendance at church, both before and after he professed religion. Rarely was his seat vacant, either at preaching or prayer-meeting. His venerable form is vividly before the imagination of the writer, at the present moment. He always occupied the same seat at church, and whoever might be absent, his gray locks were generally to be seen.

The following letter of Col. Topp to Mr. Donnell, in

reference to the same great revival, will also be read with interest :

"LEBANON, TENN., March 20, 1832.

"DEAR BROTHER :—I have for some time intended to write you an account of the interesting revival of religion that has been in progress here since Synod, and to inform you of the great desire your friends have to see you among them at this interesting moment.

"Never have I seen such a time in Lebanon. Many of our most respectable citizens have made a public profession of religion, and I have reason to believe others are engaged in a more private way, seeking the salvation of their souls. Some are much awakened on the subject of religion, but still suspend action, and I fear will endeavor to wear off their convictions.

"O, if you could visit us at this time, with what joy your friends would greet you. I have very often heard them say,— 'O, that uncle Bob Donnell would come along just now!' I believe you could do more good, just at this time, than you have done in all your visits and exertions heretofore at Lebanon put together. Come and see us at the earliest moment possible. Should you delay long, the interest may subside.

"Judge James C. Mitchell has professed religion, and joined our church. If I am correctly informed, the sermon you preached the evening after you returned from Jackson county, was the cause of his conversion.

"Col. Findley will join our church next Sabbath. Col. Caruthers, William L. Martin, Mrs. McLain, and several others, are known as seekers of religion.

"We had some happy and glorious seasons here during the winter and spring; and my heart's desire and prayer is, that they may continue. Do come, I pray you, and help us at this important crisis. I know you will be astonished and delighted at the prospects of religion in this country. Our church in this place numbers about fifty members, and I hope and trust the number will be doubled during the present year. Our dear little brother, George Donnell, is almost worn out by his ministerial labors, and he has been much afflicted during the winter, and needs help and rest.   JOHN S. TOPP.

" REV. R. DONNELL."

Col. Topp's wife professed religion during the Synodical meeting, at Lebanon, the previous fall, and he himself a few weeks afterward. Both are still living, and are active and useful members of the church.

After remaining a widower four years, Mr. Donnell was again married, on the 21st of June, 1832, to Miss Clarissa N. Lindley, (daughter of Rev. Jacob Lindley, D.D.,) a lady of devoted piety, of high intellectual attainments, and who proved a valuable auxiliary to her husband in the great work of the ministry. On the day previous to his marriage, he wrote and signed the following covenant:

"O, Lord, on to-morrow, if it be Thy will, I expect to increase my domestic obligations, and, as I hope, comforts, by uniting in matrimony with Clarissa N. Lindley. Before taking this responsible step, I would solemnly renew my covenant with Thee. Thou knowest that before I was married to Ann E. Smith, I entered into covenant with Thee, and also before her death. Thou hast promised that, as the days of Thy servants are, so shall their strength be; and that Thy grace shall be sufficient for them. By Thy grace, O Lord, I will now consecrate myself anew and unreservedly to Thy service, and promise, in my new situation, to do everything in my power, both at home and abroad, to promote Thy glory, the good of the church, and the salvation of sinners. To this solemn pledge, I now subscribe my unworthy name.

"ROBERT DONNELL.

"*June 20, 1832.*"

Under the Old Testament dispensation, vows were very common. The object seems to have been, at least in part, to render more vivid upon the mind a sense of obligation in reference to some specific duty. Whatever may be the ordinary feelings of the heart towards God, there are certain periods in every man's life, when he feels peculiarly dependent, or under special obligations for favors received ; when, although he may not enter into a formal covenant with God, as did Jacob, and others, still a secret purpose is formed to do something *for God*, that had been previously neglected, or which the individual feared he might neglect in future.

Transitions from one state or condition in life to another, are not always safe, even to physical health, much less to spiritual health. Mr. Donnell seemed to have been fully aware of this ; and to guard against the danger, entered into covenant with God, pledging fidelity to His cause, and invoking grace to meet the new circumstances about to be thrown around him.

Preachers, above all men, need God's counsel and direction in the choice of a companion for life. Not only their happiness, but usefulness, is at stake. The following sentiment of Dr. Clark, on this subject, is couched in very strong language, but certainly expresses at least a general truth : " Marriage to you," addressing preachers, " can never be an indifferent thing. It will *make* or *mar* you ; it will be a *blessing* or a *curse* to you ; it will either help you to heaven, or drive you to hell, or be a heart-rending cross to you while you live. Nor will a *bad* or *improper* marriage affect yourself alone; it may be the ruin of *every child* that issues from it. And dreadful as this is, it may not *rest* there; they may propagate the plague to interminable generations, and millions be injured, if not lost, by your improper, if not vicious, marriage. Take this step, then, with that godly fear and scrupulous caution which a man should do who feels that he has his all at stake."

CHAPTER VII.

FROM HIS SECOND MARRIAGE TILL THE ESTABLISHMENT OF A CHURCH IN MEMPHIS, TENN.

Great Revival in Memphis—Invited to become Pastor of the Church —He Declines — Reasons for Declining — Visits the City — Letter to his Son — Collects Funds to build a House of Worship — Different Pastors of the Church in Memphis.

In 1843, Mr. Donnell determined, under God, to plant a church in Memphis, Tennessee, and for that purpose commenced a series of meetings in the city. A powerful revival of religion ensued, and a large and respectable congregation was soon organized. All eyes were immediately turned to him as pastor, and he was unanimously elected to that responsible station. The following notice of the choice was transmitted to him by the Session:

"MEMPHIS, TENN., April 3, 1844.

"REV. AND DEAR BROTHER DONNELL:—At a meeting recently held by the Cumberland Presbyterian church in Memphis, you were unanimously chosen as pastor. The meeting was large, and the utmost good feeling and harmony of sentiment prevailed. All felt deeply the importance of regular service in the congregation. In both town and country, there seems to be but one desire on the subject: that is, that you be earnestly solicited to accept the appointment. You may expect hearty co-operation in all matters pertaining to the interests of the church, and a willingness on the part of the congregation to minister to your temporal wants. The doctrine of the

Now Testament, that the laborer is worthy of his hire, is fully recognized.

"We shall be glad to hear from you in regard to this important matter as soon as convenient. We doubt not that you will unite with us in fervent prayer to God that He may so guide you in your decision, that all may redown to His honor and the prosperity of the church. JOHN D. WHITE,
                                        SAMUEL D. KEY,
                                        W. B. S. GARRISON,
                                        M. B. WALDREN."

While pondering this call, and doubtless making it a subject of solemn prayer, Mr. Donnell, in the following communication, unbosomed his embarrassed state of mind to his confidential friend, the Rev. M. H. Bone:

"I am in a strait betwixt two; and as I hide nothing from you, I will tell you the cause. A call has just reached me from the congregation in the city of Memphis, to become their pastor. I know not how to refuse, and yet there seem to be inseparable obstacles in the way of my acceptance.

"In the first place, I am not qualified for the station, and the infirmities of age admonish me that the physical labor would be more than I could bear. Worldly considerations are also in my way. Many of my negroes have wives in this neighborhood, and were I to move to Memphis, would have to be separated from their families. This I could not think of doing; nor can I bear the idea of leaving my black people here under an overseer, and removing without them.

"But, on the other hand, is the voice of the church in this case to be regarded as the voice of God; and if He calls me to that field so white unto harvest, ought I to refuse? Memphis is destined to be a great city, and an important point to our church, and I know of no other preacher at present that can or will take charge of the congregation. O Lord, what wilt Thou have me to do? Pray for me, my dear brother."

10—

Mr. Donnell finally declined the call to Memphis, and made known his determination in the following letter :

"POPLAR REST, ALA., April 17, 1844.

"DEAR BRETHREN :—I have received your unanimous invitation to take the pastoral charge of the Cumberland Presbyterian church in Memphis. I regret to say, in reply, that circumstances seem to forbid my acceptance. The difficulty of moving my large family, or of dividing my servants, taking a part with me, and leaving the rest here, would be very unpleasant. My advanced period of life, and the growing infirmities of age, admonish me that I ought not to undertake the labor of pastor to so large a congregation as yours, scattered as it is over so large and growing a city as Memphis. Besides, what little skill I may have acquired in the ministry by study and experience, is more of a missionary than of a pastoral character, and I have thought that I understood better how to 'plant' than to 'water' churches.

"I have often thought of you, and tried to pray for you since I left you last fall, and hope the Great Head of the Church will send you a pastor of his own choosing. My attachments to you are very strong. Many of you were converted to God in this country, if not as seals of my ministry. Your city and country present a wide field of usefulness ; and I desire to visit you often, and should life be spared, shall endeavor to do so.

"I have arranged, if the Lord will, to be in Memphis the third Sabbath in May next—perhaps a few days before. If a house cannot be procured to preach in, can we not have a meeting in 'Court Grove?' I cannot remain with you very long, but may the visit be attended with the blessing of God !

"ROBERT DONNELL.

"JOHN D. WHITE, SAM. D. KEY, W. B. GARRISON, M. B. WALDREN."

From Memphis, Mr. Donnell writes the following letter to his son, under date 22d of May, 1844:

" DEAR JAMES :—In the midst of pressing claims upon my time, I write you a hasty line. Could I reach home by traveling two or three days and nights, I would set out immediately, having just heard that Mr. Fisher's family are afflicted with something like the black tongue, and I fear it is contagious, and may spread through the town and county. But duty will confine me here a few days, and then engagements elsewhere command my time and attention, so that I must be some weeks yet absent from home. May a kind Providence protect you.

" I shall leave Memphis in a few days for DeSota. We have a meeting next Saturday and Sabbath in Mr. Maxwell's neighborhood, and it was my intention to go to Hernando on Friday night, but hear the small-pox is still there.

" I am now trying to raise funds here to build a church. A contract has been let for the erection of the house, and it will be fit for use by October, if not sooner. The people had been begged by other denominations so much that it was thought we could not get a dollar. But we have added this week, to the amount previously subscribed, about fifteen hundred dollars.

" Dear James, let not your solicitude for the world cause you to neglect the salvation of your soul. Read and study the Bible. Make it your guide, and its Author the object of your constant trust. My anxiety for your welfare, both in this and the next world, is indescribable. But none but a father can understand or appreciate a father's feelings for the happiness of a dear and only son."

The fine Cumberland Presbyterian church in the city of Memphis, is the result of the labors alluded to in the foregoing letter.* The Rev. Mr. Dennis became the first pastor of the congregation ; who, after serving

---

* The fine house of worship in Memphis, erected through the instrumentality of Mr. Donnell, has been recently removed, and a larger one built on the same ground, to meet the wants of the congregation.

a few years, resigned. He was succeeded by the late and lamented Dr. Porter, whose labors in the city were remarkably blessed. But, unfortunately, he fell a victim to protracted efforts made during a great revival of religion in his church. The late Dr. Bryan became the next pastor, but soon felt it to be his duty to return to his old congregation, in the city of Pittsburgh. The Rev. Mr. Davis, D.D., of Lexington, Missouri, was elected to fill the vacancy, and now occupies the pulpit.

But notwithstanding the high order of talents and devoted piety that have filled the pulpit since Mr. Donnell planted the church, and acted as prime agent in erecting a house of worship, he is still recollected with gratitude, as having laid the foundation on which his brethren have built. "We feel," said one of the elders, in writing him, after he declined becoming their pastor, " that we owe you a debt that we shall never be able to pay."

It will be conceded by all acquainted with Mr. Donnell, that he planted more churches in towns and cities than any other Cumberland Presbyterian preacher of his day. Not that he neglected the country, for many flourishing congregations are now standing monuments of his labors there; but believing that town and country exert a reciprocal influence upon each other, he devoted attention and labor to the religious improvement of both.

From his example, his brethren may learn an important lesson in distributing their labors between

town and country. Both should be cared for, but
their relative importance and influence should never
be lost sight of. Towns and cities exert a mighty influence on the country and on the world. The strength
of the old world is in her cities. In our own country,
the most blasting or brightening influence emanates
from our towns and cities. Their fashions are imi-
tated; their moral habits and opinions, good or bad,
are adopted. How important, then, that great efforts
should be made for their conversion. But while this
is done, let it be remembered that our Saviour's last
command was to preach the Gospel to every creature.
The country should not be neglected.

CHAPTER VIII.

BECOMES PASTOR OF THE CHURCH AT LEBANON, TENN.

His Removal to Lebanon, Tenn.—Judge Caruthers' Letter—Great Delight of the Congregation on hearing of his consent to supply their
Pulpit—Reasons for going to Lebanon—Notes of one of his Discourses — Interest for the Students— An Extract from his first Lecture to Candidates for the Ministry—Contributes to Endow the
Theological Department.

ALTHOUGH Mr. Donnell had declined the pastorate
offered him in the city of Memphis, he was, two years
afterwards, prevailed on to take charge of the congregation at Lebanon, Tennessee. Early in the summer
of 1846, he left his quiet and comfortable home in Alabama, and all his servants, and household furniture,
and with his devoted wife, removed to that new and
interesting field of labor. The following appeal, in
behalf of the congregation, was made to him by Judge
R. L. Caruthers:

" Our pastor has determined that his duty calls him again to
the Indians, to carry out and finish the work he commenced
there. We regret very much to lose him, and differ with him
as to the field of greatest usefulness for him. But he says his
own conscience leads him to the Indians. His place here, therefore, must be filled. He suggested the Rev. Mr. Copp, and from
our recollection of him here, and his high reputation for talents
and piety, we concurred in the propriety of getting him, provided he yet entertained the Cumberland Presbyterian doctrines
in their purity. I wrote to him, and so did brother Lowry.

His reply is just received. He says such a field of usefulness as this has become, would present strong attractions to him; and clearly intimates that he would come, but for the fact that he is more Calvinistic than our church generally approve—that he is a Calvinist of the Baxter and Fuller school.*

---

* The reader may desire to know what is meant by a "Calvinist of the Baxter and Fuller school," to which Mr. Copp says he belongs. Without entering into a minute account of Mr. Baxter's views, relative to the decrees of God, or extent of the atonement, I will merely say that his theory respecting the *application* of the atonement places him in the same category with the most rigid Calvinists, so far as the salvation of sinners is concerned. No Calvinist believes more strongly in eternal and unconditional election than Mr. Baxter did. He says: "God hath positively elected certain persons, by an absolute decree, to overcome all their resistances of his Spirit, and to draw them to Christ, and by Christ to himself, by such a power and way as shall infallibly convert and save them."—*Dr. Ridgeley's Works, Vol. I, p. 537.*

Mr. Baxter believed, as Calvinists generally do, in the priority of regeneration in the hearts of the elect, leaving the non-elect without a sufficiency of grace to enable them to repent and believe on Christ.

"All men," he says, "that perish (who have the use of reason,) do perish directly for rejecting sufficient recovering grace. By grace, I mean mercy contrary to merit. By recovering, I mean such as TEND-ETH in its own nature towards their recovery, and leadeth or helpeth them thereto. By sufficient, I mean, NOT SUFFICIENT DIRECTLY TO SAVE THEM, (for such none of the elect have till they are saved;) NOR YET SUFFICIENT TO GIVE THEM FAITH, OR CAUSE THEM SAVINGLY TO BELIEVE. But it is sufficient to bring them NEARER Christ than they are, though not putting them into immediate possession of Christ by union with him as faith would do." I quote from Watson's Inst., Vol. II, p. 417.

As to Mr. Copp's other model in theology, I have only to say that I have Mr. Fuller's works, complete, in my library, and have read them with some care, and can see no difference between him and Calvin himself, on the doctrine of God's decrees. Dr. Miller once said, Mr. Fuller and he agreed on all subjects of theology, except Baptism.

The truth is, Calvinism cannot be improved, so long as the doctrine of eternal and unconditional election and reprobation is retained. Technicalities may be changed from *definite* to *indefinite* atonement, and an unlimited Gospel preached, and sinners told, in the language of Mr. Baxter, that they "perish for rejecting sufficient recovering grace," &c., still, when an explanation of this language is given, it means grace that was not intended to lead the subject of it *to Christ*, but to bring the reprobate nearer to him than they were. This is certainly what Mr. Baxter means.

"We cannot agree at this point, where so many of our young men are to be educated for the ministry, to have anything but the purest and most unadulterated Cumberland Presbyterianism taught in our pulpit. We owe this to the whole church, and particularly to those who are sustaining our institution by their money, and by sending their sons and wards to it.

"There is not, perhaps, in the bounds of our church, a position where more good could be done by a minister of talents and piety than at this point. The young men who have to carry forward the ark, and who are the future hope of our branch of the church, are here to learn the art of holy warfare, and to be supplied with weapons to fight the battles of the Lord.

"In a consultation of the elders and some of the brethren to-day, we have come to the conclusion—and in this the President of the University fully concurs—that you are the man best qualified of all others in the church for this position. Throughout the bounds of the church in every State and Territory there would be confidence, if you were here. No man would feel that his son would go much astray in doctrine or morals, if he attended the ministry of 'FATHER DONNELL' every Sabbath. Our church here, and community generally, would be much delighted at your consent to occupy our pulpit.

"I hope you will, upon a prayerful consideration of the subject, inform us with as little delay as possible, that you will come. Brother Lowry leaves in about ten days, and we desire to fill his place as soon as possible; and our minds and hearts are now all fixed on you. Before you reject our call, examine the whole ground. We know you will do what you think duty requires."

Were I disposed to adopt Calvinism as my religious creed, of any school, I would go right to Geneva, and take Calvin's Institutes as my text-book. They call things by the right name, and contain no misleading ambiguities.

Mr. Copp had *been* a Cumberland Presbyterian, and at his ordination adopted the Confession of Faith of that church.

I regret that Mr. Donnell's reply to this appeal can-not be found. The following letter, however, of Judge Caruthers, shows the great joy of the congregation on hearing that he had yielded to their wishes:

"On Saturday, your letter to brother Anderson informs us that you felt it to be your duty to accede to the petition of some of us to become our pastor, provided it should be the wish of the congregation. The Session, with some of the members of the church, met at once, and agreed most cordially and unani-mously upon calling you to this post, which you very properly denominate one of the most important in the church. We resolved, however, to take the sense of the whole congregation on the subject, and this was done after giving full notice. The same unanimity prevailed. Indeed, the whole congregation, and people generally, are very much delighted with the pros-pect of having you at this most vitally important station.

"On Monday, we determined to make up the salary, so as to have no delay or uncertainty in the matter, which was done in a few hours. It is to be paid quarterly, and we have made ar-rangements to have it collected and placed in the hands of the pastor without any trouble to him, or care of this kind upon his mind.

"We very much hope that you will be so well pleased with our village and society, that you will conclude to spend the remainder of your days with us, in some capacity of useful-ness.

"It would be very desirable to see some brother of wealth endow a Professorship of Theology in our University, and you the first Professor. We hope the Lord will put it into the heart of some one blessed with the means to perform that great and good deed before many years. But before this is done, we deem it important to have a pastor here able to instruct candidates for the ministry in the doctrines of our church; and it is agreed on all hands that no man understands our distinctive peculiar-

11—

ities better than yourself, or could teach them with better effect. But all these things can be talked of hereafter.

"I enclose you the certificate of the clerk of the Session, showing your election as pastor.

"As to the time of your coming, all I have to say is, let it be at as early a period as possible. We have had no regular pastor for several months.

"I received your letter to me, this morning; but the work was all done. I have shown it, however, to the elders of the church that I have seen, and we await your arrival with much anxiety."

The same obstacles were in the way of Mr. Donnell's removal to Lebanon, that existed when he declined the call to Memphis; but the great demand, as he thought, for his services at the former place, caused him to yield to the sacrifice of leaving a comfortable home, &c., to engage in the arduous duties that awaited him. In addition to the ordinary prospects of usefulness in the *town of Lebanon*, the University at that place presented a new and very inviting field for ministerial labor. The future guides and rulers of our nation were prosecuting their education there; and Mr. Donnell, though old in wisdom and experience, was still young in feeling and affection for the youth of his country, and knew how to appreciate revivals of religion for their benefit. He was aware, too, that at the University much might be done in turning the attention of pious young men to the subject of preaching the Gospel.

On his arrival at Lebanon, all were delighted. "We feel," said one in a letter to the writer of this Memoir, "that we have got a man from God." Said another,

in describing the character of his sermons, "you know
we always thought brother Donnell was a prodigy in
the pulpit."

In preparing his discourses for delivery, Mr. Donnell
made but little use of his pen. The following crude
notes, however, were found among his papers, and are
supposed to contain thoughts embodied in a lecture
delivered to the congregation soon after his arrival:

"MY DEAR BRETHREN:—Feelings of deep interest for the
prosperity of this congregation, have prompted me to lay before you, on this occasion, your advantages, responsibilities,
and duties:

"1. You were organized some twenty-five years ago, under
very embarrassing circumstances; without a pastor or house
of worship, and much sectarian influence and prejudice were
arrayed against you. God, however, in His providence, soon
provided for you a house, and at the first Synod ever held
in your town, blessed you with a powerful revival of religion,
in which many enterprising citizens were converted, who added
much to your strength. Revival after revival followed, affording new accessions, till your membership has grown to near
two hundred; and for many years you have had the labors of
a faithful pastor.

"2. Your location is near the centre of the Cumberland Presbyterian church, and in a country still feeling the influence of
the great revival of 1800.

"3. No town in the State of Tennessee is more highly favored
with literary advantages than Lebanon; and your institutions
of learning afford many facilities for sending abroad and into
high places of society a strong religious influence."

In addition to the arduous duties of pastor, Mr. Donnell alternated with the President of the University in
weekly lectures to candidates for the ministry.

"These lectures," says the President, "were the result of years' reflection and profound analysis, rather than the study of standard works; and embraced all the distinctive doctrines of the Cumberland Presbyterian church. His example and religious intercourse were of incalculable benefit to the literary students generally. Besides making the personal acquaintance of each, and conversing with all on the subject of religion, he often addressed them publicly on moral and practical subjects. As a pastor, he acted the part of a father to all the congregation, looking after the spiritual interests of each member with paternal solicitude, visiting the families, praying with them, and conversing with each member with a tenderness and sympathy peculiar to himself."

Dr. Anderson adds: "He regarded the institution, with its facilities for educating the youth of the country at large, and especially candidates for the ministry, as the hope of the church for whose benefit he had devoted the labors of a long life."

The following reminiscence of Mr. Donnell's intercourse with the students of Cumberland University, is furnished by Rev. J. C. Provine, who says:

"It was my good fortune to be a student in Cumberland University during the time Father Donnell was pastor of the church at Lebanon, and I can truly say that the interest he manifested in behalf of the students, gave full proof that they had a place in his heart. For them he preached and prayed, and imparted pious counsel. He sought the acquaintance of all—inquiring where they were from, whether their parents were living, whether professors of religion; and finally, whether the son had ever given *his* heart to God. He would then speak of the weekly meeting of the church for prayer, and of the Sabbath school, and of the great advantages resulting from those meetings to students. Then expressing a hope that the young gentlemen would be pleased with the University, and make rapid progress in their studies, he would retire, always leaving a happy impression upon the youthful mind.

"But while he felt an interest for the success and welfare of all the students, there was a special concern which he had in regard to those preparing for the holy ministry. Many of this class were often pressed for means to prosecute their education. For their encouragement, he would relate some of his own early trials in the ministry, and then promise to do what he could for their relief. To me he manifested all the kindness and tenderness of a father. Seldom would he permit one of us to pass him in the street without stopping for at least a brief conversation. 'Well, how do you do to-day?' he would say. 'How are you progressing with your studies? Where did you preach last Sabbath? Was there much interest among the people?' Then, with a parental kindness, he would say, 'Try to be humble and prayerful; improve your time; there is a great work for you to do; the fields are white unto harvest, and the laborers are few.'

"His regular lectures to the theological students were very interesting and impressive. His manner was plain and familiar, characterized by affectionate tenderness and sympathy, as well as an earnestness and warmth of feeling that always engaged the attention of those who heard him. In levity he never indulged, nor in any remark, either in his sermons or lectures, designed to excite mirth. He doubtless felt that

"'He who negotiates between God and man
As God's ambassador, the grand concerns
Of judgment and mercy, should beware
Of lightness in his speech.'

" His instructions to the young ministers of the University will exercise an influence that will know no end. As a stream it will widen and deepen, and gather force as it advances, until it bears out into the ocean of eternity a rich freight of redeemed souls.

" I close by subjoining the following excerpta from the last letter it was my privilege to receive from the lamented father in the ministry. It was written while I edited the *Ladies' Pearl :*

" ' I am pleased with the *Pearl*, and have promised to write a little for its columns, but have waited for time, which, like myself, is always in a hurry. * * I am highly gratified to see the ladies advance to aid the cause of Christ, by sending out the *Pearl.* If you want a tear when the heavens are hung with the emblems of mourning, call for the daughters of Jerusalem. If you want to perfume the dead body of the Saviour, call for Mary and her companions. If you would comfort weeping disciples, let Mary—last at the cross, first at the grave, and first to see a risen Saviour—go and tell his disconsolate followers that he is risen from the dead. Sisters of the Pearl, your work is not half done ; you have just commenced. Be not weary in well-doing, for in due season you shall reap if you faint not.' "

The Rev. John S. Grider was also a student of the University when Mr. Donnell was pastor of the church at Lebanon. He says :

" When I entered as a student of the University, Mr. Donnell was pastor of the church. My father had given me a letter of introduction to him, with a request that he would render some attention to my spiritual interests.

" The pastor generally saw me once a week, either at my room or boarding-house, and often propounded such questions as the following: ' Well, my young brother, how are you getting along in your studies? I hope you stand high in your class. And how is it with your soul?—you must take care of that. Come to prayer-meetings, and be sure not to neglect secret prayer.'

"I was a member, for some time, of a class of young men taught by Mrs. Donnell in the Sabbath school, from whose instruction I also derived much benefit."

The Rev. E. D. Pearson adds his testimony to Mr. Donnell's usefulness to the students of the University. He says:

"I was awakened on the subject of religion under his preaching; he received me into the church, and acted the part of a father to me, while prosecuting my education. It seemed as natural and easy for him to introduce the subject of religion in conversation as to inquire after the health of the body. His pious advice can never be forgotten."

The following is an extract from Mr. Donnell's first lecture to the candidates for the ministry:

"I am pleased to find so many young men in this institution who have devoted themselves to the great work of the ministry. In preparing for the holy office to which you aspire, your object should be to search for *truth*, the whole *truth*, and nothing but the *truth*, avoiding all speculations, either in word or doctrine, that would lead to strife in the church. To promote the peace, purity, and prosperity of the church, and to bring sinners under the influence of the Gospel, is the great business of a minister of Jesus Christ. With his office is inseparably connected, not only the progress of the church and salvation of souls, but the highest temporal good of society. No man better understood the importance of a minister's office and necessity of a thorough preparation for a proper discharge of its duties, than the Apostle to the Gentiles. Hence the frequent and solemn exhortations recorded in his epistles, both

to the churches and preachers, on the evils resulting from in-
competent and unholy teachers.

"God at the beginning made known his character and man's
duty, by direct revelations; and then good men were directed
to teach their families and others the knowledge of the true
God. The pious patriarchs were all required to impart religious instruction to their households. Noah taught the old
world the will of God. Public teachers were provided by
Divine appointment under the Mosaic dispensation. John the
Baptist, and others, received their commission from a Divine
source. When the twelve Apostles were sent forth, it was by
the special appointment of Christ.

"The christian ministry in every age of the world, since the
ascension of the Redeemer, has possessed the same Divine commission, excepting power to perform miracles. It is a *positive*
institution growing out of the *moral wants* of mankind.

"How important, then, that this office should be filled by
men who will be able to magnify and support its dignity!
But for *this office*, and the Holy Spirit's influence that attends
it, our world would be a dark and gloomy abode indeed. Ministers of Jesus Christ are highly responsible to God, and must
render a very solemn account at the last day."

Mr. Donnell took an active part in locating the theological department at Cumberland University, and contributed a thousand dollars to its endowment; and all
eyes were turned to him, at one time, as its first professor. The infirmities of age, however, caused him to
decline the appointment. In many respects, he was
just the man for the station. He possessed a clear
head and a warm heart, and his theological attainments were of a high order. No preacher was more
generally known in the church, or stood above him in

the affections of his brethren. He had borne, too, "the burden and heat of the day" in the ministry, and could have brought to the professor's chair every desirable advantage from experience. There were men in the church possessing higher scholastic qualifications than himself; but none who knew more about preaching, or were more thoroughly versed in theology; and I hope the day may never come when the trustees of the Seminary, in investing men with the high trust of educating ministers, will lose sight of the importance of a practical *acquaintance* with *the pulpit*, as well as college halls and books. Men ordained to preach, but who seldom do it, are not the men to train others to preach. Great and prospective interests to the church are involved in the appointment of theological professors. Literary attainments, in those selected, cannot be too high; but a knowledge of theology, and a practical knowledge of preaching, may be too low.

CHAPTER IX.

RESIGNS THE PASTORATE AT LEBANON, AND RETURNS TO ALABAMA.

His Labors at Athens—Meeting of Columbia Synod—Revival of Religion—Revision of the Confession of Faith proposed—His published Letter against Revision—General Remarks—Mr. Ewing's Example.

MR. DONNELL had not labored long at Lebanon, before it became apparent, both to himself and the congregation, that the infirmities of age rendered him incapable of the onerous work which necessarily devolved on the pastor. Besides, the large family of servants, left upon his farm in Alabama, needed his personal care and attention, and his temporal interests were suffering materially in consequence of his absence. So that, in view of all the circumstances, he very reluctantly came to the conclusion that it was his duty to retire from those toils which his advanced period of life rendered him unable to bear.

On his return to Alabama, he settled in Athens, and to his agency and influence the church in that town is chiefly indebted for its comfortable house of worship. The reader has already been informed of his great zeal and success in building houses for God. In the present instance, it would seem that he did not wait till he erected one for himself. The following letter indicates the manner in which the evening of his life was employed:

"ATHENS, ALA., March 6, 1851.

"BROTHER LOWRY:—Yours of the 25th ult. has been received and read with interest. I wrote you some two weeks ago, but suppose you failed to get my letter, as you make no reference to it.

"I am unusually busy, finishing my own house, and building a new church in this place.

"A late storm swept away one-half of the buildings of Fayetteville, including the Cumberland Presbyterian church; and a storm last fall blew down our church at Mooresville—both of which we must try to rebuild this year. I must send Professor Safford a little money for his department in the University, and also the interest on my endowment note, the first safe opportunity.

"The ladies have formed here what they call an 'Effort Society,' for the benefit of our church, and I hope they will do good.

"I tremble for our approaching General Assembly, and desire to attend, but fear I shall not be able to travel so far.

"R. DONNELL.
"REV. D. LOWRY."

The following letter, which I find published in the "Banner of Peace," shows the success of Mr. Donnell's labors at Athens:

"ATHENS, ALA., November 15, 1852.

"MESSRS. EDITORS:— The new Cumberland Presbyterian church of this place, was dedicated the first Sabbath of last month. The Columbia Synod met in it on the previous Friday, and closed its business harmoniously on Saturday evening.

"There was considerable religious interest during the meeting among the people; and what was remarkable, there seemed to be a revival from the commencement of Synod among the ministers and elders. They caught the fire first, and then the good work began in the community. About eleven persons professed religion, and several joined the church. The communion on Sabbath was a glorious one, and perhaps the last that some of the preachers and people will ever be at in this world. Several of the brethren remained some time after the close of Synod; among whom were brothers F. Johnson and Mitchell. The latter staid two weeks.

"After remaining one week at Athens, brothers Johnson, Roseborough and myself commenced a meeting in Mooresville, which continued two weeks. A revival ensued, in which thirteen professed religion, and nine were added to the church. The brethren evidently preached with the Holy Ghost sent down from heaven.

"Brother Johnson has determined to travel extensively, if the Lord spare him, and the people will sustain him. He ought to be constantly in the field. We need ministers to visit the churches, and see how they do, as well as preach to sinners.

"R. DONNELL."

While our General Assembly was in session at Princeton, Kentucky, in 1853, the subject of revising the Confession of Faith was presented, whereupon a committee was appointed to take the matter into consideration, and report to the next General Assembly. The subject had been agitated at former Assemblies, and discussed through the press, and serious apprehensions were entertained as to the consequences that might follow. Mr. Donnell was not insensible to the danger to be apprehended; and though in his last affliction, he addressed a very conservative and impressive letter, through the "*Banner of Peace,*" to the

Assembly at Memphis, in 1854, setting forth the danger and impropriety of the proposed revision. His letter was read in open Assembly, while the subject was being discussed, and it produced a most salutary effect upon the members. When the vote was taken, the report of the committee was not concurred in.

I regret that the letter referred to cannot be found. The following communication, however, addressed to Dr. Bird, and published in his paper just before the Assembly convened in Memphis, contains the substance of that letter :

"ATHENS, ALA., May 4, 1854.

"BROTHER BIRD :—Though extremely feeble in my physical nature, still I am capable of some mental exercise ; and in the range of thought in which I have indulged, since I have been confined to my room, I have thought of you often as an editor of a religious journal, and as a brother and friend. I have thought much about the church of Christ, and particularly that branch of the church for the defense of whose doctrines and interests you are set as editor. I have long thought and labored for it also. Now, unable to labor, I can do little else than think. Could I even write, I might employ my thoughts to some profitable results to the church. But I can only submit them, in a feeble voice, to an amanuensis, to be committed to paper.

"I have often felt a great desire, during my protracted confinement, to send the result of some of my reflections to you for publication in your paper. There are many things appertaining to our church, about which I feel greatly, and think often and intensely. And as the subject of a proposed revision of the Confession of Faith of our church is producing much interest and feeling among our people, I could not be expected to remain insensible to the importance of this question. And as I am one of the few who remain of those who compiled that book, many have sought, by frequent private correspondence, to know my views; and one writer in the *Cumberland Presbyterian*, has recently spoken out through the columns of that paper, and appealed to the surviving fathers on the subject. But I have been at a loss to know how to respond to such calls, inasmuch as those who originated the question of revision have not told us particularly what parts they wish revised; and the last General Assembly having referred the question to a select committee, to report to the next General Assembly, and that committee not having, through any medium to which I have access, reported anything as to what they are doing, or what they intend to do in the premises, I could say nothing, because I knew nothing pertinent to the subject. As to the abstract question of revising our Confession of Faith *at all*, I have never had but one mind, and have heretofore endeavored to express that opinion in more than one way, and at different times and places.

"As you have declared the columns of the *Evangelist* open and free to the discussion of this subject, in the proper spirit, you are at liberty to make what disposition your judgment may dictate of these thoughts, with more which will follow. Though they may be imperfect in themselves, and imperfectly expressed, one thing I feel conscious of: that is, my motive is good in entertaining and expressing them.

"I have before conceded that in the Confession of Faith of our church, there are some 'words and phrases' used that in the compilation of the work might be expunged, and others substituted in their stead, and still the system of doctrines to be set forth by the compilers preserved inviolate. The compilers endeavored so to revise the Westminster Confession of Faith as to leave out the doctrines therein taught of limited atonement, *particular* and *personal* and *unconditional* election and reprobation, and such other tenets as belong to ultra Calvinism, and to set forth instead thereof, the doctrine of general atonement, with its concomitant adjuncts. The compilers were aware that they used some words and phrases in their book, which are used by ultra Calvinists in teaching their system. But they found those very words and phrases in the Bible, as well as in the Westminster Confession of Faith. They would not expunge them from the word of God, because they had been misapplied by the Westminster divines, and in connection with other words and phrases, made to teach a doctrine which is not contained in the Holy Scriptures. These words and phrases retained in the Confession of Faith to which some take exceptions, as taught by Mr. Calvin, may, to the mind of any one who has been in early life indoctrinated into that system of theology, appear to teach and inculcate the whole of the Calvinistic system. But it is not necessarily so, nor did the compilers of our Confession of Faith so regard it. For if the use of such terms as '*election*,' '*reprobation*,' '*decrees*,' '*effectual calling*,' &c., as found in the Westminster Confession of Faith, necessarily teach the doctrine of particular and personal election, *from all eternity*, then the same must be a Bible doctrine, for the words and phrases are also in the Holy Scriptures.

"There are some men, perhaps, in all the churches, who are restless spirits, and are always looking up something with which to find fault. There have been some in our church; they may be styled 'heresy hunters.' One of such left our church some time ago, not because there was not enough of Calvinism in our Confession of Faith, as he conceived, for he thought it full of it, but he left us with our book under his arm, simply because we did not live up to the letter of our own book. Another left our church, because he had become decidedly Calvinistic in his theology, and therefore must part forever from our Confession of Faith, because he could not find Calvinism taught there. Another who, perhaps, had no matured system, and incapable of maturing theological matter so as to form any settled and fixed notions of divinity, left us because he could find no 'stand points' of doctrine in all our Confession of Faith. But he rather concluded it was entirely Armenian so far as it had any points at all in it.

" Thus, you see, that if we should attempt to revise our Confession of Faith, so as to meet the objections of such 'heresy hunters,' as thus so palpably conflict and disagree among themselves as to what is taught in it, then verily we would have a little more to do than we could soon accomplish.

"Candid and honest men—men who are disposed to deal fairly—have never been at a loss to determine clearly the distinctive doctrines and religious tenets taught in the Confession of Faith of the Cumberland Presbyterian church, which make up and constitute their system, which differs essentially in many of its features from any other system extant at the time when that book was compiled and published to the world. It is the middle system between ultra Calvinism on the one hand and ultra Armenianism on the other. It is Bibleism; it is Cumberland Presbyterianism. Others in making out or amending their systems, may adopt it in part or in whole. Still, Cumberland Presbyterians are the first to embody it in their Confession of Faith, and must be acknowledged its originators as a system of correct and harmonious doctrines founded upon the Word of God, and which commends itself to every man's conscience in the sight of God.

"I am of the opinion that if our ministers and people will take this system of doctrine as it is clearly set forth in our Confession of Faith, and strive together ' in the unity of the Spirit and in the bonds of peace,' that it will still prove mighty in their hands through God to the pulling down of the strongholds of error and sin.

"My mind is tranquil in the full confidence that God will preserve and prosper our infant branch of His church, as He has done in all our former struggles.

"I rejoice at the success which has attended the united efforts of our church during the last year. Let every one attend to his appropriate work, and fill his appropriate place this year, and every succeeding year, striving together—not to find fault, not to divide and pull down—and our church will not fail to accomplish, in the United States and in the world, what the Great Head of Zion designed in our organization--the abundant glory of His name, and the salvation of multitudes of immortal souls.

"Let our ministers be emulous only for truth. Let our editors guard the sanctity of the religious press, and direct that mighty engine for the defense of the truth as it is in Jesus. Let them carefully avoid political questions which engender strife. Let them, and all our institutions of learning, guard against all appearance of local jealousies, and the gates of hell shall not impede the velocity nor diminish the power of the ball now in motion, and which received its projection when the Westminster Confession of Faith was so revised as to be divested of ultra Calvinism, and sent out into the world by the distinctive name of Cumberland Presbyterianism.

"Sincerely your brother,

"ROBERT DONNELL."

The above letter was published in the " *Watchman and Evangelist*," of May the 12th, 1854, accompanied by the following brief editorial:

"This beloved and highly esteemed father in the ministry has been unable to preach during the last winter. He is still quite feeble in body, but his condition is thought to be some better than it has been. It was his desire to meet once more with his brethren in the General Assembly, but the Lord has otherwise directed, and he feels to say in his heart the will of God be done.

"It is his earnest prayer that the Divine Spirit may preside over the deliberations of the Assembly. Of this we have a heart-stirring expression in a private note. We should have felt certain of this, even without receiving this candid revelation of his heart from his pen.

"Rev. R. Donnell has lived a long and useful life. His life and labors are identified with the history of our church from its commencement to the time being. Many facts and incidents

13—

are inscribed on the pages of his memory, that would be of interest to our church, and the common cause of religion. We cherish the hope that they may be embodied in a form for preservation, before he goes hence to his home in the bright spirit land. If it be the will of Heaven, we trust he may yet be spared for a time, and see the church of his prayers, labors and tears, continue in harmony and prosperity, maintaining its distinctive doctrines, and cherishing the revival spirit in which it took its existence and was baptized.

"As a people, we have not been given to change, nor employed in heresy hunting. It has been our absorbing work to make known the fullness and unsearchable riches of Christ, and beseech sinners to be reconciled to God. So may it continue while the world stands.

"The views in Father Donnell's letter will be subservient to the good cause, and we hope will assist in rightly disposing of the revision question which will engage the attention and action of the Assembly. It is a matter in which a very general interest is now felt. Brethren whom we esteem very highly in love, for reasons satisfactory to themselves, advocate the revision of our Confession of Faith; but to others, and in our opinion a large majority of the church, those reasons are insufficient, and they are decidedly in favor of maintaining the Confession of Faith as it is.

"We close these remarks by requesting members of the Assembly to watch and pray that they enter not into temptation; that they be kind and courteous, forbearing one another in love. Our heart's desire and prayer to God is, that wisdom from above may influence every breast."

It will be proper here to state, that the points proposed for revision were of subordinate importance in the Confession of Faith, and might be expunged without touching the vital parts of our system of theology; still, there was a diversity of sentiment in regard to them; besides, the book in its present form had been adopted as a bond-of union in the church, and it was therefore deemed unsafe to attempt a change.

One of the points, about which there is some diversity of opinion in our church, is the influence of Adam's sin on his posterity—a question that has been debated more or less in all churches, but which still remains unsettled. It was one of the causes of the late unhappy division in the Presbyterian church, and now threatens to disturb the peace of the Methodist church North.* Our Confession of Faith is very explicit relative to the condition of infants; but it is thought by some that its language savors too much of those objectionable points of Calvinism which the compilers of our book aimed to expunge.

So far as I know, it is conceded by all evangelical churches of this country, that mankind, without exception, become *sinners* before they are regenerated, and that the first responsible act put forth by a child is sinful. This act, of course, takes place under some *"master principle"* of soul that exists antecedently to moral agency. What, then, it may be asked, is gained by disputing about the moral condition of infants prior to the time when they become personally accountable, if, under a natural constitution over which they have no control, the first responsible deed they perform involves them in condemnation? It may be urged, that

---

* A writer in a late number of the *"Quarterly Review,"* contends that infants are born, not only in a justified, but regenerated state.

children could avoid coming into condemnation, by embracing the Saviour. But if not condemned till they commit sin *personally*, where is the inducement to accept the offer of mercy in the absence of condemnation ?

Unfortunately for the cause of religion, all ecclesiastical, as well as secular, organizations, are liable to be divided into parties, and this tendency generally increases as churches expand and gain numerical strength. While weak and persecuted, there is less danger of division.

Perhaps *entire unity* of sentiment, even in the same church, ought not to be expected, while men are imperfect. They have always differed, more or less, in minutæ on all subjects to which their attention has been directed. In matters of religion, the great fundamental doctrines should be carefully guarded; but on points not essential to salvation, a little latitude of construction might be safely tolerated. Those who differ from their brethren in minor points of doctrine, ought to exercise a wise discretion in pressing their *peculiar* views, either from the pulpit or press, upon public consideration. "Hast thou faith, have it to thyself," is a maxim which may be adopted under apostolic authority, for the sake of peace in the church.

The late Mr. Ewing left an example on this subject, worthy of permanent record. He had completed his lectures, but previous to their publication, he selected a committee to examine them. The committee convened at the house of Col. Young Ewing, near Hopkinsville, and the author was several days reading the manuscript. An objectionable sentiment was at length discovered, and a discussion ensued, but on failing to convince the committee of the correctness of the sentiment, Mr. Ewing, without hesitation, erased it from the manuscript. I had frequently heard him preach it from the pulpit, but never heard it afterward. Such a spirit of concession and compromise is indispensable to harmony in any church, and without it discord and jargon will ever prevail among brethren, to a greater or less extent.

But, some one will ask, must I sacrifice *truth* to preserve peace in the church? This would depend on the degree of importance belonging to the truth in question. It is a truth that our Savior was crucified under the reign of Pontius Pilate. It is also a truth that He died for the sins of the world; but who would think of attaching the *same* importance to each of these statements?

CHAPTER X.

CORRESPONDENCE.

Letter to Rev. William Harris—To the same—From Rev. Finis Ewing —From Samuel Donnell—From Mr. Donnell's Mother—From Samuel Donnell to Mr. Hugh Bone—To the same—To Mr. Erwin—To the same.

MR. DONNELL TO REV. WILLIAM HARRIS.

Madison City, Ala., December 23, 1814.

Dear Brother:—I have just met with an unexpected opportunity of writing to you, and gladly embrace it.

I am now in Madison county, and shall remain here till spring. The country is very destitute of preaching, and religion at quite a low ebb. The hearts of the people are carried away with the world, so that they talk of little else but corn, cotton, the price of land, &c. Land is selling from ten to fifteen dollars per acre, and the price of all kinds of produce very high.

As to myself, I am tolerably well in body, and sometimes feel well in soul; but am often much discouraged. It will not do to quit preaching, and yet to continue and do but little, if any, good, is very distressing. O, Lord, revive Thy work in my own heart, and throughout the world.

I know, however, that the foundation of God standeth sure, both as it respects the church and individual chris-

tians; and I am sometimes enabled to draw comfort
from His promises and supporting grace. But for this
comfort, I should sink under my discouragements. I
think I am trying to "walk uprightly," both as a private christian and minister of the Gospel; knowing
that my labors in the pulpit can be of but little service
if contradicted by my private life.

On to-morrow, brother Stewart and myself commence
a two-days' meeting at Canaan, near Huntsville. Some
are preparing for the meeting, and others for a ball on
Christmas. What a strange and wicked perversion of
the reputed birth-day of our blessed Saviour! It is
bad enough to dance on any occasion, but doubly so
when done in memory of the advent of Christ. O,
Lord, save the wicked. Let us, my dear brother, pray
and preach for their salvation.

Write to me soon.

R. DONNELL.

REV. WILLIAM HARRIS.

[When the above letter was written, the heart of the
writer was panting for a revival of religion. He saw
that the influence of the world was predominant in
the church, and christian energy greatly paralyzed
thereby, and that nothing but a revival of religion
could restore the living pulse of piety. When the
church is in this condition, public morals always dete-
riorate, so that the house of God is forsaken, and
the ball-rooms, and other places of sinful amusement
become crowded. Over this state of things, the

preacher's heart ought to mourn, and if he understand the nature and responsibilities of his office, *he will mourn.* But how cheering is a revival of religion under such circumstances! It excites new hope, and prompts to new effort on the part of the weary, discouraged laborer. Every minister of Christ, who has been long in the work, can appreciate the sentiments and feelings of Mr. Donnell.]

A SECOND LETTER TO MR. HARRIS.

FAYETTEVILLE, TENN., January 23, 1815.

DEAR BROTHER :—I am all anxiety to hear from our troops at New Orleans. Many brave men of my acquaintance are there. At our last advices, they had been engaged in skirmishing, but no decided battle had been fought. Before this reaches you, we shall have further intelligence. May the Lord give success to our arms! Peace with England, I think, will depend upon the result of the battle now pending.

I have lately seen several of our preachers, among whom were King, Bell and McGee. All were well except McGee.

R. DONNELL.

REV. WILLIAM HARRIS.

REV. FINIS EWING TO MR. DONNELL.

EWINGSVILLE, KY., February 11, 1815.

MY DEAR BROTHER DONNELL :—Three days ago, I received your favor of the 25th ult. I am really grateful for your attention ‘to me on the score of writing, and have often felt anxious to reply, but know not where to direct my letters. You once told me that a letter would find you at a certain time at Shelbyville, and I accordingly wrote to you at that place, but I got no answer from you. You now urge me to write, but say nothing about your postoffice. I therefore send this letter, as it were, hunting you. Tell me where to direct my letters, and I will, with great pleasure, correspond with you often.

With respect to our Confession of Faith, I will just say it is printed. Brothers Barnett, Kirkpatrick and myself, examined it in committee. But owing to ill health of the binder, it will be some time yet before all will be bound.

I am pleased that the people in the South approve of my "National discourse." It is an evidence to me that they are good Whigs. I have had flattering letters from other quarters; but having advanced considerably in life, these things have not the same effect on my mind now that they might have had at an earlier period. I am gratified, however, to hear that any of my well-meant performances are approved by the wise and good; and hope the discourse may be of service to many, by giving them just views of what is at stake in the present war with Great Britain, and stimulating christians to frequent and fervent prayer for the success of our arms.

I am glad you are yet blowing the gospel trumpet, and that you and brother Calhoun contemplate a visit

14—

to East Tennessee. I would be glad to accompany you, but fear it will be out of my power.

We hear the General Assembly has dealt harshly with us, and that the Synod of Kentucky will repeat the blow next fall at Nashville. But these things give me but little uneasiness. The present state of religion among ourselves gives me much more concern than anything the old church can do or say. But thank the Lord, his Spirit is still present in some of our congregations. Brother Barnett frequently has very good meetings; and what is the greatest wonder of all, God now and then gives *my* poor soul some sweet repast on his love.

A strange epidemic is now prevailing in this country, sweeping many after a few hours' sickness, into eternity.

You have, ere this, heard of General Jackson's victory at New Orleans. I have read a good deal about war, but do not recollect of any parallel to it, except the old wars of Israel, when God wrought miracles for them. Let us say, "not unto us, not unto us," &c. With my whole heart, 1 desire to thank God for such obvious interpositions of His power. Many citizens of this county were in the hottest of the battle.

Your friend and brother,

FINIS EWING.

REV. R. DONNELL.

SAMUEL DONNELL TO MR. DONNELL.

WILSON COUNTY, KY., August 19, 1815.

DEAR BROTHER:—I am still living, but my health is rapidly failing, and I feel that my time on earth must be short. O, that I may be enabled to glorify God in sickness as well as in health, in death as well as in life. I have been spending some time at Medical Springs, of this county, but received but little benefit.

I feel under great obligations to you, as well as many other kind friends, and should like to see you once more. Can you not visit this country and preach to the people? They would be greatly delighted to hear you. I suppose you have heard of Col. Doak's sudden death. I hope it will produce a good effect upon the neighborhood.

I was truly pleased to hear of the success of your tour, in connection with brother Calhoun, to East Tennessee. It is a matter of rejoicing, too, that signs of revivals are appearing elsewhere. O, that they may be multiplied and extended throughout the world!

I have lately seen a book, called the *Body of Christ*, with which I am much pleased. The writer urges, in a very clear and forcible manner, the propriety and necessity of all evangelical denominations of christians uniting on a doctrinal basis, embodying only the fundamental doctrines of religion. The author also dwells upon the moral government of God, and shows most clearly that salvation was provided for all who fell under the curse of the Divine law.

Our relations are all well, so far as I know, and anxious to see you.

Your affectionate brother,

SAMUEL DONNELL.

REV. ROBERT DONNELL.

[The writer of the foregoing letter was the oldest brother of the subject of this Memoir, and brother-in-law of the late Rev. David Foster. I find the following statements respecting him, in Mr. Donnell's own handwriting, among his papers:

"Samuel Donnell, my oldest brother, died August 12, 1817, sitting in his chair, in Caldwell county, Kentucky, far from home, among strangers. He was an elder in the Spring Creek congregation, when under the pastoral care of the Rev. Samuel Donnell. He was truly a revivalist, and active in promoting the work of God. He joined Cumberland Presbytery as a candidate for the ministry in the Presbyterian church, and was one of the young men arraigned for trial before the 'Commission of Kentucky Synod.' He was licensed to preach soon after the organization, in 1810, of the first Presbytery of the Cumberland Presbyterian church, but never preached much, owing to pulmonary affection, with which he was attacked in 1800."]

FROM MR. DONNELL'S MOTHER.

WILSON COUNTY, TENN., December 29, 1815.

MY DEAR SON:—I have heard of your affliction, with much sorrow, and would be glad to have it in my power to nurse and take care of you; but the journey to Alabama would be too great for me to undertake it. I hope the Lord will supply my place with kind friends, and that you will not suffer for the want of attention. Should you be spared, write us so soon as you get able, and come and see us when you can.

I will send you some articles of clothing by the first

opportunity. My health is about as when I wrote you last. Give my love to Mrs. Taylor and family.

Your affectionate mother,

MARY DONNELL.

REV. R. DONNELL.

SAMUEL DONNELL to MR. DONNELL.

WILSON COUNTY, TENN., July 30, 1816.

DEAR BROTHER:—I am now returning from a camp-meeting, and embrace the opportunity of sending you a few lines by brothers Farr and Stewart.

My health is about as it was when I last saw you. Alternate hopes and fears still make up a large portion of my religious experience. Comforts at times I have, which I would not exchange for anything the world can give; but I also have my dark moments, when doubts and fears annoy me. Impatience sometimes yields to submission, and sometimes overcomes it. Are such strange vicissitudes common to christians?

But the bearer waits for my letter, and I must close it. The brethren can tell you about our camp-meeting. Fail not to write me soon.

Your affectionate brother,

SAMUEL DONNELL.

REV. R. DONNELL.

MR. DONNELL TO MR. HUGH BONE.

FALL CREEK, TENN., December 29, 1817.

DEAR BROTHER:—I have been trying to preach through your county for several days, but have not had the pleasure of seeing my good uncle Hugh at one of my appointments. I am now on my way to Madison county, Alabama. O, that the Lord would go with me!

The Lord has helped me to preach since I saw you, and we have had some good meetings; but I have also had some dark hours.

Since I came into the bounds of your Presbytery, I have been trying to kindle some missionary fire in the hearts of God's ministers and people. I find that you have not one circuit-rider in all your bounds this year. You appear to be well supplied with Apollos to "water" your churches, but there are no Pauls to "plant." I find, however, that some of your preachers have caught the flame, and are willing to go if the people will open the door.

Now, my good brother, the elders represent the people, and have an equal voice in our judicatures with the preachers. Will you not, at your next Presbytery, unmuzzle the ox and let him go, (I. Cor. ix: 9); or, to speak without a figure, will you not, at your next session, devise some means to support the itinerating system? To this system our church is greatly indebted for past success, and if we would continue to prosper it must still be supported. The church is everywhere waking up to the importance of sending the Gospel to the destitute. Will this Presbytery be idle? True, you are preaching the Gospel at home to your organized congregations; but, brother, try to introduce some plan by which you may be able to speak with more than one tongue.

The Russian Bible Society have recently sent off sixteen wagon loads of Bibles and Testaments, to different parts of the empire. Cannot the Nashville Presbytery send one or more laborers into the vineyard of the Lord, at your next meeting? Think, O, think, brother, of the value of one precious soul; it cost the precious blood of the Son of God. O, does God love sinners; does Jesus Christ love them; does the Holy Ghost love them; is the sacred Trinity engaged for their salvation, and can we be idle? While you reflect on this subject, pray for me, that I may not preach in vain; and may the Lord bless you and yours.

R. DONNELL.

MR. HUGH BONE.

[This letter presents one prominent trait in Mr. Donnell's character. While he labored to convert sinners, he endeavored to develop an active, practical piety in the church. His theory was, that spiritual life, in one respect at least, is like material life—must have exercise. This is true to the letter. And one great reason why there is so little enjoyment among christians is, they do so little to promote the cause of Christ. They "shall *eat* the fruit of their doings," is God's promise to the righteous; but the idle christian—if we can conceive of one—has no fruit to eat.

"Apollos to water, but no Pauls to plant." Might not this language of Mr. Donnell be still, by way of complaint, addressed to the Cumberland Presbyterian church ? Is she not more anxious to settle pastors to preach to organized congregations, than to send out preachers to the destitute ? Without aggressive operations, no church can prosper. Keep the fort, but at the same time invade the territory of the enemy.]

MR. DONNELL TO SAME.

MR. HILL'S, TENN., March 27, 1818.

DEAR BROTHER:—I did not call on you the other morning, as you requested, owing to a hurry of business. The objects, however, that then claimed my attention, have been disposed of, but other duties are now pressing me. Indeed, there seems to be constantly something of importance to be done, just before me, so that the performance of one duty prepares the way to another which is immediately presented ; and a leisure moment is rarely found for the gratification of mere social feeling.

But in addition to business pertaining to time, death, judgment and eternity are just before me, and if I will not be attentive to them, they will soon arrest and *command* my attention. May my work for both worlds be accomplished when death comes to summon me to the bar of God.

On Tuesday, the 17th inst., the marriage covenant between Miss Ann E. Smith and myself was sealed. What a solemn thought ! Nothing but death is to break the bond now formed between us.

On next Sabbath, I have an appointment to preach

on Spring Creek.   The Sabbath following, at Winchester, and the next in Madison county, Alabama.   Calls for preaching are daily reaching me from various quarters.   Several private letters, and a petition from many of the citizens of Nashville, urge me to preach there one Sabbath in each month.   May the Lord direct me unto that part of the great harvest-field where my labors are most needed, and call and send more laborers into his vineyard.

R. DONNELL.

Mr. Hugh Bone.

[Though Mr. Bone was not a preacher of the Gospel, most of the ministers who knew him corresponded with him, and often sought his advice.   His theological knowledge was of a high order, and his talents as an exhorter were unsurpassed.   Indeed, it was the opinion of his brethren generally, that he ought to have preached.   The writer has heard him deliver some as rich and powerful exhortations as he ever heard fall from the lips of either layman or preacher. But he was modest to a fault, and rarely ever spoke in public when ministers were present.   Occasionally, however, he would consent to do so on Sabbath mornings, before breakfast, at camp-meetings, and never failed to interest the audience, and often produced great excitement.   He raised a large and respectable family, and two of his sons are now useful ministers of the Gospel—Rev. M. H. Bone, of Tennessee, and Rev. Thomas Bone, of West Tennessee.

15—

The Rev. H. B. Hill, of Tennessee, is a nephew of Mr. Hugh Bone.* Mr. Hill had a brother, who was also a useful preacher in Kentucky. What a powerful influence is exerted by such families in the church of God! A sketch of Mr. Bone's life will be found at the close of this Memoir.]

MR. DONNELL TO MR. ERWIN.

MR. TAYLOR's, April 17, 1820.

DEAR BROTHER:—I left home yesterday morning, and preached yesterday at Canaan, and last night in Huntsville. It is after 12 o'clock, and raining, and yet if the Lord will, I must go home to-night. A want of time, therefore, will not permit me to call to see you. Yet I confess I should not like it were you to come so near to my house without calling to see us. When you recollect, however, that I am so much from home, I hope you will excuse me.

We expect a sacramental meeting at Canaan on the third Sabbath of May. I hope you and sister Erwin will attend. We had times of refreshing from the presence of the Lord at Elkton, and at Presbytery. Glory to God! I hope the Lord will revive His work this year. Pray for me and mine.

R. DONNELL.

MR. R. ERWIN.

---

* Since the above was written, Mr. Hill has closed his labors in the church below, and gone to his reward in the church above.

MR. DONNELL TO SAME.

WINCHESTER, TENN., October 25, 1821.

DEAR BROTHER:—Little Francis bid us a long adieu last Saturday night, and was laid in the grave last evening. I have preached the funeral of many children, but had to attend to the funeral of my own child myself.

Mrs. Donnell wishes you to send James to Winchester by brother and sister Deckerd, who are now at Concord camp-ground. His mother wants him very much. Her health is very precarious, and he would be company for her. We shall probably go to the Springs to-morrow.

I cannot tell when I can return home; shall try to be at Cane Creek camp-meeting, and I may go home before my wife leaves the Springs. The people have great confidence in those waters. .

Remember me and mine.

R. DONNELL.

MR. ROBERT ERWIN.

CHAPTER XI.

CORRESPONDENCE.—CONTINUED.

Letter to Mr. Erwin—To Rev. William Harris—To Rev. Thomas Calhoun—From Rev. John Morgan—From the same—From the same—From the same—From Mrs. Nancy Watt—From Col. James W. Smith—Mr. Donnell to his Wife—From Rev. John Morgan—From the same.

MR. DONNELL TO MR. ERWIN.

BEECH HILL, TENN., October 29, 1821.

DEAR BROTHER:—We arrived here on Thursday last. Our little son's health improved on the journey, but he is still very weak, so that I cannot leave him as yet, and it is uncertain when I can. My wife's health is not as good as when we left home.

I cannot now say when I shall be able to return home, or whether my family will be well enough to accompany me. My own health is improved, so that I preached on last Sabbath in this neighborhood, and expect to preach again on next Sabbath.

I have not yet heard from Synod, but feel much solicitude on that subject.

Col. Smith's family are well, but there is much sickness in the country. Though still under the chastening rod, I trust I am submissive, and thankful for remaining blessings.

R. DONNELL.

MR. R. ERWIN.

MR. DONNELL TO REV. WILLIAM HARRIS.

HAZELGREEN, ALA., October 1, 1823.

DEAR BROTHER:—It is quite uncertain now whether I shall go to Synod or not. My family are at Col. Smith's, in Tennessee. I left them five weeks ago, in fine health; but a letter just received, sealed with a black wafer, announced the death of a dear child, and informed me that my wife was not well. I intended visiting my family on my way to Synod; but since the reception of this melancholy news, think it doubtful whether I shall leave them after reaching my wife's father's, till I bring them home.

I send you, by brother Gibson, fifty dollars for your hymn books. All you sent me are not yet sold, but there is no doubt, I presume, but a sufficient number will be disposed of to make up the amount remitted.

I have not time to say more now, as there is a glorious revival of religion going on at the stand while I write.

R. DONNELL.

REV. WILLIAM HARRIS.

———

MR. DONNELL TO REV. THOMAS CALHOUN.

NEW SALEM, ALA., August 12, 1829.

DEAR BROTHER:—I have been intending to write you for some time. We have had a glorious revival of religion in this country since I saw you.

At New Salem camp-meeting, between thirty and forty professed religion, and the work is still going on in the neighborhood. Winchester has also been visited with a refreshing shower. Twenty-nine have, at that place, been converted — twenty-eight of whom joined the Cumberland Presbyterian church. Fayetteville, too, has been highly favored. Fifty have professed faith in Christ in town, and about the same number in the country. The work began in Fayetteville, on the fourth of July. Our meeting was in the Court-house. I collected twenty or thirty mourners in the jury box on that day, and several professed religion. There has been a meeting there almost every day and night since. Every kind of vice was prostrated. The dancing-master has hung up his fiddle, and horse-racers have set out for life and glory. Eternal honor to God!

I never was so busy in all my life; feel almost worn out, and get no time to rest. The great and good work in my Presbytery will prevent me from attending yours as I had intended. I will try to visit your country, however, some time during the fall. I feel great solicitude for my relations and acquaintances in that country, especially for my Lebanon friends, and want to see a revival of religion in the town.

In great haste, and "less than the least of all saints,"

R. DONNELL.

Rev. Thomas Calhoun.

[The foregoing letter was written about two years before the great revival of religion at Lebanon, out of whose fruits the Cumberland Presbyterian church of

that town grew. The connection of Mr. Donnell's
anxiety and prayers and labors with that revival, eternity alone can unfold. His youthful days had been
spent in the vicinity of Lebanon; his parents and
many relations are buried near that place; and such
associations could but create peculiar solicitude for the
salvation of the community. Mr. Calhoun, in conversation with the writer, has often referred to his—Mr.
Donnell's—solicitude for the conversion of that people.
On one occasion, he closed a most powerful sermon,
upon his knees, praying them, "in Christ's stead, to
be reconciled to God."]

REV. JOHN MORGAN TO MR. DONNELL.

COLUMBIA, KY., January 11, 1832.

DEAR BROTHER DONNELL:—I suppose by this time
you wish to know what has become of me; and having
a few minutes' leisure before dinner, I will improve
them in writing you a short letter, hoping you will
favor me with a speedy answer.

After your departure from Nashville, I preached
several times, and visited several families. My congregations were generally large, attentive and feeling;
but, on visiting families, I found that some of the members of the church did not even know each other, and
among some that were acquainted, a very bad state of
feeling existed. Finding this to be the condition of
things, I appointed a meeting, requesting all the members of the church to attend. They were generally

present. All were examined on experimental religion and the practical duties of christians, &c. I hope the effect was good.

Our meeting at Franklin, Tenn., was very interesting. We had several mourners, and I baptized two adults, who joined the church at the meeting.

On the following Monday, we had a meeting at Major Allcorn's, and I have not seen such a time since I left Pennsylvania. Twenty or thirty mourners appeared, among whom was the Major himself. After leaving Nashville, we preached at Gallatin and Glasgow, and then came on to Edmonton; assisted brother Weeden at a communion meeting. Some seriousness among the people, but nothing indicating a revival. We shall now hurry on to Pennsylvania as fast as possible. My health has been good for some time. Pray for me and our success in the good cause.

        Yours in Christ,

                        JOHN MORGAN.
REV. R. DONNELL.

SAME TO SAME.

CHILLICOTHE, OHIO, June 25, 1832.

DEAR BROTHER DONNELL :—You will no doubt feel astonished when you learn that we have got no further on our journey than this place yet. But I was detained two weeks in Nashville, waiting on brother Sparks; and an attack of cholera has detained me some time in this place. But I hope our detention was of the Lord, for it has afforded us an opportunity of preaching here, which we would not have done had I not been confined by affliction. Brothers Woods and Sparks commenced preaching on Friday night. They also preached on Saturday night and Sabbath morning. By the evening service, I was able to attend, and at the close of the sermon, exhorted. Several mourners distinguished themselves. The excitement was general and powerful. We intended to have set out this morning for Athens, but the people have prevailed on us to remain and continue the meeting.

I find the Presbyterians in this country much divided. I presume you have seen the proceedings of their General Assembly.

The cholera has created great alarm in this country, and is much more fatal than it was in Asia or Europe.

Pray for me, and remember me affectionately to all; and believe me, as ever,

You sincere brother in Christ,
JOHN MORGAN.

Rev. R. Donnell.

SAME TO SAME.

Newport, Ohio, September 2, 1832.

DEAR BROTHER DONNELL:—For some time past, I have been so constantly at meeting, and other business, that I have scarcely had time for a thought about home, much less to write a letter to a friend. But being now on my way, in company with brother Aston,

16—

to Athens, to hold a camp-meeting, form a church, &c., and having an appointment at this place to-night, and there being a little time between this and the hour of preaching, I will improve it by writing to *one* who is near and dear to my heart.

Since my arrival in Pennsylvania, I have attended a four-days' meeting or camp-meeting every week, and to God's glory be it said, we have had an interesting time at each of them. At one camp-meeting at Ten-mile, about thirty professed to find the Saviour, and many left the ground under serious concern for their souls. At a meeting near Washington, fifty professed religion, and one hundred left the ground under serious conviction. At another meeting near Jefferson, Green county, between eighty and ninety were converted, and perhaps one hundred and fifty mourners left the meeting at its close. A large number professed religion at a four-days' meeting near Union Town, and forty-five joined the church.

Our Presbytery closed at Union Town on last Saturday. The session was small, but very harmonious in all its deliberations. We ordained brother Chapin, from New York, and received two candidates for the ministry; both very promising. Our membership is now about one thousand, and generally of the most respectable order of society. We have several large and comfortable meeting-houses nearly completed, and our congregations seem disposed to support the Gospel.

After closing the camp-meeting at Athens, we shall

return to Pennsylvania. Brother Aston will spend
the winter in New York. I expect to take charge of
Washington and Ten-mile congregations; brother
Woods will spend the winter in Green county, and
brothers Sparks and Bryan in Fayette county; brother
Bird has gone South, on a visit to his father, and will
not return till spring. Brother Bryan has been sick
for some time.

Notwithstanding the hard labor through which I
have passed, my own health is very good. I am
anxious to see you all, but cannot say when I shall
have the privilege. It seems impossible for me to get
away from this country. If spared, however, I may
visit Alabama next spring or summer. You know that
I love you and Clara, and that it would give me great
pleasure to see you; but the Lord's cause should be
dearer to us than earthly friends.

JOHN MORGAN.

Rev. R. Donnell.

SAME TO SAME.

Washington, Pa., October 26, 1832.

Dear Brother Donnell:—After a long delay, which
has perhaps tried your patience, I again write you. I
hope, however, that you will not attribute my silence
to a want of affection for you. My apology is camp
and protracted meetings. We have just closed an interesting meeting in Ohio, where about one hundred
professed religion; and we organized a church of one
hundred and fifty members.

The cholera is raging in many parts of this country, and many are dying. This is our fast day in reference to it. O, that God would sanctify his judgments to the good of our nation!

I have at last settled the question in relation to my remaining in this country. Duty says stay, and the voice of duty must be obeyed, though it cross our inclinations. How astonishing the providences of God! When I think of home and friends in Alabama, from whom I am now to be separated, my feelings almost overcome me. But God's will must be done.

How this climate will agree with my constitution, has yet to be seen. My health, however, is better now than it has been for some time. May the Lord bless my dear friends!

JOHN MORGAN.

Rev. R. Donnell.

MRS. NANCY WATT TO MR. DONNELL.

Rockingham County, N. C., November 13, 1832.

Dear Brother in the Lord :—I received your kind letter some time since, but bad health has delayed my answer. Never has such a revival of religion been known in this country, as has been in progress since the visit of yourself and brother Burrow. It has been quite common for one hundred persons to profess religion at a camp-meeting. Many of my dear relations were among the converts, for which I feel that I cannot be sufficiently grateful. Several of them date their first impressions, to seek the Lord, under your preaching and Mr. Burrow's.

Much solicitude is felt for a Cumberland Presbyterian preacher, to be sent to this country. Could regular preaching be had, a great many would join your church.

I was much delighted with the pamphlet you sent me. All who have read it are much pleased with it.

May you be prospered in your labors, and happy in this world and the world to come, is the prayer of your sincere friend,

NANCY WATT.

REV. ROBERT DONNELL.

COL. JAMES W. SMITH TO MR. DONNELL.

BEECH HILL, April 15, 1833.

DEAR SIR:— In consequence of business, both at home and abroad, demanding my attention, two mails have passed before I could find time to answer your last letter. As it respects dear little James, I think he is entirely too young to send to Lexington to prosecute his education this year. Better keep him at home, or near home, where his studies can be directed and morals guarded by those who feel a solicitude for his welfare, that strangers cannot feel. He is a promising child, every way obliging in his disposition, and I think possesses elements that, if properly developed, will one day make a useful man. I know the dear child feels the loss of his mother, and in consequence of that bereavement a greater obligation now devolves on his father to care for and watch over him.

My dear wife is in a very low state of health, so that I am almost afraid to leave home to attend to business.

O, that I had more of the spirit of my Master, and resignation to the will of God.

You, my dear sir, have for many years given evidence that you are called to preach the everlasting Gospel; and God, in a very special manner, has stood by and blessed you. I hope you will not let the affairs of this world cause you to neglect His work. If you do, God will forsake you.

If I know my heart, I desire to see our church prosper. When recently in North Carolina, my friends often laughed and told me my countenance indicated interest whenever your name or Cumberland Presbyterians were mentioned. Great revivals of religion followed the tract of Mr. Burrow and yourself in that country, but other denominations gathered the fruits of your labors, because we had no preachers to take charge of the work.

Much love to yourself, Mrs. Donnell, and dear little James.

JAMES W. SMITH.

REV. R. DONNELL.

MR. DONNELL TO HIS WIFE.

NASHVILLE, TENN., May 18, 1836.

DEAR CLARISSA:—The General Assembly was organized yesterday. Father King preached the opening sermon. Only about fifty members present. Brother Burrow was chosen Moderator. We shall probably have a long and busy session. My hoarseness continues, and I am much troubled with a bad cough; yet

I have been appointed on nearly all the committees, and expect no rest till I get home, where I know I am needed and desired.

I cannot express the solicitude I feel for you and the family, and the church in my own country.

I preached yesterday, and am to preach again to-day.

Your affectionate husband,

R. DONNELL.

MRS. CLARISSA N. DONNELL.

[This short letter presents, without intention on the part of Mr. Donnell, the importance attached to his services in every department of his church. "On almost every committee, and preaching every day." Whether at camp-meeting, Presbytery, Synod or General Assembly, he was looked upon as the file leader, in business, and expected to preach as often as physical strength would permit.]

REV. JOHN MORGAN TO MR. DONNELL.

UNION TOWN, PA., July 6, 1838.

DEAR BROTHER DONNELL :—Your letter of last month was received yesterday, and its perusal called up reflections both pleasing and painful. Never while memory continues, and affections are permitted to operate, can I forget the scenes and associations of my early life. And there is no man living in reference to whom there are more heart-stirring associations in my short history, than yourself. Distance, change of circumstances, the existence of new relations and duties, may produce a temporary silence; but not even a diminution, much less a total extinction, of that warm glow of friendship which has ever been felt in my bosom for you from our first acquaintance.

Many events, of thrilling moment to church and state, have transpired since we last interchanged thoughts, either by word or letter. My mind, in view of them, has often been the seat of great anxiety, when I desired much the counsel and tender sympathy of my old companion and father in the ministry.

I have looked at the contentions of our mother church, and ultimate separation, with astonishment and regret. I have seen, too, marks of a restless spirit in our own church; some want her name changed, &c. I have thought on the abolition question with deep concern. But, after all, three things have been particularly impressed on my mind: 1, I am more than ever convinced of the truth of the doctrine of our church; 2, I am a more decided friend of colonization; 3, I believe more firmly in the wisdom and goodness of God.

The fate of our paper is yet uncertain. We will not commence it without patronage, and will not seek patronage at the expense of the peace of the church.

Our college is in a very flourishing condition, having a president and three professors, and one hundred and thirteen students. The State has made a donation to the institution annually, for ten years, of one thousand dollars, which, in connection with funds on hand before, will enable us to make a considerable deduction in the price of tuition.

My labors in the ministry are very great. I preach and lecture from six to eight times a week. Calls from a distance are frequent. I have just returned from Brownsville, whither I was called to deliver an address in behalf of the Colonization Society.

My health continues good, and I believe an active life agrees best with me.

Remember me to sister Donnell, and all the old friends, and accept my best feelings and wishes for yourself.

JOHN MORGAN.

Rev. R. Donnell.

SAME TO SAME.

Washington, Pa., December 28, 1832.

Dear Brother Donnell :—Your long desired letter of the 10th instant, was received this morning, and although it is now 11 o'clock at night, I sit down to answer it. I have some news for you that I never had before. I do not know whether it will be pleasing or painful, but I am certain it will be new.

One week ago to-night I was married. This was to me a most solemn and responsible event, and I hope the step was not taken without the Divine approbation. At any rate, I tried to make it a subject of serious reflection and solemn prayer. In my courtship, I lost no time from preaching; have preached twice

17—

since my marriage, and am now on my way to Pittsburgh to attend a four-days' meeting.

I have already informed you that I had determined to remain in this country. I regret that I shall be so far from you, and my dear parents, and many other friends in Alabama. But duty to the interests of religion seems to require me to stay here. I think I am willing to sacrifice earthly comfort and social feeling for the cause of my Divine Master.

The cause of religion is not so prosperous in this country as it has been; but in Ohio it is still advancing. I received a letter this evening, pressing me to return to that State. Dr. Lindley has been there four months, and it seems as if he could not leave.

I have never enjoyed as uninterrupted health as I have this winter, and yet I have never labored harder in the ministry.

Pray for me, my dear old friend and brother, every time you bow before a throne of grace.

JOHN MORGAN.

Rev. R. Donnell.

CHAPTER XII.

CORRESPONDENCE.—CONTINUED.

Letter to his Wife—From Rev. Samuel King—To Rev. R. Beard—From Col J. W. Smith.

MR. DONNELL TO HIS WIFE.

OWENSBOROUGH, KY., May 18, 1841.

MY DEAR CLARISSA:—I reached Fayetteville late in the evening the same day I left home, and preached to a large and attentive congregation. Brother Chadick set out with me next morning, and we arrived at Murfreesborough that night, and again preached. The next day being Sabbath, we remained in town, and preached twice. On Monday we rode to Alexander Marrs's, preached on Tuesday at Bethesda, and at night at Lebanon, and also the next day. Brother Burrow and others met us there, and we went on the same evening and preached at Gallatin. The next day we preached near Russellville, and the day following at Greenville. Here brother Chadick and myself remained and preached Saturday and Sabbath. Brother Burrow and others went on to Rumsey and preached, where we overtook them on Monday, and preached again. We arrived here on Tuesday, and organized the General Assembly.

Up to this date, we have progressed in business slowly, but with considerable harmony. The subject of a church paper has been up for discussion, and the Assembly has decided not to publish one. Brothers Cossitt and Morgan will publish upon their own responsibility. Whether they will succeed or not, time will prove.

We have only about seventy members in attendance at this Assembly, but so far as I know they are strictly Cumberland Presbyterians.

This is a new but pleasant town. I am boarding with Hon. Phillip Triplett, a member of Congress. He is now at Washington.

We have an intelligent and religious congregation here, and a comfortable house of worship. I had the pleasure of dedicating it on last Wednesday. There are some indications of a revival at the Assembly. A good work is now going on at Cumberland College. About twenty students have professed religion, and several citizens of Princeton.

I am a member of the committee on Education, and now seated in a fine room, on the bank of the Ohio river, where steamboats pass nearly every hour. But this is not "home, sweet home." I am much fatigued, but have no time to rest. Even while writing this letter, other duties are claiming my attention.

Your affectionate husband,

R. DONNELL.

CLARISSA N. DONNELL.

[The reader can but be struck with the extraordinary industry of Mr. Donnell in the ministry, as presented in the foregoing letter. In the language of Dr. Burrow, "he always seemed to be ready for his work;" and I will add, delighted to engage in it. He perhaps came as near obeying the injunction of Paul (II Tim. iv: 2,) as any preacher since the days of Timothy. In season and out of season, by day and by night, at home and abroad, he scattered the Word. He was not one of those ministers whom you never can get into the pulpit, unless they have had time to make elaborate preparations, so as to astonish the audience with a display of learning and research. Such men are too common in the church. They may attract attention, and even admiration, but are rarely blessed with a revival of religion. They are not the men for the age. They neither "plant" nor "water" churches. Mr. Donnell often preached with labored preparation, and no man could excel him in making a popular impression on great occasions; but he was always ready and willing to preach on ordinary occasions, without preparation, when emergency called for it.]

REV. SAMUEL KING TO MR. DONNELL.

At Home, August 3, 1841.

Brother Donnell:—You have, no doubt, heard of the death of brother Ewing. This solemn event has spread much gloom and sorrow over our State. It occurred on the 5th of last month. I conversed with

him frequently, during his sickness, respecting the
state of his mind, in view of death. He expressed
strong confidence in the truths he had preached, and a
firm reliance on that Saviour he had so often recommended to others. When the trying crisis came, those
who witnessed his departure had every reason to believe that he felt ready to go.

He left one thousand dollars to his Presbytery, the
interest of which is to be expended in the support of
circuit preaching—which shows his full confidence in
that mode of disseminating the truth.

Could I see you, we would talk much on this and
many other subjects; but the infirmities of age render
it more than probable that we shall never meet again
in this world. I often think of the happy meetings
and glorious revivals of religion we have enjoyed together in Tennessee; but those happy days are passed.
I have confidence, however, that we shall meet and
worship and praise God together in heaven.

I bless God that my faith in Christ grows stronger
as the evening of life grows shorter. May my kind
Lord be near to comfort me when earthly friends can
do little else than weep at my bed-side.

Old and infirm as I am, I have been requested to
preach brother Ewing's funeral, and I must try to do
it. It will be a great undertaking for me; but our
long acquaintance, and the part we have acted in our
church together, seem to make it necessary.

But my hand trembles so that I must close my letter.
Love to all who love the Lord Jesus.

In Gospel bonds,

SAMUEL KING.

REV. R. DONNELL.

[The writer of the above letter, it will be recollected,
united with Messrs. Ewing and McAdow, in 1810, in
organizing the first Presbytery of the Cumberland
Presbyterian church. He had been ordained as a
member of the Presbyterian church, previous to the
action of the Kentucky Synod in 1805, and was a distinguished instrument in the great revival of 1800.

Mr. King was the first man that ever preached the
Gospel to the Choctaw Indians. Under his first sermon, the mother of the Rev. Israel Folsom professed
religion, who was the first Indian woman of her nation
that ever wore the dress of the white woman. I have
heard, with much interest, Mr. King describe the meeting. He preached through an interpreter; and when
Mrs. Folsom began to rejoice, his interpreter, an irreligious man, became so affected that he could not
speak; and to use Mr. King's own words—"there,"
said he, " I stood without a tongue." The first time I
ever saw Mr. King, he alluded to that meeting. His
remarks were made to the Synod of 1822, then in session at the Beech meeting-house, Sumner county, Tenn.
He dwelt at some length on the obligations of the
church to civilize and christianize the American Indians. Among other reasons, he told us it was more

than probable they were descendants of the ancient
Jews; and that *we* Gentiles had received the Bible
from their ancestors, and ought now to give it back to
those children of Abraham.   It was the first missionary speech I had ever heard, and it made a most vivid
and lasting impression on my mind.

As a preacher, Mr. King differed widely from Mr.
Ewing; but perhaps that difference only fitted them
the better to act as colleagues in the great work they
undertook.   Mr. Ewing possessed a logical mind; was
a profound and independent thinker, wielded a strong
pen, and was irresistible in argument, both in preaching and writing.   Mr. King was not a writer, nor were
his reasoning powers equal to Mr. Ewing's; but he
was a more powerful declaimer, and excelled in rousing
the feelings of an audience.   In the delivery of a sermon, Mr. Ewing proceeded slowly and cautiously until
the object of his discourse was brought clearly to view,
and free from all doubt in the minds of his audience;
while Mr. King moved off rapidly, regardless of sophis-
tical objections, and if any crossed his pathway, he
threw them aside as with the arms of a giant, and continued on to the end of his sermon, ordinarily closing
with an irresistible appeal to the hearts of his hearers.

A general remark here will not be out of place, respecting the first preachers of the Cumberland Presbyterian church.   But few such men are now to be found.
Physically, they were strong, most of them living on
farms, and accustomed to labor, more or less, with

their own hands. Their preaching excursions were performed generally on horseback, and meetings were often held in the open air. Their voices were strong, and adapted to out-door preaching. Though they preached often and *loud* and *long*, I never heard of bronchial disease among them. Most of them lived to a good old age, and enjoyed life till the last, because they continued to labor in their Master's cause. They appeared before their hearers, not with paper batteries or *written discourses*, but always preached without being confined, as mere readers of sermons, to their manuscript. The memory of such men would adorn the history of any church of any age.

Many of their sons in the ministry may possess higher literary attainments, but do not surpass them in Biblical knowledge. They may be said to have been men of one book, and that book was the Bible. Their mission was to *plant churches*, and they fulfilled that mission well. They were men of extraordinary industry in the Lord's vineyard. They were at home in revivals of religion, and excelled, under God, in producing revivals. *Present effect* was their great object; and nothing short of that satisfied them. May their memory be preserved, and their example prove a blessing to the church till the end of time!]

MR. DONNELL TO REV. R. BEARD.

Pontotoc, October 22, 1842.

DEAR BROTHER:—I am now at this place, at Synod, 18—

and have but a moment to write you, as brother Muse is about to leave, and I wish to send my hasty note by him.

I have long wanted to see you, and have often thought of writing you.

This Synod is now discussing the propriety of establishing an institution of learning, to aid young men in preparing for the ministry. Should it determine to do so, you may be called to take charge of it. How would such a position suit your views?

You have seen the strife in the *"Banner"* and *"Evangelist."* I hope it will soon cease. The old leaven ought to be purged out.

We have had some precious revivals of religion in our Presbytery, and many accessions to the church.

There are encouraging prospects of a revival at the present Synod. I have to preach in a few minutes. My health has not been good for the last three months. May I not expect a letter from you soon?

Your brother in Christ,

R. DONNELL.

REV. R. BEARD.

———

COL. JAMES W. SMITH TO MR. DONNELL.

BEECH HILL, TENN., March 24, 1843.

REV. AND DEAR SIR:—Your highly esteemed favor of January last, though long on the road, was received and has been read more than once with warm feelings of love and gratitude.

It would have been answered sooner, but writing has become such a burden to me that I almost dread to begin a letter. I think I love my children and relations as much, or more, than when I was able to visit and write to them. It is now more than a year since I was able to ride, or even walk, without the aid of crutches. I have lost the use of one thigh entirely, from the hip down; it has become much smaller than the other, and I can bear no weight on it at all. In addition to this affliction, I have had very sore eyes all winter, so that it has been with difficulty that I could see either to read or write. Several of my negroes have also been sick, so that but little business has been attended to, except to feed the stock and provide firewood. Kind feelings to friends, too, have led me into difficulties at a period of life when I am illy able to bear them. I have, in several instances, allowed my name to be used as indorser, and shall have the money to pay. In the midst of all my troubles, however, I try to be resigned, and wish not only to feel, but say, O Lord, thy will be done!

On reviewing my past life, I see but little to approve and much to mourn over, and I am made to wonder at and adore the forbearing mercy of God in not cutting me off as an unprofitable servant, in the midst of many imperfections. But I desire to feel grateful for that grace that disposes me to look to that great atonement made by Jesus Christ, as the only foundation of hope for fallen sinners. I hope, too, that I enjoy at times much pleasure in the service of God, and love his people wherever I find them.

We have had no stated preaching at our church since last fall. Brother Calhoun, who had preached to us regularly once a month for the last thirty years, then informed us that the distance he had to ride was so great that the infirmities of age would oblige him to discontinue his service. We regretted much to give him up, but felt that his reason for retiring was good. Some effort has been made, but as yet without success, to fill his place.

The Cumberland Presbyterians have had a considerable revival at Carthage, and also at Mr. Allen's, in which many accessions were made to the church.

I am yours in the bonds of christian love,

JAMES W. SMITH.

REV. R. DONNELL.

[Mr. Donnell's first wife, it will be remembered, was a daughter of Col. Smith. The family moved to Tennessee in 1811. The following statement was furnished by the Colonel but a short time before his death:

"In North Carolina, I was a member of the Presbyterian church, and belonged to what was called the Grassy Creek congregation, in Granville county. On removing to Tennessee I settled near old Mr. Williamson's, in the vicinity of which I I now live.

"On the 21st of February, 1818, the Rev. Robert Donnell organized a church, at what was then called Concord meeting-house. He presented the following bond of union, which was adopted by the members on that occasion:

"'We, the professors of the religion of Jesus Christ, living on Martin and Indian creek, feeling it to be our duty to be under the care of some church, that we may regularly enjoy the means of grace and ordinances of religion, and approving the doctrine and discipline of the Cumberland Presbyterian church, do now unite as a congregation, and agree to be governed by the rules and regulations of that denomination.'

"The following names were on that day enrolled : James W. Smith, Mary Smith, William Sadler, Patsey Sadler, Michael Williamson, Sally Williamson, Ann Smith, Joseph Williamson, Elizabeth Williamson, Henry Sadler, Robert Anderson, James Sadler, Hugh Stewart, Malinda Williamson, Polly Appleton, Jane Stewart and Robert McKinley."

Col. Smith will long be remembered in Tennessee as one of her useful and enterprising citizens; and the congregation of Smyrna, Jackson county, will cherish his memory with the most profound respect. For many years he was an elder of that church.]

CHAPTER XIII.

CORRESPONDENCE.—CONTINUED.

Letter to Rev. Thomas Calhoun—To Rev. M. H. Bone—To Rev. M. Bird
—To Rev. M. H. Bone—From Mr. J. D. White—To his Wife—To Rev.
Jacob Lindley—To his Wife—To Rev. Thomas Calhoun.

MR. DONNELL TO REV. THOMAS CALHOUN, SR.

POPLAR REST, ALA., January 30, 1844.

DEAR BROTHER:—I am some younger than you, at least in the ministry; and I feel it my duty to renew the friendly correspondence between you and myself, that has been too long suspended. I have often thought of my negligence with shame. Surely, we have grown cold in religion, as well as old, or we could not have remained silent so long.

Those whom we call the founders of our church, are nearly worn out and gone. The next class of ministers, such as Porter, Bell, yourself, and a few others, are rapidly declining, and will soon also be numbered with those that have been. Then the interests of the church will fall into the hands of our sons in the ministry. How they will guard and conduct them, we know not. We know not what a day may bring forth; much less can we tell what years may do. One thing I can say: I believe most firmly the great leading doctrines of our church, and that they will be transmitted to coming ages. If we remain humble and united, a bright future is before us. But if we fall out by the way, and divide and devour each other, our system may pass into other hands that will prove more worthy of it.

You remember the advice of some of the founders of our church when the Confession of Faith was adopted —which was, never to dispute about small matters, nor divide, though we might not be able to split every hair in theology alike. I have ever acted under this advice, and shall continue to do so. It is the only principle that can keep any church together.

I think I shall not be at the next General Assembly, unless pressed by my Presbytery to go. I wish to live in peace, and promote the work of God the balance of my days, without contention.

Much is now being said about the best plan of conducting religious newspapers. The point at issue is, whether they should be the property of associations or individuals. Much may be said for and against both plans. Both have been tried by other churches, and their advantages and disadvantages are now before the world. Less harmony prevails in those churches that have not controlled their papers, than where the supervision has been held by the church. Will you give me your opinion on this subject?

R. DONNELL.

Rev. Thomas Calhoun.

[It appears from the date of this letter, that at the

time it was written, trouble in the church was apprehended, from the influence of the Rev. James Smith, who subsequently joined the Presbyterian church. The cause of his dissatisfaction may be seen in the "Life of the late Rev. George Donnell," by President Anderson. Mr. Smith, however, on leaving the church, only took one preacher with him, so that the danger apprehended soon passed away.

The conservative advice referred to by Mr. Donnell, when our Confession of Faith was adopted, was no doubt given by Mr. Ewing. It was characteristic of the man, and I often heard him, in substance, repeat it after I entered the ministry. No man studied more the peace of the church than he did.

The subject in reference to the best and safest policy of publishing and conducting religious periodicals, was very much agitated in 1844. Some contended that they ought to belong to the church, and be made a source of revenue. Others thought that a paper owned and conducted upon individual responsibility, would be equally as useful, and less annoying to the church; and that their yielding a revenue, would be doubtful. The former policy has never been practically tested; but there are still those in the church in favor of it. The individual plan has not worked well. In several instances, a paper has been commenced, and discontinued for the want of patronage. Others have repeatedly changed owners, indicating thereby that the income they afforded was not very tempting.

The profits of a paper, whether belonging to the church or an individual, must depend, first upon its intrinsic merits, and secondly, on the promptness of its readers in paying for it. A large list of subscribers would only accelerate the downfall of a paper, without punctuality of payment.

There is one general principle that will hold good in all enterprises, whether religious or secular. A defective plan of operation will work better in *good* hands, than a more perfect plan in *bad* hands; and very often failure is attributable, not so much to *plan*, as to the manner in which it is conducted.]

MR. DONNELL TO REV. M. H. BONE.

MOORESVILLE, ALA., June 24, 1844.

DEAR BROTHER:—Your letter was received to-day, for which I thank you. Had it not reached me at the time it did, I should have written first, as I was just about commencing a letter to you. I would have written you while absent in Mississippi, but had not time.

I left home on the 28th of April, and after traveling one thousand miles, returned on the 20th instant. I had good health during the whole journey, for which I think I feel grateful. I did not preach as much as I desired to do, owing to the state of the weather, condition of the roads, &c.

A Cumberland Presbyterian preacher is much needed in Memphis. I found the brethren there greatly dis-

19—

couraged, in consequence of my declining to accept their call, and had almost given up the idea of building a church. I told them, however, that I would never visit Memphis again, if they did not go on with it; but that if they would build a good house by October next, that I would come down and preach for them during the winter. Before I left, we had in all subscribed about five thousand dollars. If they finish the house, and no other preacher can be had, I must go and occupy their pulpit, as promised.

I want you to meet me at a two-days' meeting here or at Salem, embracing the third Sabbath in July, and remain for a camp-meeting, on the fourth Sabbath, at Salem.

I did not see Smith. He left Memphis two days before I got there. It is generally understood, however, that he intends joining the Presbyterian church, and our brethren say they hope he will.

But I cannot write everything now. Come to my meetings as requested, and we will then talk face to face.

Tell all Huntsville—sisters and brothers—that I love them.

R. DONNELL.

REV. M. H. BONE.

MR. DONNELL TO REV. M. BIRD, D.D.

POPLAR REST, ALA., November 25, 1844.

DEAR BROTHER BIRD:—Your favors of the 13th and 14th inst., were received yesterday, and the contents have employed and interested Mr. Lindley and myself to-day.

So far as I can learn, our church is now in a more prosperous condition than it has been for years. Tennessee Presbytery has been greatly blessed this year with revivals of religion. Our doctrines are well received, and both preachers and people are coming up to the proper standard.

I expect shortly to set out for Memphis, to remain there until spring. A Cumberland Presbyterian church is now being erected in that city, and will be finished, or fit for use, in a few weeks.

I have always endeavored to maintain a conservative position, both in church and State—believing that extremes are generally dangerous. Those questions which are now rending other churches, I hope will not get into ours; but that we will continue to maintain the unity of the spirit in the bonds of peace.

R. DONNELL.

REV. M. BIRD, D.D.

———

MR. DONNELL TO REV. M. H. BONE.

POPLAR REST, ALA., December 5, 1844.

DEAR BROTHER :—Your letter of the 3d instant, was received yesterday.

I intended to have set out for Memphis on the 12th of last month, but heard by letter from brother White, one of the elders, that the church would not be ready for use until some time in next month. He also advised me not to go down till January. I shall therefore expect to leave for Memphis early in that month.

I received a long letter last week from brother Bird. He thinks our church has not been in a more prosperous condition for years than it is now. He wishes a new edition of "Miscellaneous Thoughts," and speaks of publishing a magazine, devoted to doctrinal, experimental and practical religion.

My time is very much occupied in answering letters, just now, so that I cannot write you at length. I wish we could be together about twenty-four hours. Perhaps I may visit you before I leave for Memphis.

R. DONNELL.

REV. M. H. BONE.

MR. J. D. WHITE TO MR. DONNELL.

MEMPHIS, TENN., December 26, 1844.

DEAR BROTHER DONNELL:—I have delayed writing you longer than I intended, but am better prepared to give you all the particulars relative to our house of worship now being erected in this place. You know a few of us shouldered the burden, and pushed it ahead, and I fear we shall soon be in a close place. The building is now nearly done, except pulpit, seats, and plastering, and heavy payments will be due in a few days; but many of the subscribers say they are not ready to pay. The unfinished part will have to be delayed till we can liquidate the debt for which we are now liable.

I hope you will not fail to be here early in next

month; all expect you, and you can afford much aid in collecting funds to pay the debt of the church. I never saw more plainly the need of a leader to our little flock. We are so scattered that it is difficult to secure a united effort. You are the only man that can help us in this close place. We shall look for you at the time just indicated.

Yours truly,

J. D. WHITE.

Rev. R. Donnell.

MR. DONNELL TO HIS WIFE.

Memphis, Tenn., February 21, 1845.

My dear Wife:—Your kind letter of the 10th inst., has been received.

I expect to set out for home about the middle of next month, and may return here in April again. I think I never saw a wider and more promising field of usefulness, than is presented here to a Cumberland Presbyterian preacher. The people are extremely anxious for us to move to Memphis, and settle for life; but I cannot promise to do so.

We have appointed a communion meeting on the second Sabbath in next month. Brothers Cowan, Dennis and Birney will aid me. I lecture every Wednesday night. My last lecture was on the Trinity.

Since I came here, I have written several letters for our papers, and one for the temperance paper published here, and am to lecture next Tuesday night on the subject of temperance—so that, although it is much needed, I have no time to rest.

Tell the brethren to have the pulpit made, church finished, &c., by Presbytery. I want our little church to look well, and the congregation to do well. I think I shall spend my days in that country, and should like to go to a comfortable church while I live, and to die in a good congregation.

Your affectionate husband,

R. DONNELL.

Mrs. Clarissa N. Donnell.

MR. DONNELL TO REV. JACOB LINDLEY, D.D.

Memphis, Tenn., February 7, 1845.

Dear Sir:—Having a leisure moment, I will send you a few thoughts, to occupy your reflections in the morning, as you are in the habit of rising at an early hour. But what subject shall be submitted for meditation? Perhaps the late progress in the march of improvement in the arts and sciences, will not be unacceptable.

At the beginning of the present century, the power of steam had been thought of, and some experiments made; but the practicability of applying it to machinery was not fully tested, till the launching of Fulton's boat in 1807. What wonders have been accomplished by steam navigation since that time!

At a later period, the world was astonished by the application of steam to propel the rail-car; and now

the surface of both Europe and America is checkered
with railroads, on which millions of tons of produce
are every year carried to market.

Labor-saving machines, too, have without number
been multiplied, both in the shop and on the farm, until one man can now accomplish in one day as much
as ten could before their introduction.

The last wonder that I will mention, and perhaps
the greatest of all, is telegraphic communication, which
enables men to communicate in an instant with each
other, though thousands of miles apart.

Within the last fifty years, educational facilities have
increased with astonishing rapidity. At the beginning
of this century, there were about twenty-five colleges
in the United States; now it is believed there are
more than six times that number. Theological seminaries, law and medical schools, have been provided.
Normal institutions and female seminaries have been
added. The benefits of education, within the present
half of the nineteenth century, have been placed within
the reach of the masses, by the introduction of free
schools.

Religion has shared largely in the benefits of all these
improvements. Indeed, religion has been the nursing
mother of them all; and has a right to be benefited by
their fruits.

But extraordinary revivals of religion commenced at
the beginning of the present century, and are still in
progress; and new facilities, such as Sabbath schools,

&c., to aid in spreading the Gospel, have been introduced.

I have many things to do and say in this country. Never have I seen a brighter prospect for usefulness to our church than is now presented here. Our new house of worship is ready for use, but not finished. Since my arrival, I have begged $53, to aid in paying for a pulpit, and expect in a few days to double this amount. I am urged to remain here till the house is completed and paid for—or, until they can get another preacher. I expect to preach in the church on next Sabbath for the first time. I shall not dedicate the house to God, but the people who occupy it.

I feel great solicitude about home, but must leave all in the hands of God.

Love to Mrs. Lindley, and all the family.

R. DONNELL.

REV. JACOB LINDLEY, D.D.

MR. DONNELL TO HIS WIFE.

MEMPHIS, TENN., May 2, 1845.

MY DEAR WIFE:—I have remained here longer than was expected when I wrote you last; but shall leave on Monday. This is Saturday night, and I shall not mail my letter till Monday morning, hoping in the meantime to hear from you.

The church here still urge me to become their pastor; but there are insuperable difficulties in the way, and I must decline. Brother Dennis is willing to accept the appointment, and I think it had better be made.

We had our first communion on last Sabbath in our new and fine house of worship. Several new members were added to the congregation, and there is a bright prospect here for accomplishing great good, if the people had a preacher. I love this people, and think it probable if you were here, and saw the prospect for usefulness, you would advise me to become their pastor. But the people of Alabama are dear to me too, and I have it in my heart to live and die with them.

I feel great solicitude about home. Hope religion is still prospering in the church in Alabama, and although it is out of my power to preach to the people, other preachers will.

Monday morning.—Your kind and welcome letter has been received, and I have this moment finished reading it. Am glad to hear that you are all well. I shall leave for Raleigh in a few minutes, and will try to get home in time to rest a few days, on my way to the General Assembly.

Brother Aston requests an appointment in the city of Nashville, and I have agreed to preach there the Sabbath preceding the Assembly.

Love to all—your father, mother, James, and family, and all the black people; and receive for yourself that love which is stronger than death, from

Your husband,
R. DONNELL.

CLARISSA N. DONNELL.

[Mr. Donnell came on to the General Assembly,
20—

which met at Lebanon, Tenn., a short time after the above letter was written. A love of ease and domestic enjoyment would have said, remain at home and rest; but devotion to the interests of the church, led him to forego that pleasure. The writer was present at that Assembly, and had not seen Mr. Donnell for twelve years previously—having lived, during that time, among the Winnebago Indians. Toil and age had produced a great change in his appearance, but he was still burning with zeal for the salvation of sinners, and devoted to the welfare of the church. He took no part in trifling debates; but when a vital question came up, all eyes were turned to him, and he was expected to give direction to the decision.

At that meeting of the General Assembly, he preached the funeral of Rev. Samuel McAdow, who, in connection with Ewing and King, had organized the first Presbytery of the Cumberland Presbyterian church.]

MR. DONNELL TO REV. THOMAS CALHOUN.

POPLAR REST, ALA., November 29, 1845.

DEAR BROTHER:—We remember the days of old and years of former generations. Allowing twenty-five years to an age, we are now living in the third generation since we were born. I am very sensible of life's decline; perhaps the more so on account of my long labors in the service of the church. But I cannot now labor as I once did; and yet I see more to be done, and want to do more, than I ever did.

To forget you, would be impossible. To love you not, would be not to love myself. We have labored together in weakness and fear, and much trembling; and know how to sympathize with each other.

I have just determined to write you, brothers James B. Porter and Bell—three of the oldest living ministers of our church. Many who, like them, bore the " burden and heat of the day," are now dead. Who will go next? Lord help me to " finish my course with joy."

How pleasing the contrast between the present state of our church, and when you and I were young ! Then we had no institutions of learning, and a religious newspaper was not known among us; but now, we have both in abundance. Let us keep humble, and try to encourage among our people the piety of 1800 ; and never suffer a love of numbers, and wealth and influence, to induce us to depart from the spirit, simplicity and power of the Gospel.

My general health is at present pretty good, though a sore foot confines me to my room. I was, however, quite unwell for two months or more last summer, after returning from the General Assembly.

Tell father Aston I still keep him enrolled among my friends on earth.

R. DONNELL.

Rev. Thomas Calhoun.

[Mr. Donnell alludes, in this letter, to the piety of the great revival of 1800. He and Mr. Calhoun were both converted in that revival; and there is no doubt but a power attended the Gospel then that does not generally appear now. Perhaps the extraordinary work of God that has been going on in Ireland, for some time past, is more like the revival of 1800, than any known on the pages of history. Conversions, at the time alluded to by Mr. Donnell, were generally decided—preceded by deep and thorough conviction, and followed by the most satisfactory evidences of true piety. It is not unusual now to see persons professing to pass from a state of nature to grace, apparently with the same composedness of mind with which they attend to ordinary business. Such was not the case at the time of which Mr. Donnell speaks. Conviction for sin was then a matter of *deep feeling,* as well as of judgment.

It is true, the piety of *this age* discloses some elements not seen at the beginning of the present century, particularly in efforts to send the Gospel to the heathen. This, however, may be owing to the *opportunity* now existing, that was not known to the church when Messrs. Donnell and Calhoun were converted. A missionary spirit, in a very large degree, was then *felt;* but access to the heathen was not so readily obtained as now. In many countries, the door was entirely closed. The aggressive power of religion in the revival of 1800, was confined to the home field ; and many and great were its achievements. The laity were all at work. Even females were more useful then than the elders of the church are now, with some few exceptions. A female was the honored instrument in the conversion of the late Rev. James B. Porter, and I regret that her name is not certainly known. It ought to be recorded in letters of gold. The mothers and daughters of 1800 knew how to pray, and to speak to sinners, and were not ashamed to do it.]

CHAPTER XIV.

CORRESPONDENCE.—CONTINUED.

Letter to Rev. J. Kirkland—To his Wife—To Rev. R. Beard, D.D.—To
Rev. D. Lowry—To Rev. M. Bird, D.D.—From Rev. Samuel McSpedden—Mr. Donnell's Reply—From Rev. Thomas Calhoun.

MR. DONNELL TO REV. JAMES KIRKLAND.

NASHVILLE, TENN., June 10, 1846.

BROTHER KIRKLAND:—I have occupied our pulpit here for the last few days and nights. Congregations have not been large, owing in part, I suppose, to the volunteers for the war with Mexico being encamped near the city, and leaving almost every day for the field of contest.

I hope the war is over—at least, on our frontier. General Taylor may carry it into the enemy's country, and even into the City of Mexico.

The people here have laid out for me work enough for several strong preachers. They forget that the infirmities of age are upon me.

I cannot leave Lebanon at the time of which you speak, and be absent till after the camp-meeting in Limestone. I try, however, to remember the churches and people there in almost every prayer.

Have as little to do as possible with ——. Controversy is their element. They study nothing else.

Take from them their "hobby," and they have but little to say in the pulpit. Out-preach, out-pray and out-live their preachers, and you will have nothing to fear from them.

But I have so many calls to make in the city, that I cannot write more now.

R. DONNELL.

Rev. James Kirkland.

[Another evidence of Mr. Donnell's unexampled industry in the ministry. Though pressed with the weight of years, and worn down with preaching, &c., in his congregation at Lebanon, we find him in the city of Nashville, in the heat of summer, holding a protracted meeting, and improving a moment while going "from house to house," for the purpose of stirring up the minds of the people on the subject of religion, in dropping a word of counsel to one of his sons in the ministry. Such an example deserves to be placed on permanent record, and transmitted down to the latest period of the church. Its weight and influence will increase as time advances, and generations yet unborn will refer to it as a fit model for imitation.

But how little does the world know or care for such a toilsome life! Even the church fails to appreciate it. Bonfires are kindled in honor of the military hero; and counties and cities are named to perpetuate the memory of the statesman; while he who labors to promote men's eternal interests, is forgotten.]

MR. DONNELL TO HIS WIFE.

LEBANON, TENN., September 1, 1847.

MY DEAR WIFE:—I arrived safely here a few days ago, and in good health; but my bowels have since become deranged, so that I am now scarcely able to sit up. I shall, however, try to get to the country for a short time, and hope to be better. Since my return, we have had a communion. Mrs. Lindsey joined the church, and her husband appeared quite serious.

I wish you to remain in Alabama as long as you feel like it, however lonesome it may be here without you; for I know your presence there is greatly needed. I feel great uneasiness about everything in North Alabama—James, the family, the church, and yourself, all press upon my mind. And then the church here—what is to become of it? I feel that I am unable to perform the labor that ought to be done; but who can be got to relieve me? I think I want to do the will of God, if I can know what that will is.

I feel that I have great cause to mourn over my imperfections, both as a christian and minister of Christ. Neither in the pulpit nor out of it, am I what I should be. May the Lord hide my weaknesses and sins from His pure eyes, by the merits of his Son.

My love to James, and family, and brethren generally. Tell my servants that I love all who love the Lord Jesus. I hope to receive a letter from you soon.

Your affectionate husband,

R. DONNELL.

MRS. CLARISSA N. DONNELL.

[The complaint of Mr. Donnell, as expressed in view of his imperfections, is characteristic of a true christian. The man of the world knows nothing of such a feeling. If he renders any attention to his heart at all, it is to plead his frailties as an excuse for his sins. A christian's great difficulty is with his heart. " He hates vain thoughts." The very thought of evil, though checked in a moment, gives him pain.

In the performance of religious duty, the true christian finds in himself much cause for self-accusation, and for the adoption of the prayer of the Psalmist, "Cleanse thou me from secret faults." Though sincere in his attempt to worship God, he feels that he is far below that standard of devotion described in the Bible. Paradoxical, too, as it may seem, just in proportion to a christian's progress in the divine life does he become conscious of his imperfections. As a knowledge of God increases, and he approaches the divine perfections, and beholds their glory shining around him, he understands more perfectly, and feels what David meant when he said, "I remembered God, and was troubled." Ignorance led the Pharisee to say, " God, I thank thee that I am not as other men;" while knowledge prompted Paul to exclaim, "Oh, wretched man that I am!"]

MR. DONNELL TO REV. DR. BEARD.

LEBANON, TENN., September 1, 1847.

DEAR BROTHER:—Your letter of the 30th ult., was received on my return from North Alabama to this place.

21—

I hope you will go on and write the history of our church, and that you will also publish a volume containing a selection from your sermons and addresses. Such a book would be bought and read with interest by the church. Our own preachers must write for our own people. Parents know best how to nurse and correct their own children. I am still hoping to find time to revise and enlarge my " Miscellaneous Thoughts."

We have lately lost a very promising candidate for the ministry—brother B. Foster. He expected to go to Texas this fall; but God, in His providence, has seen fit to call him from the church below to the church above.

My own health is not good at present. Mrs. Donnell is in Alabama, and the scattered and deranged state of my family gives me much concern.

R. DONNELL.

REV. R. BEARD, D.D.

MR. DONNELL TO D. LOWRY.

LEBANON, TENN., October 27, 1848.

DEAR BROTHER :—Your letter of the 29th of August last, was duly received, and ought to have been answered ere this; but I have been very busy, and absent part of the time since it was received.

The University has resumed its duties with fine prospects, and the Female Academy has a larger number of students than was expected.

I have preached here but seldom recently, and seen but few of the members of the church. There have, however, been some conversions lately, and a few accessions to the church. We have had, in many parts of the country, glorious revivals of religion this year; and I think our ministers and people are waking up. Our Synod will meet here in next month, and we may hold a protracted meeting then, if the Lord will.

My old Tennessee Presbytery met last week. I was at the meeting. Most of the members were present, and congregations generally represented. The Lord has done a great work in the bounds of that Presbytery this year.

I attended a camp-meeting, in August, near Winchester. The Lord was present, and we had a good meeting.

I have just written to brother Bird, who wishes to publish "Miscellaneous Thoughts," that I have no time to enlarge the work now, as has been requested; but that I would endeavor to collect and revise some of my doctrinal pieces, that have appeared in the papers, which he might add; and that if I live, and have time, I will enlarge the work hereafter. I wish you were here to counsel and aid me. I never was so busy in all my life. You ought to be here. The people expect you. I shall have to be absent in the winter, at least several weeks.

Write me soon.

R. DONNELL.

Rev. D. Lowry.

MR. DONNELL TO REV. M. BIRD, D.D.

ATHENS, ALA., November 12, 1851.

DEAR BROTHER:—I have been unusually busy for several months past, so that I had neither time nor place to write to my friends. I have at length got my house finished, and a comfortable room to study in; but am still scarce of time.

I am pleased to hear of the prospects of old Cumberland college, and hope to be able soon to afford it a little pecuniary aid. At present, I am obliged to give to my means another direction.

You assumed a heavy responsibility in becoming the President of that institution; but I hope a bright prospect of usefulness is before you, and that the college over which you preside will be the means of much good, not only to the cause of religion generally, but to our church in particular.

I am not able to labor much now, but am pleased to see and hear of others laboring. As years increase, I feel more and more concerned for the prosperity of the church. I think I have learned more fully than ever the import of the words, "The zeal of thy house hath eaten me up."

I trust our Book concern will do well. Yourself and others ought to write books and tracts for publication. Our church needs reading matter from the pens of its own ministers.

The congregation here want to procure a preacher. A new and comfortable house of worship will soon be completed; but we have no preacher to occupy the pulpit. Can you tell us where one of fair talents can be obtained? Let me hear from you soon. A letter from you will always be welcome.

R. DONNELL.

Rev. M. Bird, D.D.

REV. SAMUEL McSPEDDEN TO MR. DONNELL.

MOUNTAIN CREEK, TENN., January 5, 1854.

DEAR BROTHER DONNELL:—In your obituary of Bro. Bell, you speak of Kirkpatrick, Porter, Calhoun and McSpedden as your seniors in the ministry. Permit me to correct a small mistake in that statement. *I* am not older than you in the ministry, though your senior in age. I was an elder of Big Spring congregation, and a representative in Presbytery at that place, when you were licensed to preach, and remember well the remark of Mr. Ewing on the discourse you read. He said it was a very short sermon for so long a man, and a very little sermon for so large a man.

I was not licensed till the last meeting of Cumberland Presbytery, when it was divided, and Nashville, Logan and Elk Presbyteries formed. The name Cumberland Presbytery was changed to Nashville Presbytery. Your brother Samuel was licensed at the same time.

By the blessing of God, my health has been very good for the last two years, until about five weeks ago, when a fall from a horse, I fear, rendered me a cripple for life. I am, however, able to sit up and walk about my room, but suffering very much in my back, shoulders and breast.

In addition to this affliction, my voice, for the last four years, has been almost entirely gone, so that I have not preached, and rarely been able to pray in public, or speak above a whisper.

But, I thank God, I can still enjoy the pleasure of reading, and secret devotion; and love occasionally to put my thoughts on paper.

The late discussion in our church on the subject of faith, has called up some reflections. The point debated was, whether it be proper to call faith, in the language of our Confession, " the gift of God?" Now, I have ever regarded faith as *an act;* but that the sinner never would believe in Christ without Divine influence. Repentance is also an act, or a series of acts, put forth by the mind; yet it is said to be a *gift;* and as repentance and faith both take place on the same principle, so far as philosophy of mind is concerned, I can see no more impropriety in calling faith " the gift of God," than repentance.

But the subject of revising or changing our Confession of Faith has also been discussed in the papers of the church. This has, from the first, been to me a source of much anxiety; for should it be attempted, I confidently expect a division in the church. What your views are on the subject, I know not; but you may rest assured most of the Presbyteries in our Synod will oppose it. I hope and pray that the Confession of Faith may remain as it is. I am sure this would be the wish of Ewing and King, and McAdow and McGee, were they alive.

I was, not long ago, severely tried on the score of my personal religion, under the following circumstances: There was a good Methodist circuit-rider, who had several preaching places near me, which I was in the habit of attending, and enjoyed as I thought the sweet comforts of religion. On one occasion, unusual power seemed to attend his preaching, and christians became very happy. Tears of joy flowed freely, and some shouted. I for a time rejoiced with them. But at length the thought occurred : " these people have religion, and are happy ; but with you it is mere sympathy." In a moment, I felt miserable, left the house and went home, and have had many dark hours since ; but feel now a stronger evidence of my acceptance with God, than I have since the meeting alluded to.

It is very probable that my few remaining days will be attended with much pain of body, and confinement at home. Be it so, if it will " work out that exceeding weight of glory," of which the Apostle speaks.

SAMUEL McSPEDDEN.

REV. R. DONNELL.

———

MR. DONNELL TO REV. SAMUEL McSPEDDEN.

ATHENS, ALA., January 12, 1854.

DEAR BROTHER :—Your letter of the 5th instant, was received yesterday, and it was like cool water to a thirsty soul. Very lately, the impression has been strong on my mind to write you, but I have been indisposed for the last five or six months, and my correspondence has consequently been much neglected. I am, I hope, better, but not able to preach, and scarcely able to write. Hard preaching in the open air at campmeetings, &c., has perhaps brought on a disease, from which I shall never recover. Although the evening of life has come, and my labors probably ended, I fear I have done but little good; but I think I tried to give my time, &c., to God; and had I my life to dispose of again, I would cheerfully spend it in His service. I have come through great affliction, and met with many trials; still, God's mercies have outnumbered them all.

On the subject of revising our Confession of Faith, to which you allude, I have to say that I am satisfied with it as it is. It is not perfect, no more than any other human production, and perhaps some would like to have a few phrases altered; but while the change would please them, it might displease others. Our system of doctrine is fully set forth in the book, taking all its parts together: and we have adopted it as it is, and had better let it alone. Thus far, the Lord has been with us, and I trust He will be with us to the end.

You and I can look back to the period when the church was unknown. We saw the bright morning that gave it birth; were acquainted with its struggles in infancy, and its prosperity in riper years. Oh, how humble we ought to be! We are not able to labor

now; but others have taken the field, and Cumberlandism is still prospering.

The Lord saw, in 1800, that a more conservative
system of doctrine than was then extant, was needed,
and therefore raised up in this great valley the Cumberland Presbyterian church to introduce that system.
May our church never let go her distinctive system,
nor lose sight of the end to which she was appointed.

I am pleased with your views of faith. It is the
creature's act; but the ability by which the act is performed is of God, and without which the act would
not take place. We are, therefore, debtors to free
grace for that ability.

You speak of trials. Who is without them? It
would seem that we are old enough to know something of the wiles of the devil; but he is older and
wiser than we are, and knows how to adapt his temptations to our peculiar circumstances. Let us try to
meet him with "the whole armor of God." Then we
shall be able to stand in the evil day.

Let us exchange letters often. My contemporaries
in the ministry are nearly all gone, and I am as a
stranger in a strange land. A letter from one who
was the companion of my youth, and who has labored
with me in middle and old age in the ministry, will
always give me pleasure.

I desire much to attend our General Assembly next
May, in Memphis, but fear I shall not be able.

R. DONNELL.

Rev. Samuel McSpedden.
22—

[Mr. McSpedden is still living, and as the reader will see, has furnished me valuable aid in preparing this Memoir; but is not able to preach. He is, however, much revered and respected by all who know him, and takes great delight in visiting the house of God, and especially in attending the judicatures of the church. He seldom fails to answer to his name at Presbytery, and to participate in the business. He has still sufficient physical strength to preach; but, as he states in his letter to Mr. Donnell, has lost his voice so that he cannot speak above a whisper. The hard and protracted labor which this minister has done in the church, will long be remembered on earth, and never be forgotten in heaven.

Since writing the above, I see Mr. McSpedden's death announced in the *"Banner of Peace."*]

REV. THOMAS CALHOUN, SR., TO MR. DONNELL.

[*Without date.*]

DEAR BROTHER DONNELL:—It is now about fifty years since we began to worship God together, and wrestle with him in prayer. We were then young, and able to work in His vineyard. When reviewing the past, I have often been astonished at the amount of labor we have performed. Surely God was with us by His supporting grace, or we could not have endured the toils through which we have come.

I am not able to preach much now; but I attend the

house of God regularly, and occasionally exhort, and administer the ordinances, and hope to find work in the church suited to the evening of life.

But the main object of this letter is to call your attention to the subject of revising our Confession of Faith. Some good brethren, you know, have been writing on that subject, and seem to think it indispensable to the prosperity of the church. My own opinion is, that should it be done, it will divide the church; and I look to you, as you were one of the compilers of our book, to interpose your influence against this measure. The churches, so far as I know, are satisfied with our Confession of Faith as it is, and if let alone, would never think of revision. I have confidence in you, that you will do what you honestly believe to be right in this matter, and hope you will look over the whole ground, and consider the subject in all its bearings.

You are aware that our General Assembly will meet in the city of Nashville. As the place of meeting is in the vicinity of most of the first preachers of our church, who are still living, I hope they will be present, and that *you* will be among them. Will you urge brother Bell to come? I shall not be a member, but will endeavor to attend.

Everything that is kind to your dear wife, and for yourself the best wishes of an old brother,

THOMAS CALHOUN.

REV. R. DONNELL.

CHAPTER XV.

SELECT THOUGHTS.

Theology and Philosophy—The Decrees of God—Difference between God's Fore-knowledge and Decrees—On the Trinity—on the Holy Scriptures.

THEOLOGY AND PHILOSOPHY.

THEOLOGY teaches the nature and character of God and his operations on the rational and moral universe; while mental philosophy teaches the nature of rational and moral beings, and how far their powers extend. Theology presents God as the creator, preserver and governor of man—having a right to his services, and to dispose of him according to immutable principles of rectitude. It also teaches what God has done, and is now doing, that man may be saved. Philosophy teaches what man can and must do in order to be saved. If our theology teach the operations of God on or in man, in such a way as to destroy his free agency, that theology is wrong. If our philosophy teach that man has power to save himself, independent of Divine influence, that philosophy is wrong.

Some men study theology before they study philosophy, and then make the latter bend to the former. Others arrange their system of mental philosophy first, but fall into errors equally as fatal, by making their theology yield to it.

Much of the theology and philosophy of the present day have doubtless been gathered from the pagan world. The ancient heathen generally believed in a plurality of gods, and placed all the passions and actions of men under their control, and thereby closed the door effectually against all reformation—for a sinner will not reform till made to feel guilty, and he cannot feel guilty while he believes his heart and life are under the sovereign control of the gods. Another extreme among the heathen, was the belief that man controlled his own actions and destiny, independent of the gods; and that whatever he made of himself, the gods are entitled to neither praise nor blame for it.

Now, whether we believe in one God, or many gods, we are but little removed from heathen theology and philosophy, while we embrace systems that involve errors akin to theirs. To believe that God so governs the world as to make every volition and action of man the result of a *Divine* efficiency, or that, after creating mankind, and establishing fixed laws, he retired to a state of inactivity, leaving these laws to execute themselves, and man to form his own character, and secure his own happiness without Divine aid, or direct influence of the Holy Ghost, is nothing more nor less than a religion of paganism.

THE DECREES OF GOD.

By the decrees of God, I understand his predetermined purposes or appointments. Rational beings are always influenced in their actions by motives. God,

therefore, in all his decrees, must have acted in view
of motives. A being, self-sufficient and independent,
never can go out of himself for a motive to action ;
hence our Catechism says, " He according to the counsel of his own will hath foreordained to bring to pass,"
&c. The glory of God constitutes the highest motive
to action that can be presented ; and he always con-
templates the happiness of his creatures, when it can
be secured, on the principles of good government. All
the volitions of God must be holy, like himself ; therefore, sin among his creatures can never be to him an
object of choice or desire, and, of course, could not be
decreed.

That man should exist, was an object of choice and
desire with God ; that he should exist, just as he was,
in his primitive state ; but the fall of Adam constituted
no part of the Divine decree—it was the result of
man's own free choice, uninfluenced by any act on the
part of his Creator. God chose, or ordained, to give
man a second probation, by the appointment of a mediator. This he did upon sovereign principles. He
might have punished the first transgressor without
mercy, but he did not choose so to do. He forbid man
to sin, and it would be incompatible with his nature to
forbid what he desired to have man do, or to command
that which he did not wish to be done. The idea that
God has a *secret* and *revealed* will, opposite to each
other, in reference to the same thing, has no foundation in truth. It is equally absurd to suppose that a

holy God could choose disobedience, rather than obedience, among his creatures. But it may be asked, Had not God power to prevent sin from entering into his universe; and did not a neglect to exert that power imply a desire that it should enter? It will be a sufficient answer to this inquiry to say, that God does not choose to govern mind, as he does matter, by mere physical force. No one could suppose the Ten Commandments adapted to govern the planetary system, or that the laws by which those heavenly bodies are regulated, should be imposed on mind. God's physical and moral government must never be confounded.

THE DIFFERENCE BETWEEN GOD'S FOREKNOWLEDGE AND DECREES.

Knowledge is a perfection of the Divine Being; decree is an act of his will. The Bible settles the question as to whether knowledge is founded on decree, or decree on knowledge. "For whom he did foreknow he also did predestinate," &c., (Rom. viii: 29.) According to Paul, God did not decree and then know, but he knew and then decreed. His knowledge is infinite, but his decrees are limited to certain events and things. He must know all he does, but he need not necessarily do all he knows. Everything that God purposes and does, has holiness stamped upon it; but many things have not this image, therefore they do not belong to the divine operations. *"An enemy hath done this."*

ON THE TRINITY.

I wish to offer a few practical remarks on the doctrine of the Holy Trinity:

1. A knowledge of God is indispensable to true religion. "This is life eternal, that they might know THEE, the only true God, and Jesus Christ, whom thou hast sent." The doctrine of the Trinity can only be learned from the Sacred Scriptures. Here we find many passages, to which no rational interpretation can be given, without admitting the doctrine in question.

2. Those who believe, and those who reject the Trinity, must worship different gods. The character of the DEITY we worship, must give character to the devotion rendered. If the doctrine of the Trinity be true, those who deny it do not worship the God of the Bible, and, of course, are guilty of idolatry. It cannot, therefore, be a matter of small moment whether we believe the doctrine of the Trinity or not.

3. He who denies the doctrine of the Trinity, denies the doctrine of the atonement of Christ, and consequently must regard sin as a mere trifle. This may account for the fact that in every age where the unity of God in opposition to the Trinity has been taught, infidelity has expressed much friendship for the system. There must be something in it agreeable to the carnal heart, and contrary to the word of God.

ON THE HOLY SCRIPTURES.

A book which teaches, as the Bible does, a system of morals and religion so pure and elevated in their nature, so honoring to God, and so well calculated to meet all the wants of man, must be more than a human production. It must be Divine.

He who excludes God and the Bible from his creed, must be in theory a deist, in experience a pagan, and in practice an atheist.

CHAPTER XVI.

SELECT THOUGHTS.—CONTINUED.

The Doctrinal Position of Cumberland Presbyterians—A few Theological Questions and Answers—A Thought on Romans vi: 11—On the Will of Man.

CALVINISM and Armenianism have long been taught as systems of theology. Either creed contains truth enough to save the world; but rivalry and collision have always paralyzed the usefulness of both Calvinists and Armenians. A medium system, therefore, seemed to be necessary—combining the excellencies, and excluding the errors, of the other two. Baxter felt the importance of such a system; so did the Tennents and New School Presbyterians; but all failed in their attempts to form such a system. This responsible work was, in the Providence of God, assigned to Cumberland Presbyterians, and their Confession of Faith shows how far they have succeeded. Dr. Bascom once said, in conversation with me, that "Cumberland Presbyterians could do what no other church could—unite the christian world."

Armenianism embraced in its creed an atonement as broad in its provision as the wants of mankind, and a divine influence co-extensive with the atonement. This article of faith Cumberland Presbyterians have adopted. The doctrine of "passing by" a portion of the human race, and "foreordaining them to dishonor and wrath," as taught by Calvinism, Cumberland Presbyterians have rejected. They have embodied in their system the final perseverance of the saints, a sentiment found in the Calvinistic platform, but do not connect it with eternal and unconditional election, as does the Presbyterian Confession of Faith. It is connected with faith in Christ. "*After that ye believed, ye were sealed with the Holy Spirit of promise.*" (*Eph. i: 13.*)

Cumberland Presbyterianism, it is thought, commends itself more *readily* and *directly* to the judgment and conscience than any other scheme of doctrine. Our Calvinistic and Armenian brethren may be appealed to on this subject: On what doctrines do they rely with most confidence to produce revivals of religion, or to encourage and promote them when in progress? Not on a limited atonement; not on eternal and unconditional election and reprobation, as taught in the Westminster Confession of Faith; nor yet on that of falling from grace, as held by our Armenian brethren.

Our system also accords more fully with christian experience, than either of the creeds alluded to. Every christian, when first converted, feels that salvation is free for all men; nor would it enhance his happiness to be informed that he is yet liable to fall from grace, and be lost. A disposition, too, to commune at the Lord's table, with all his people, is felt by every new-born soul. It may be safely asserted, therefore, that the entire Cumberland Presbyterian *system* has its foundation in the nature of true religion.

The system of doctrine taught by our church, has thus far met with unexampled success. When first organized, she had barely preachers enough to form a Presbytery, and a membership not exceeding 1,000. Now she numbers about as many preachers as her laity then amounted to, and her congregations have multiplied till her membership has reached 100,000—all in less than half a century._ Add to the present living members, the thousands that have died in the church below and joined the church above, and you have a brief view of the short but successful career of Cumberland Presbyterians. Should they continue to increase in proportion to their numerical strength, for the next fifty years, as they have done up to the present time, who can estimate the brightness of the future that is before them? The next generation of Cumberland Presbyterian ministers and members may save a million of souls.

A FEW THEOLOGICAL QUESTIONS AND ANSWERS.

Q. What constitutes the rule of action to created intelligences?

A. The will of God.

Q. What constitutes the rule of action to God?

A. His own holiness.

Q. Does the will of God alone constitute everything right that he wills?

A. He wills a thing, because it is right. The simple act of choice, without holiness, as a rule of action, could not make a thing chosen right.

Q. But is it not written, " He worketh all things after the counsel of his own will?"

A. Yes; but it is also written, "Shall not the judge of all the earth do right?" "The Lord our God is holy in all his ways, and righteous in all his works." His will operates independent of his creatures, but not independent of his holiness. He could not, therefore, will sin into the world; the holiness of his nature forbids such volition.

A THOUGHT ON ROMANS VI: 11.

" Likewise reckon ye also yourselves to be dead indeed unto sin ; but alive unto God through Jesus Christ our Lord."

Paul in this chapter confirms the doctrine taught in the preceding chapter, viz: that salvation is by grace through faith, and that this doctrine, so far from leading to licentiousness, stimulates to good works. In view of this great cardinal truth, the Apostle propounds the question, " How shall we, that are dead to sin, live any longer therein?" It is every way important to understand the nature of the relation sustained by the christian to Christ. His sufferings and death met the claims of the law; and when a sinner believes in him, faith receives that which meets the demands of divine justice, and releases the believer from condemnation. He becomes identified, in view of law, with Christ.

After satisfying the law, Jesus Christ rose from the dead, to die no more; so the believer, being raised from spiritual death, dies no more *spiritually*, but "walks in newness of life." He can never fall back into his former state of condemnation. " He that believeth on him that sent me, hath everlasting life, and shall not come into condemnation, but is passed from death unto life." (*John v : 24.*)

The sentiment is universally received, that our bodies shall be raised by virtue of Christ's resurrection, and when raised, can die no more; so a soul, raised from death to life, cannot again die. The Bible gives no account of a *second* spiritual resurrection.

So close and permanent is the christian's connection with Christ, that the believer is said to be a "member of his flesh and of his bones;" and that his "life"— spiritual life—"is hid with Christ in God," and that none shall be "able" to "pluck" that sacred deposit from the position in which it is placed.

ON THE WILL OF MAN.

Man is a compound being, possessing a soul and body. The body is material and divisible, but complete in its organization. The soul is a spiritual, immaterial substance, and though comprising several faculties, it is a unit and indivisible. Matter, however sublimated, refined and divided, is matter still.

The union of soul and body constitutes human identity, or is the distinctive characteristic of human nature. This, however, does not preclude the idea that soul and body possess each a separate identity. The soul, though immaterial, may be approached through the senses of the body. It is likewise susceptible of impressions from God, independent of physical organization. Its powers are intellectual and moral. The intellectual perceives, judges, and chooses; the moral loves, hates, &c. The intellectual, however, governs the moral in matters of choice.

Mind possesses a positive moral character. An accountable being cannot exist in a negative state; there must be an inclination either to good or evil. But that inclination does not *necessitate* choice. When man was created, his inclination was to good, for he was made upright; but he was nevertheless free, and could and did choose evil, contrary to the inclination to holiness with which God had created him, and thereby became corrupt and sinful. As Adam chose evil before he lost his purity of heart, so man, now placed as he is under an economy of grace and divine influence, can "choose life" before his heart is changed, and depravity removed; or, in other words, a sinner can seek regeneration before he is regenerated.

To be accountable, man must be free; he must possess determining power over volition and action. His choice must not be *necessitated* by any other agent or inherent quality of nature, nor yet by an overbalance of motive. Adam received his moral quality of soul from God, but fell and became corrupt. We inherit his depravity, but placed as we are under an economy of grace, we are not compelled to choose evil.

[It will be seen, that the position here assumed by Mr. Donnell, with regard to the will of man, places the power that determines volition *in the mind*, and not *out of it*. He discards the "divine *efficiency*" scheme, which is, that God, by a direct agency, determines the will of man, either to good or evil. This was the theory of Drs. West, Hopkins, Emmons, and others, who held that the human mind cannot act any more than matter can move, without a divine agency acting upon it. This is one of the cardinal points in Hopkinsianism. True, the distinguished Hopkinsian writers use the phrases, "power to choose," "liberty," &c., when speaking of volition, that Mr. Donnell would but attach to these words quite a different meaning. When they speak of the mind's power to act, they mean what Mr. Locke calls "passive power"—a *susceptibility* to be acted upon. When they speak of the mind being the author of its own actions, they mean that the will *chooses*, when acted upon by an "*extrinsic efficiency*." Dr. West says: "Men may be said to have powers of will," &c., as they are subjects fitted to have certain "effects take place in them, or as they are adapted to receive or to be subjects of that kind of influence which is the cause of human will." He further illustrates, by representing "air as being fitted to receive an influence," that expands or compresses it. It is the air that *expands or contracts;* but the power that acts upon it is the cause of it. So the mind acts in choosing, as the air in expanding, &c., when acted upon. (*See Christian Spectator, Vol. 8, No. 1, p. 173.*) Mr. Donnell regarded this theory of the will as unphilosophical and absurd, destroying man's accountability, and making God the author of sin.

He also rejected the theory of Mr. Edwards, that the will is "determined by motive." This he regarded as differing from the Hopkinsian theory only in appearance, not in reality. To place the *efficient* cause of volition *in motive*, and *that motive* under the control and power of an agency, outside and independent of the mind, is substantially the same as putting the will under the control of *divine efficiency*, for God is still the agent, acting upon the mind through the instrumentality of motives, and without whose agency the motives could have no influence.

While Mr. Donnell admitted the connection of volition with motives and surrounding circumstances, he denied that their power over the will was *absolute* and irresistible; but maintained that they were mere occasions of volition, without necessitating the mind to act in any particular direction. This power, or liberty of choice in man's primitive state, was a derived power, imparted at his creation, and was distinct from his dependence as a creature upon God for his continuance in being. Many writers have confounded man's dependence upon his Maker as a free moral agent, with his dependence for a physical existence.]

24—

CHAPTER XVII.

SELECT THOUGHTS.—CONTINUED.

On Saving Faith—Practical Religion—They were of One Heart, &c.—
Pastoral Visitation—The Fathers and Founders of the Cumberland
Presbyterian Church—Infant Baptism—The Widow's Two Mites—
The Gospel of Christ—Prayer—On the Death of Rev. W. McGee.

ON SAVING FAITH.

1. "FAITH in Jesus Christ, is assenting to the truths
of the Gospel. 2. Consenting to the terms of the Gospel. 3. A reliance on, and confidence in, the promises
of the Gospel. It is yielding to the instructions of
Christ as a Prophet, accepting the atonement he has
made as a Priest, and submitting to him as a King.
Faith does not constitute a justifying righteousness,
but receives a justifying righteousness wrought by
Christ. Faith simply receives what is done for us. It
does not result from, nor depend on, regeneration. It
has its own work to do, and must not be confounded
with its antecedents or sequents. It is called a grace,
because a sinner could not and would not believe without the light and influence of the Holy Ghost. Faith
is entering into covenant with Christ. Justification,
adoption, regeneration, sanctification and glorification,
are blessings embraced in the covenant, and are sequents of faith. The influences of the Spirit, and
means employed to awaken the sinner to a sense of

guilt, &c., are antecedents of faith. Faith itself is a simple act of the mind, giving itself away to Christ for time and eternity. We are indebted to the Spirit for aid in believing, and to Christ for the blessings bestowed after believing."

[I have never seen a better definition of faith, than is here given by Mr. Donnell. He makes it more than a mere assent of the mind, that "Jesus is the Son of God." He was also a firm believer in the imputed righteousness of Christ, as the ground of a sinner's justification. He also rejected the sentiment that regeneration *precedes* faith in Christ, as taught by Calvinistic writers. He shows, too, very clearly, in what sense faith is to be understood as "the gift of God." His view differs widely from Calvin, who taught that not only "the ability to believe" is given by Divine agency, but "faith itself."—*Inst., Vol. 2, p. 181.*]

PRACTICAL RELIGION.

This is the religion the world needs. Fruit, in accordance with profession, is called for. The church is praying, "Thy kingdom come," &c. This is right, for we are taught so to pray by Christ. We ought to be, in great earnest, ardently desiring the cause of the Redeemer to prosper. But prayer is not all that is required to advance the kingdom of Christ. Various other means are enjoined. The Gospel is to be sent to destitute portions of our own country, and to the heathen world.

For what should christians desire to live, and how can they best promote the great design of their existence? I suppose all will say, we ought not to live to ourselves, but to the glory of Him who died for us. This is just what the Bible teaches; and can we think of any object so glorious and important as living for Christ? Is not this just what we said we would do when we gave our hearts to Him? Think of that memorable moment, when near despair, beyond the reach of help from man, and feeling that God alone could save! When deliverance came, did we not lay our all at the feet of Jesus—time, talents, influence, substance, were all at his command—and how happy were we in this surrender! Now, if these feelings are realized by all christians at conversion, ought not their practical influence to be seen in after life?—and without such development, are we not liable to the charge of inconsistency? Can any man make the world believe that he is in earnest, and that he is a christian in heart and principle, when he is not willing to deny himself, and make sacrifices for Jesus Christ?

What would be thought of a man, in this day of political excitement, who would expect to be highly honored by the President of the United States by some gift of office, though he is doing nothing to promote his election? How, then, can the professed followers of Christ expect to be rewarded by him at the close of an inactive life? But to labor for the salvation of souls, should be looked at in the light of a great privilege, and not as a burden. The feelings and views of those are not to be envied, who complain when God presents work for them to do. How unlike the spirit of Christ, who, though he was rich, yet for our sakes he became poor, that we, through his poverty, might be rich! Oh, how low is the standard of piety in the church! How shall christians be stirred up to live for Christ, to send the Gospel to the ends of the earth?

THEY WERE OF ONE HEART AND ONE SOUL.

This was emphatically true of the first christian church. All were interested for the cause of religion, and labored to promote it.

I remember well when this spirit was more prevalent among Cumberland Presbyterians, than it is now. They were then few in number, and of one mind, and all at work. When people are lawfully employed, they are apt to be united, for they feel that there is no time for disputation. It is the idle professor of religion that engenders strife in the church. A single idle member or minister can do more harm, by producing faction in the fold of Christ, than half a dozen faithful christians can remove.

Let us then all go to work in the right cause, and in the right way, and we shall be a united and happy people. Our field of labor is large, and white unto the harvest, affording work enough for all to do. The present condition of the church and world ought to be sufficient to call forth our energies, and stimulate all

to christian effort.   Waste places of Zion at home need
building up, and the heathen are perishing abroad.
"Oh, that my head were waters, and mine eyes a fountain of tears, that I might weep day and night for the
slain of the daughter of my people."

PASTORAL VISITATION.

It is the duty of a pastor to see the people of his
charge, at their respective homes, as well as at the
house of God. The pulpit is his chief but not his only
place of usefulness. A good physician will watch the
effects of his medicine upon his patients; so a good
pastor will try to ascertain, by personal interview, the
impressions his sermons make upon the minds of his
hearers. Some preachers have less skill and taste for
this kind of labor than others; but whether possessing
two or five talents, the gift should be improved, and
this department of service faithfully attended to.

Pastoral visits should be frequent, and never confounded with social calls. Too many, having the name
of pastors, pay nothing but social visits to their flocks,
spend their time in light and worldly conversation, and
then depart, without prayer, or saying a word on the
subject of religion. Such a visit would not be strange
from a doctor or lawyer, or a mere politician in search
of votes; but it will not do for a minister of Jesus
Christ, professedly laboring to save souls.

THE FATHERS AND FOUNDERS OF OUR CHURCH.

Fathers McGee, McAdow, Ewing and King are no

more. Their preaching, and prayers, and tears, are still remembered, but their voices are no longer heard. They planted many churches, and laid a good foundation on which others are building. May those who have succeeded them, be as faithful in watering, as our fathers were in planting, churches. They were prominent instruments in the great revival of 1800—which, though it began in that year, is still progressing, and affecting, more or less, all the churches of the United States, and even in Europe its influence is felt, to some extent.

INFANT BAPTISM.

We have often been most solemnly impressed with the beauty of the scene, while witnessing the consecration of an infant, by christian parents, to the Lord Jesus Christ. The minister, in the holy name of the Trinity, applies the sacramental water, and then the whole congregation unite with him in prayer for the child thus dedicated to God. What a privilege to live in christendom, and to be born of christian parents, and to have the fervent prayers of the church recorded before the throne of grace in early childhood!

We have often thought, too, of the fearful responsibility of parents who thus offer their infant offspring to God. They thereby give them up to Him, and virtually declare that, above all things next to their own personal salvation, they desire the salvation of their children. And as it is on their moral culture their eternal happiness so much depends, they promise that they will endeavor to employ all the means for their religious education that may be in their power.

Though we most sincerely believe in the doctrine of infant baptism, and would not only defend it, but urge it upon all the members of our church, yet we are far from believing that parents have discharged their whole duty to their children, when they have had them baptized. But baptism is the commencement of parental duty, and should be followed up by a faithful discharge of other obligations. Where this is neglected, the covenant is practically denied, and parents have no assurance that God will be a God to their children. If the children of such parents are saved at all, it will be through the influences and instruction of others.

THE WIDOW'S TWO MITES.

We learn from this narrative, that our Lord has a treasury upon earth, and that it is the duty of every one of Adam's family, rich and poor, to put something into that treasury. There is no man so poor, if he has health and is able to work, but may have something to give to promote the cause of truth. The Lord's treasury is raised, and is to be expended by the church for the advancement of the kingdom of Christ. God designs the earth to help the woman. The gold and silver are His, as well as the cattle on a thousand hills.

I am aware, that some think the church should have nothing to do with the management of money; that her work is purely spiritual, &c. If she was not in this world, and did not need instrumentalities, there would be some plausibility in this sentiment. But it cost the church a great deal of money or property to inform the world that Christ *was* coming to seek and save the lost. It will cost a great deal more to tell the world that he *has* come, and is ready to save sinners. The church must have much to do with money, both for religious and educational purposes.

THE GOSPEL OF CHRIST.

The Gospel is a remedy for the evils introduced by sin. The existence of sin is seen in its effects, and those effects show that their cause could not have originated in God. The Gospel also produces wonderful effects, and the nature of those effects proves that a sinful world did not originate the Gospel. Created agency, by an abuse of derived power, introduced sin. Divine agency, upon the principle of sovereign love, introduced the Gospel. In the fall of man, no redeeming qualities were left in his nature; he could destroy, but was unable to help himself. But in the Gospel, a redeeming power is published; hence it is called glad tidings of great joy to all people.

The Gospel, as a provisional system, proposes a remedy to all men for all the evils that sin has introduced. It publishes an election of all men to a day of grace, or to a second probation in Christ—"chosen in Christ *before the foundation of the world.*" It also publishes a full and complete atonement for all mankind, together

25—

with Divine influence sufficient to enable all men to embrace the offers of mercy. This election to a day of grace is general and unconditioned. There is a second election, however, which is personal and conditional, embracing the believer only. The first election is to a state of trial; the second is to a state of glory.

The Gospel sustains every principle of the Divine government. The law is not brought down in its claims to suit man's fallen nature, but man is elevated by virtue of the atonement, and the operations of the Spirit to the holiness of the law. The Gospel is an administration of the law in a way of mercy through a mediator. The principles of the law are not changed, only in their mode of administration.

PRAYER.

Some have supposed that prayer for others is of no avail, unless the persons prayed for hear the prayer. But we are not to pray to be heard of men, but to be heard of God; and God commands us to pray for all men, whether they be present or absent.

ON THE DEATH OF REV. W. McGEE.

Our beloved brother McGee is dead. The spirit from the body has fled. The silver cord and golden bowl are broken. Horses and angels were employed at his death—the former bore the body away, the latter carried the soul; the horses moved toward the grave, the angels toward heaven. The body is at rest; but the soul is still employed. One lies in the dust, the other lives with God. But soon the day will come when both shall meet again triumphant in the skies, with Jesus the Lord to reign.

CHAPTER XVIII.

SELECT THOUGHTS.—CONTINUED.

The Atonement—The Church needs more Ministers—This is my Beloved Son, &c.—Unsearchable Riches of Christ.

THE ATONEMENT.

An atonement, in a theological sense, signifies a covering, and always supposes a difference between two parties. In the case of God and man, the latter had offended, and could not be forgiven on the principles of good government without an atonement. Had the offender been disposed to repent—but he was not so disposed—his crimes were too heinous in their character to be forgiven without an atonement. Repentance could, at best, only be regarded as a pledge of obedience in future, but could not serve as an atonement or covering for past disobedience. Man ought never to have trampled on Divine authority; and although he might, by repentance, be restored to a right state of mind for the future, that could not be considered as a ground of pardon of former offenses. If he, therefore, as a sinner, ever be justified in the sight of God, it must be by or through an atonement made by another.

Let us now consider the character requisite to make an atonement. The sins committed were against high authority, and the personage undertaking to repair the breach must possess great dignity of character, so that he may approach acceptably the offended party, and at the same time sympathize with the offender. While he offers an atonement to the offended party, he must have sufficient influence with the offenders to induce them to become reconciled. Moreover, as death was the penalty of the law violated, the person who makes an atonement must possess a body that he may die— voluntarily die. But he must not only die, but be able to rise from the dead, and appear as mediator in the presence of God. Such a personage was the Lord Jesus Christ, who was both God and man, in two distinct natures.

The atonement was made to law, to sustain law; while pardon might be offered to the sinner. Had the sin of man been the result of a Divine decree, it could have been willed out of the world without an atonement. But it was man's voluntary act, uninfluenced by Divine agency; therefore, the law, and not mere sovereignty, required an atonement before pardon could be offered.

A word here on the extent of the atonement. First, the atonement was made for the sin of the world—or Adam's first sin—which was a public or representative sin, rendering the whole race guilty; and therefore the atonement could not be limited to a part of mankind, when all sustained exactly the same relation to the Divine law. The first idea of the atonement, then, is that it was made for a great public offense, which was Adam's sin. But it was also made for all men personally, and for personal sins. "But not as the offense, so also is the free gift: for if through the offense of one many be dead, much more the grace of God, and the gift by grace, which is by one man, Jesus Christ, hath abounded unto many. And not as it was by one that sinned, so is the gift: for the judgment was by one to condemnation, but the free gift is of many offenses unto justification." (*Rom. v : 15, 16.*)

THE CHURCH NEEDS MORE MINISTERS.

But she wants holy ministers who know how to behave themselves in the house of God. Prudent, humble, watchful, faithful, zealous men, who will hazard life, fortune, everything in this world, for the cause of Christ, and the salvation of souls. Men who will preach not themselves, but Christ Jesus the Lord; men whose hearts feel, and eyes weep, when they preach; men who are not afraid to lift up their voice like a trumpet, and show the house of Israel their sins, and warn sinners to flee from the wrath to come; men who will teach publicly and privately, going from house to house, believing and feeling what they teach. Such men, and enough of them, would soon convert the world.

THIS IS MY BELOVED SON, IN WHOM I AM WELL PLEASED.

We are not to understand, when "Son" is applied to Jesus Christ, that his essence or personality in the

Godhead is in any way an effect of the Divine will. This would destroy his equality with the Father, besides involving the absurd idea that *infinity* produced *infinity*. The essence and personality of the Son belong to the being of God; hence we are taught to worship the Son, which would be idolatry were he a mere delegated God, or a God by office.

Perhaps, strictly speaking, the term "Son," as applied to the second person in the Trinity, has reference to the office he fills as mediator, to which he was appointed by the Father. Personality and essence belong to the being of God, while *office* pertains to his operations. We are not to understand, therefore, that the Son, in essence or personality, is *inferior* to the Father, but that he is *subordinate* in office.

As mediator, the Son of God is the only medium of Divine communication with our fallen world. (*I. Tim. ii: 5.*) He is made Head of all things for the church. By and through him, every difficulty in the moral universe is to be adjusted. On entering the office of mediator, it became necessary that flesh should be assumed—that "a body should be prepared." (*Heb. x: 5.*) This was necessary, that he might sustain a personal relation to this world, as well as to the Godhead.

But it is said, the Father is "well pleased in the Son." He is well pleased with his personal identity in the Godhead, and with the relation that he sustains as mediator to this world; and also with the manner in which he filled that important office. He gave his life for the life of the world, and thereby rendered it just for God to pardon sinners who repent and believe. The Father is pleased with the revelation the Son has made to mankind, and with the Divine influence which accompanies the word, and with the terms on which salvation is proposed. The Father is also well pleased with the prospects of the Son's administration, and views the period as near at hand when "all the people shall praise him," and all nations serve him.

UNSEARCHABLE RICHES OF CHRIST.

The unsearchable riches of Christ may be applied to his atonement. The atonement was rich in itself—richer than gold or silver. More precious than rubies is the precious blood of Christ; rich in its provisions. The atonement was made for all Adam's race; made for the whole and every part of the great whole; extending back to the first sin of Adam, and forward to the last sin of his fallen race, both representative and personal. It can save from the deepest hell, and raise to the highest heaven. It embraces the infant of a day, and sinners of a hundred years old.

The riches of Christ are seen in the Divine influence provided to enlighten and convert the world. Under the operations of the Holy Spirit, every sinner *may* be saved.

The unsearchable riches of Christ may also embrace the means of grace. The Bible was given to the world through the intervention of Christ. And what a book!

Think of its doctrines, principles, precepts, promises, all through Christ! Think of the world without the Bible—how dark, and gloomy, and miserable! Add to the Bible the millions of other religious books that have blessed mankind. A living ministry is also produced by Jesus Christ. Their indefatigable labors add efficiency to all other means.

Ask the christian to describe the possessions received through Christ. He speaks of a title to heaven—justification, pardon of sin, regeneration, adoption, the work of sanctification in progress, and finally, a certain prospect of glorification. Christ has not only provided for the believer a title to and qualification for heaven, but grace to sustain him on his way to heaven—strength equal to his day. "Because I live," says Christ, "ye shall also live." Christ is the believer's life, and his life is not derived, for he has life in himself. The fullness of the Godhead dwells in him, and of his fullness have all we received, and grace for grace.

Jesus Christ is rich in power, and will ultimately destroy the works of the devil—even death itself shall be swallowed up in victory, and not a vestige remain. The time will come when neither old man nor child shall be found in the grave. All that are in their graves shall come forth.

CHAPTER XIX.

REMINISCENCES AND GENERAL REFLECTIONS ON THE CHARAC-
TER AND USEFULNESS OF MR. DONNELL.

His Personal Appearance and Social Habits—Physical Constitution—
Intellectual Character—Religious Character—A Christian at Home
—A Peace-maker—Denominational but not Exclusive in his Feelings—Public Spirit and Liberality—A Friend of Education—In Favor of an Educated Ministry—Conduct in reference to Politics.

It was impossible that the personal appearance of
Mr. Donnell would ever be forgotten, after seeing him
in the pulpit. He was a man of large frame, well pro-
portioned, and somewhat inclined to corpulency. His
countenance, though expressive of great intelligence,
was marked rather with a calm dignity and solidity
than vivacity. His eyes, when in repose, presented
the appearance of a slumbering intellect; but in the
heated action of his mind, under excitement, they exhibited, particularly in the pulpit, a dazzling glare, indicating a heart softened under the influence of truth,
and deeply impressed with the importance of the work
in which he was engaged.

His social habits were no less attracting than his
personal appearance. In company, his manner was
easy and pleasant, but always marked with unaffected
dignity.

Dr. T. C. Anderson says: "He was the most unex-

ceptionable model of ministerial propriety I ever knew.
He made no effort to be sociable, impressive or prepossessing. All seemed to be natural and unpremedi-
tated. He was at ease in every circle of society—
never reserved, but always familiar, kind and affectionate. His sympathies embraced all human kind.
Prattling childhood and decrepit age, shared alike his
kind attentions. For the gay, or the serious, the master or the servant, the sage or the simple, he always
had a word in season."

Rev. J. H. Erwin says, that "Mr. Donnell always
took peculiar interest in catechising children, and was
a special favorite with the youth of his acquaintance.
Familiar, yet always preserving a becoming ministerial
gravity, so that young people both loved and revered
him."

Mr. Donnell inherited a sound and vigorous constitution, to which the early training and discipline of
his youth added a firmness and elasticity that rarely
fall to the lot of man. His early days were not passed
in the shade, devoted to ease and pleasure; but on the
farm, for the support of a widowed mother and bereaved sisters.

The early development of his capacity to perform
and endure physical labor, is graphically set forth in
Mr. Doak's letter, published in a former part of this
Memoir. Think of a young man splitting one thous-
and rails in a day! Mr. Doak also says that he built
a grist-mill, with his own hands, without ever having

studied any mechanical profession. This course of discipline developed the physical man, and qualified Mr.
Donnell to endure an amount of labor in the ministry
which astonished all who knew him. For fifty years
in succession, he attended camp-meetings, and upon an
average, not less than twelve each year—preaching
once or twice a day at every meeting, besides praying
with and instructing mourners, exhorting sinners, &c.
Mr. McSpedden says, he has known him to preach four
times, in one day, at a camp-meeting; that on such
occasions his voice was often heard from four to six
hours in the congregation, singing, praying, exhorting, &c. Mr. Donnell, not long before his death, said in
conversation with the Rev. B. C. Chapman, that he had
often labored through a whole camp-meeting almost
entirely without sleep.

Rev. T. C. Anderson says: "The first time I ever
saw Mr. Donnell, was at a camp-meeting. On Sabbath
morning he occupied the pulpit before breakfast, then
at 11 o'clock, and also at 3 o'clock in the evening."
He further states, that "in the fall of 1832, he traveled
with him from his own house to Synod, which met at
Tuscumbia; that he preached twice in one day, on the
journey—at 12 o'clock, then rode twelve miles, and
preached at night." These were not isolated cases in
the history of Mr. Donnell, but of frequent occurrence;
and nothing short of extraordinary physical powers
could have borne such labor.

The intellectual powers of Mr. Donnell were as extraordinary as his physical energies. He was not educated, in the popular acceptation of that term, but by self-directed mental labor, he became a respectable English scholar, and his Biblical knowledge was very profound. It has already been stated that his mother taught him the shorter Catechism of the Presbyterian church, before he was seven years old, and caused him to read the Bible through four times before he reached his twelfth year. When a boy, plowing in the field, he carried his book in his pocket, and when his horse required rest, he employed the time in reading. His leisure moments, by day and night, were devoted to mental culture; and when he set out upon his circuit as a preacher, he carried his books in his saddle-bags, and read and studied in the morning and evening, as well as while riding from one appointment to another. He also had the head of his cane so constructed as to furnish an inkstand, and when a thought occurred, while riding, worthy of preservation, it was reduced to writing.

In the study of theology, the Bible was his textbook. Aside from the Scriptures, his reading, until he had formed his doctrinal sentiments, was confined almost entirely to the Theological dictionaries of Brown and Buck. He seemed to possess the extraordinary power of placing every new acquisition of truth in its proper place in his *"great mental storehouse,"* to be drawn upon at pleasure, as necessity demanded. Like a rich banker, who can furnish a large or small check, to suit customers, Mr. Donnell was always ready for a popular effort on a great occasion, or an exhortation at an ordinary meeting. To repeat the language of Dr. Burrow, "*he was always ready for the work.*" He committed to memory much of the Bible, which enabled him not only to express his thoughts in the most suitable language, but, as it were, "to dove-tail" all his doctrinal statements with appropriate texts of Scripture.

He began at an early period of his ministry to arrange what he very properly termed a "system" of religious truth, embracing the cardinal doctrines of the Bible. These he held with a firmness which nothing could shake, and he dwelt upon them, in public and private, in a manner which indicated that they were incorporated with all his habits of thought and feeling. The intrinsic merits of this system were so universally acknowledged, that he was prevailed on to publish it for the instruction of the church at large; and his sentiments thus given to the public were soon recognized in the sermons of many of his sons in the ministry.

In metaphysics, Mr. Donnell was his own philosopher —rejecting all theories of mental philosophy, whether ancient or modern, which he believed to be in collision with the Word of God, and tended to destroy man's accountability. The Bible, and exercises of his own mind, were his guide, and his conclusions respecting the determining power of the will, were formed as an independent thinker.

The religious character of Mr. Donnell, in the private walks of life, commanded the respect of all who knew him, whether religious or irreligious. The following incident, related by Dr. Blair, of Athens, Ala., will corroborate this statement: "At a camp-meeting in Lawrence county, Alabama, the church put on her armor, and God, in a remarkable manner, revived his work. Christians concluded, on a certain evening of the meeting, to retire to the woods to pray; and the grove at once became vocal with the voice of supplication. A band of thoughtless, wicked young men had just assembled in that grove, to indulge in drinking and dissipation; but finding themselves surrounded with praying christians, and prompted by feelings of derision, the ring-leader called on his companions to kneel for prayer too. He commenced by saying, 'I beseech thee, O Lord, to have mercy on us, and come down and save our poor souls; but if it is not convenient for thee to come now, send Bob Donnell, for there is no two ways in him.'"

Dr. Blair says this incident was related by one of the party, who afterward became religious; and that, notwithstanding there was great irreverence toward God in the conduct of the young men, still it indicated their confidence in the uncompromising piety of Mr. Donnell.

The following incident is furnished by Mrs. Beard, (wife of Dr. Beard,) and serves to illustrate the christian character of Mr. Donnell: "While traveling on a preaching tour, Mr. Donnell called at my father's, for dinner, and to rest for a short time. Before leaving in the evening, he proposed praying with the family. All were assembled, and after reading a portion of Scripture, he commenced his prayer in these words: 'O, Lord, we are traveling a long journey, never to return,' &c. The impressiveness and solemnity of his manner, and the adaptedness of his whole prayer to his moving position as a traveler, and especially its opening expression, produced such an effect on my mind, that I could not refrain from weeping; and for months afterwards, that solemn and emphatic expression, 'we are traveling a long journey,' seemed to ring in my ears, and with unusual interest I still recollect that prayer."

The Rev. J. C. Provine says: "Mr. Donnell often visited my father's family in the days of my childhood, and well do I remember those visits. Impressions were then made upon my mind that time never can destroy. He had a peculiar art of attracting the attention of children, by relating stories, singing songs, and propounding Bible questions. In this way, he would interest their feelings, win their affections, and make lasting impressions upon their tender hearts. He rarely ever visited a family without introducing the subject of religion. His fervent prayers, expositions of the word of God, and pious counsel to each member, are still recollected with interest by many households."

To be fully acquainted with a man's whole character, it is necessary to know him, not only in the public walks

of life, but in the more private circles of home. Let us,
therefore, contemplate the character of Mr. Donnell *at
home*. Though a christian everywhere, yet if his piety
was more attractive and impressive at any one place
than another, that place was in his own family. The
following account of him, when freed from the restraints
of society abroad, and quietly enjoying the pleasure of
home, is from the pen of Dr. T. C. Anderson:

"In the fall of 1832, I visited Mr. Donnell at his own
residence, in Alabama. He was then the proprietor of a
cotton farm, regarded in that State rather as a medium
size. On this farm he employed about fifteen hands. It
was the picking season, and all were in the field with
their baskets. About the setting of the sun, each laborer
came in with his day's work, and had it weighed. While
this process was going on, feelings of emulation were
freely indulged by the company. During the evening,
the younger servants played '*baste*' in the yard, while
the older ones sat in the doors of their cabins, singing
religious songs. The bell rang at an early hour for
prayers, when all assembled in the family room. A
chapter was read, explained, and applied to practical
life; then all joined in singing a hymn with much animation, which was followed by a prayer, expressing the
daily wants of the family in a spirit that moved the
hearts of all present. In the morning, ere the sun had
risen, the bell rang again, and all promptly appeared for
family devotion, as on the previous evening. Then came
breakfast; and so soon as it was over, each cotton-picker
27—

repaired to the field, as though anxious to be first at work."

Mr. J. H. Bradley, a ruling elder of the Cumberland Presbyterian church, corroborates the statement of Dr. Anderson, respecting the domestic piety of Mr. Donnell. He says:

" For several years I lived on Mr. Donnell's farm, and attended to his business. Never have I known a man more uniform in his domestic habits. He was patient and forbearing toward all; more especially toward his servants. His custom was, when any of them transgressed, to produce penitence, if possible, by kind remonstrance; and when successful, to remit the offense. He never disclosed the fault of one servant to another, when concealment was possible.

" It was his invariable custom to call his servants into his dining-room, every morning and evening, for family devotion. He would first read a portion of Scripture, giving a brief explanation; then all joined in singing a hymn, and after the prayer, he would deliver a short lecture. An hour in the morning was frequently spent in this way, before I could get the hands to work. I at length told Mr. Donnell that it would be impossible for me to cultivate his farm, unless he would shorten the time spent in devotion. He replied, that we were dependent on God for a crop, and he would rather have less done in the field, than to curtail his worship in the family."

Mr. Donnell maintained family devotion during the

greater part of his last affliction. When he became too feeble to bow down upon his knees, he sat in an easy chair, or lay upon his bed, and led in prayer. How important that such an example, as this venerable man of God maintained in all the relations of life, should be preserved and handed down to posterity! There is nothing equal to the power of consistent conduct, as an argument to prove the truth of christianity.

Mr. James, in his work on domestic religion, mentions a man who, at his ordination to the ministry, stated that at one period of his life he was inclined to the principles of infidelity; but that there was one argument in favor of the christian religion which he could not refute—"the consistent conduct of his own father."

Mr. Donnell's character as a peace-maker in the church deserves a passing notice. No man deprecated more than he did, divisions of feeling among brethren, or labored more assiduously and skillfully to heal a breach when it occurred. His plan of adjusting difficulties of this sort, was to go immediately and talk separately to the parties concerned—always defending the absent person, so far as truth would permit. In this way, he rarely failed to bring about a reconciliation.

Strife among brethren is always injurious to the cause of religion. It gives its enemies occasion to triumph, and its friends cause to mourn. A fruitful source of dissension, both in the church and out of it, is envy—a passion every way degrading to mankind. It is not so much a desire to benefit oneself, but to pull down and injure a supposed rival. Love of pre-eminence is natural to the human heart. Even among the disciples of Christ, there was a dispute about who should be the greatest in the kingdom of heaven. Would that this vile passion were confined to the laity: but it is too often to be seen among ministers of the Gospel.

Looseness in pecuniary transactions is frequently the cause of much difficulty also, both in the church as well as in the world. Bargains are indefinitely made; the memory is relied on to keep accounts; settlements are improperly postponed, and the result is, a misunderstanding in the final adjustment.

A slight discrepancy of religious sentiment, too, sometimes leads to unhappy divisions among brethren—a discrepancy that sustains no important relation to the great system of fundamental truth revealed in the Bible, but consists in mere metaphysical subtleties and distinctions which are impalpable to the common christian, and tend only to perplex the church. Ecclesiastical history furnishes many examples of division in the body of Christ that ought never to have taken place.

Mr. Donnell never would become a partizan in church difficulties; but always occupied the high position of mediator between contending parties. Said a preacher, who was in collision with some of his brethren, and desired to enlist the feelings of Mr. Donnell on his side of the controversy,—"As for Donnell, he will lie down and be trodden upon, and walked over, rather than participate in a dispute."

Mr. Donnell possessed well-defined and established religious sentiments, and did not hesitate to preach the distinctive doctrines of his church, when deemed necessary; but his denominational attachments never degenerated into sectarian bigotry. While he followed his own preference, respecting modes of worship, forms of government, and shades of sentiment, he did not exalt them into such undue importance as to overshadow the essential doctrines and duties of religion, or consider them indispensable to the character of the true church. He did not believe that Presbyterians are saved by their Presbyterian peculiarities, or Methodists by theirs, or Baptists by theirs; but that all are saved by what they hold in common; and thus believing, he was ready and willing to meet them at the Lord's table, in the pulpit, or on any other common ground, for christian communion and co-operation. His own church, however, being the division of the great army of Christ, in which he had enlisted to fight the battles of truth, he felt, as a matter of course, an anxiety for her success and prosperity; but this he never sought by proselyting from other denominations. To the world he looked for converts to build up his church. His denominational attachment was increased by the consideration that he had nursed his church in her infancy, and toiled with and for her in her riper years, and believed she had a great work to do in the world for the cause of Christ.

Every enlightened and faithful minister of Jesus Christ is a man of public spirit. His first and direct efforts are to save the people of his immediate charge; but he desires, at the same time, to live for the salvation of the world, and in proportion as his success is seen at home, will he be active in devising ways and means to send the Gospel abroad. Some men are always behind the age in which they live; others are barely up with it, while a few are occasionally to be seen in advance of it, serving as file leaders in the progress of society. The latter was Mr. Donnell's position; and such was the confidence of the church in him, *as a leader*, that when any new enterprise was presented, with *his sanction*, the practical utility of the measure was rarely doubted. He was president of the first Missionary Board ever organized in the Cumberland Presbyterian church; and one of the first Vice Presidents of the American Tract Society.

His rule of spending money for benevolent purposes, was to discriminate between the merits of objects presented, and give accordingly. He considered himself merely as a steward, and riches as a talent, to be accounted for at the bar of God; and that he was not at liberty to contribute irrespective of a prospect of usefulness. I am not aware of but one man of the church to which he belonged, that contributed, while living, more than he did to the cause of benevolence. To the Bible and Tract Societies, he made annual donations, besides responding to various other calls outside of his own church.   •

It is pleasing to reflect upon the great change that has taken place, on the score of liberality, in the church at

large, within the last fifty years. Time was when the
Methodists could raise but $600, and that they had to
borrow to commence their great "book concern." Near
the same time, an effort was made by a Synod in the
Presbyterian church, to raise funds to print "Dodridge's
Rise and Progress of Religion in the Soul;" and after
trying several years, the project failed. When the
American Board of Missions determined to establish the
first foreign mission, they were afraid to proceed without
soliciting aid from the London Missionary Society. It
is easier now to raise $1,000 in the Cumberland Presby-
terian church, for benevolent purposes, than it would
have been to raise $100 forty years ago.

Next to the progress of the Gospel, and the planting
of churches, there was nothing in which Mr. Donnell
felt a deeper interest than the cause of education. He
was a leading member of the Synod, then the highest
judicatory of the body, when it was determined to establish the first college of the Cumberland Presbyterian
church. Revs. John Barnett and F. R. Cossitt, and
Ephraim M. Ewing, Joseph D. Hamilton and Joseph M.
Street, Esqs., were appointed commissioners to locate
the institution. They placed it at Princeton, Kentucky.
Mr. Donnell was never pleased with the location, but
acquiesced in the decision of the commissioners, and gave
to the college his hearty co-operation, until the church
despaired of its success. A fundamental error had been
committed, in attempting to combine manual labor with
literary instruction; which, together with other minor

causes that more properly belong to the secular historian to record, operated in diminishing public confidence, and it was ultimately deemed advisable, by the General Assembly, to establish an institution upon a different basis. Mr. Donnell was placed at the head of a committee for that purpose, and Lebanon, Tennessee, was selected as the most eligible site for Cumberland University. Soon after the location, he donated $1,000 toward an endowment fund, and then exerted a happy influence in developing the liberality of the church for the same object.

Mr. Donnell felt not only a great interest in the general diffusion of education in the country at large, but especially for the intellectual improvement of candidates for the ministry, both in literature and theology. Respecting his solicitude on this subject, President Anderson says:

"In the summer of 1833, I became connected with the ·*Revivalist*,' the only paper then published in the church. Mr. Donnell was a regular contributor to its columns, and at that day he seldom discussed doctrines, or engaged in controversy, but generally dwelt on subjects relating to church policy. The establishment of Presbyterial schools, for the literary and theological instruction of probationers for the ministry, was with him a favorite theme. His communications called out opposing views, and a discussion ensued upon the relative merits of Presbyterial schools, compared with one institution of a high order for the *whole church*. After mature deliberation, a majority of the leading members of the body

seemed to favor the latter. Mr. Donnell promptly sig-
nified his readiness to co-operate with the majority upon
any feasible plan that would call forth the energies of
the church in its support. The final action of the General Assembly, however, on the subject, was not obtained
till 1848, when he introduced a resolution to establish a
theological department in Cumberland University. The
resolution passed, and was carried into effect in 1852,
when Mr. Donnell gave his note for $1,000, to endow
the first professorship.

"When called to the pastoral charge of the church at
Lebanon, his solicitude for the University was the principal cause of his acceptance. While pastor, he delivered a course of lectures on theology to candidates for
the ministry, which were the result of years' reflection
and profound analysis. The course embraced all the
distinctive doctrines of the Cumberland Presbyterian
church, and afforded much valuable information to the
young men for whose benefit they were delivered."

The following is an extract from his introductory
lecture :

"The doctrines of religion are very correctly called a
system of truth. This system, of course, has its parts,
sustaining a relation to each other. To understand the
system correctly, each part should be carefully studied.
Though called of God to preach the Gospel, you are not
to expect knowledge by intuition. 'Study to show thyself approved, give attention to reading,' &c., are Divine
commands, binding on ministers of the Gospel now as
28—

much as in the days of the Apostles. That which man can do for himself, God will not do. Having given him a capacity to think, investigate, and reason, his Maker expects him to acquire knowledge by mental application.

"The idea that learning is prejudicial to religion, and unnecessary to a minister of the Gospel, was never entertained in the Cumberland Presbyterian church. Our first preachers were unable to command those literary advantages that have been provided for you; but they were all in favor of high intellectual attainments in the ministry.

"The importance of a theological seminary is now under consideration in the church, and it is hoped one will soon be established. It is true, there is some diversity of opinion with regard to *the best plan ;* but none question the necessity of a profound knowledge of theology. The best method of obtaining it, is the question of debate. Some urge as an objection to theological seminaries, the evils which seem to have grown out of them in other churches; while others contend that if an institution is not to be tolerated unless it be perfect, all civil governments would cease, for none are perfect.

"All other professions are generally studied in a systematic way, before their duties are undertaken; and I cannot see why the same necessity does not apply to ministers of the Gospel. True, some men have become eminent lawyers and physicians, without seeing a law or medical school; and I rejoice to know that many preachers have been eminently useful and an honor to

the church, without the advantages of a theological
seminary. Still, in all such cases, books were read and
studied, that had been written by men who had gone
through a systematic course of education."

Mr. Donnell's conduct in reference to politics, deserves
a permanent record. Such was his weight of character,
that his opinion in political matters was often sought
for party purposes. In 1840, when political excitement
was carried to very great extremes, he conversed so
little on the subject, that his sentiments were known to
but few. He was waited on by a committee, for the
purpose of ascertaining his position, to whom he replied;
"I am in favor of the missionary cause." A second
effort was made by another committee, and the question,
"What are your politics?" directly propounded, to which
he responded, "Go ye into all the world and preach
my Gospel to every creature." Though disappointed,
and perhaps a little chagrined, yet the parties treated
Mr. Donnell's prudence with respect, and even admiration; and as evidence of their feelings, presented him a
handsome walking cane, with his last answer inscribed
upon it. The likeness of Mr. Donnell, accompanying
this Memoir, holds also the likeness of that cane in
hand.

Perhaps Mr. Donnell's taciturnity on the subject of
politics, was never more severely tried than at the General Assembly, at Owensborough, in 1840. While dining
on a certain day of the meeting, the question why so
many preachers belonged to a certain political party

arose. The lady of the house, at the head of the table, answered this question by saying, it was to be attributed to their superior intelligence. Mr. Donnell, though in politics opposed to the party referred to, and seated near the lady, blushed, but said nothing.

CHAPTER XX.

REMINISCENCES AND REFLECTIONS.—CONTINUED.

A Friend of the Missionary Enterprise—Recommends the Itinerant Mode of Preaching—Visits East Tennessee in 1818—Great Effects of his Preaching—Anecdote from Rev. J. B. Logan.

I HAVE already stated that Mr. Donnell was President of the first Missionary Board that was ever appointed in the Cumberland Presbyterian church. The special object of that Board was to educate and christianize the Chickasaw Indians, then occupying a portion of what is now the State of Mississippi. The late Rev. Robert Bell was the first missionary sent among those Indians by the church. He opened a school for their benefit, on the 13th of November, 1820, one mile from the Tombigby river, and two miles below Colbert's old cotton gin; and continued with the nation till their removal to the Indian territory, west of the Mississippi river.

Mr. Donnell, under an appointment of the Board of Missions, with the assistance of Revs. James B. Porter and William Barnett, held a camp-meeting at the above station, in the month of May, 1824. The following reference to this meeting is from the pen of the Rev. Israel Pickens, who says:

"Mr. Donnell, on Saturday evening, made a general request that all should retire to the woods and pray for the success of the meeting. This request produced an unusual effect upon my mind. I had been under conviction for some months, but my efforts, up to this time, seemed to be unavailing. I had never seen Mr. Donnell before, and so soon as he arose in the pulpit, I was struck with his appearance. His remarks, in connection with the request, were very appropriate and impressive, and I went with the multitude to pray, and returned with an increased purpose to seek religion. On Sabbath, Mr. Donnell preached a very powerful sermon, on the valley of dry bones; and on that night I embraced religion; and I have ever regarded him as the means of my submission to Christ."

Mr. Donnell was in full sympathy with the foreign missionary enterprise, from the commencement of his ministry; but the infancy of his church forbade a practical development of his feelings. Indeed, the great revival of 1800, at the beginning of which he was converted, was the dawn of the foreign missionary spirit upon the churches of America. Isolated efforts had been previously made, by Elliott. Brainard, and others, to convert the heathen; but there was nothing like a general interest felt on the subject. In 1801, the year after Mr. Donnell's conversion, Samuel J. Mills obtained religion, and fixed his heart on the work of a foreign missionary; and history will ever award to him the honor of being the first mover in forming the American Board of Foreign Missions. Soon after his conversion, he became a student of Williams college, and disclosed

his missionary feelings to Gordon Hall and James Rich-
ards, and to his astonishment, as well as gratification,
he found that their minds had been turned in the same
direction as his own. Those three young men were in
the habit of retiring frequently to a certain hay-stack
for prayer, and mutual consultation relative to the work
on which they had fixed their hearts. Soon the missionary spirit they had imbibed, expanded till it resulted
in the organization, in 1810, of the American Board.

Mr. Donnell, in the meantime, was diligently employed
as a home missionary, planting churches and introducing
men into the ministry, preparatory to a commencement
of labor in the foreign field; and so soon as numerical
strength justified it, he called the attention of the church
to the duty of sending the Gospel to the heathen. Here
is one of his appeals:

"Our church is not doing all she can to promote the
cause of Christ in our great missionary field at home—
the valley of the Mississippi. The whole world is now
a missionary field, white unto the harvest. Some are
doing but little for the heathen, for want, as they say, of
a suitable system of operation. I will not say we have
the best system; I believe it can be greatly improved;
but this must be done *practically*. Our General Assembly is a missionary society, and has its missionary board;
and there are regular channels of communication to that
board from all the congregations. He that wants to aid
the cause of missions, can find a way to do it. May the
Lord stir us all up to suitable action."

Mr. Donnell gave an unqualified expression of his feelings in favor of circuit preaching, but a short time before he died, by saying, he "regarded that mode of preaching as one of the most valuable auxiliaries of the church, and desired that it should be revived in every Presbytery where it had been discontinued, and that new life and energy might be infused into it where it was still practiced."

No man was better prepared to give a correct opinion relative to the advantages of circuit preaching. He had himself, for several years, in the earlier part of his ministry, been a circuit-rider; so had all his cotemporaries. The following is a brief reference to them, by Mr. E. Currey:

"In the year 1805, we were made glad by a visit from Rev. James Farr, who was traveling through the country, seeking the destitute, and leaving appointments for circuit preaching. On the day appointed, Rev. Samuel King came to my father's, in Williamson county, Tenn., and preached with such life and power, that it caused considerable rejoicing in the house. I recollect a very wicked old man started off, apparently in a great rage, and said he would as leave be among a pack of wolves, as at such a meeting. Poor man! in a few days after he was a corpse. I have often thought of his wicked look when he left. Next to King, came Alexander Anderson, a man of sober habits and pleasant conversation, of whom it was said, he had not an enemy on earth. Then followed David Foster, a heart-searching preacher, who could paint the hypocrite in glaring colors. After him, came Thomas Calhoun, who was called by some Boanerges; others said he taught as one having authority, and not as the Scribes. Then came James B. Porter, a most soothing minister of the Gospel, and well calculated to do much good in the church. After him, came Alexander Chapman, a man of serene countenance and pleasant address, calculated to promote peace and harmony on the circuit. Then followed Robert Donnell, who was noted for his wisdom and zeal. Then came William Bumpus, a man that was severe on the infidel and skeptic; who could trace them to all their lurking-places. After him, Robert Bell, a meek man, and acceptable preacher. Then followed Robert Guthrie, a great reasoner. Then came Hugh Kirkpatrick, who dwelt much on the prophecies."

To the itinerating system, Cumberland Presbyterianism is, under God, principally indebted for its early prosperity. Many of the old congregations, yet living and flourishing in the great valley of the Mississippi, can bear testimony to the truth of this statement. Alabama, Tennessee, Kentucky, Indiana, Illinois, Mississippi and Arkansas, are all still feeling the effects of circuit preaching.

Mr. Donnell, in company with the late Rev. Thomas Calhoun, Sr., went on a preaching tour to East Tennessee, in 1818; and it will be in place here to refer to the results of that expedition. The following account I find in the "Life of Rev. George Donnell," p. 157 :

29—

"They had sent on a series of appointments, and when they reached the first one, at Washington, they found a vast multitude congregated in a grove—there being no house in the place of sufficient capacity to receive all that had assembled. Mr. Donnell preached, expounding the distinctive doctrines of the new church with a lucidness and suavity that enchained the multitude for two hours; then closing with a pathos and solemnity that moved the hearts of all.

"The assembly was bathed in tears; expressions of rapturous joy welled out from many christian hearts; while sighs and groans heaved the bosoms of sinners, who had never before been known to manifest any religious interest. This was the first sermon ever preached by a Cumberland Presbyterian in East Tennessee.

"From Washington, the evangelists passed to Morgantown. Here both preached to a large assembly; much excitement prevailed, and many seemed to be amazed at the novelty and the solemnity of the scene. The next appointment was on Baker's creek, where the congregation were interested with the impressive manner of the speaker, and the reasonableness of the doctrines. On Sabbath, Donnell preached at Maryville, in Dr. Anderson's church. The audience was convulsed with feeling. Descending from the pulpit, singing as no other man, even in that day of song, could sing, and shaking hands with the people, some shouted for joy, and many flocked around him, bidding him a cordial welcome, and entreating him to make another appointment. Calhoun preached the next day to a crowded house, and great solemnity pervaded the audience. Donnell preached the day following, at Mr. Houston's, a few miles in the country. Some of the old men shouted for joy. Dr. Anderson called on one of them to pray—hoping, as it was thought, to stop the shouting. But the old man prayed with such power and heavenly-mindedness, that the shouting greatly increased, and the Doctor was constrained to let the Spirit work in his own way.

" From Maryville, they proceed to Knoxville, and preached to a very attentive and interesting audience; and lodged with Dr. Nelson, by whom they were kindly entertained. Passing to Campbell's Station, Mr. Donnell preached with unusual power and spirit. Great excitement prevailed ; some shouted, and others were affected with the jerks. One man was jerked under the benches, and continued jerking while under there, till he was extricated by his friends.

" This strange affection was common in East Tennessee, as elsewhere, during the prevalence of the great revival in 1800; and had been occasionally witnessed from that date up to the visit of Donnell and Calhoun, in 1818. It is said that Dr. Samuel Doak, who was much prejudiced against the exercises, was sometimes subjected to it; and that, on one occasion, while in the pulpit, he was seized with a paroxysm, and jerked so violently as to throw his wig from his head into the congregation.

" From Campbell's Station, the missionaries passed to a vacant church on Bull Run, where Calhoun preached with such power, as to leave an impression that subsequently resulted in the organization of a Cumberland Presbyterian church at that place. At Kingston, Donnell preached to a vast multitude, assembled in a grove. Great excitement prevailed in the congregation, and at the close of the sermon, Calhoun rose from a sick bed, and, with a fever upon him, delivered a most powerful exhortation. Donnell preached the next day at Post Oak Springs, and as Calhoun was still sick, they set out for home, traveling slowly—Donnell preaching at Washington, and other places, on the road."

The following incident, which occurred during this preaching tour, is related by the Rev. J. B. Logan, whose father was present at the meeting where it took place :

" Messrs. Donnell and Calhoun had sent on a request to the session for the liberty of preaching on a certain day in what was called the old Baker's Creek church. Quite a number of respectable families belonged to the congregation, though somewhat rigid in their notions of Presbyterianism, customs of the fathers, &c. When the request reached them, the elders held a meeting on the subject; and after some discussion, it was agreed that, as the appointment was on a week-day, the church might be occupied. When the day arrived, there was a large congregation in attendance ; but strange to say, the elders and old members of the church, for the most part, refused to go into the meeting-house, for fear they might encourage *heresy*, &c. But their pews were filled by the young people of the neighborhood, and with strangers. It was the custom of the times to have two sermons in succession. Calhoun preached first. My father, who was then a young man, was outside of the church, standing by the door, unable to get a seat in the large house. On the other side of the door, stood one of the elders. As Calhoun advanced in his subject, the old elder moved up a little closer to the door. The speaker preached with great fervor and eloquence, and closed with the tear drops in many eyes, and a profound impression for good in the minds of the vast audience. The old elder, in the meantime, had gotten *inside* the door, and was standing in the aisle.

"When Donnell rose to follow, there seemed to be depicted in many countenances a feeling of regret, for they evidently thought his effort would be far inferior to the one just closed. It was in Donnell's palmiest days. He rose in the pulpit with great solemnity and dignity, and made one of his happiest efforts. At the close of his sermon, he said he expected to get to heaven, and wished to know how many of those present felt a sure evidence that they would meet him and all God's people there? During the progress of the discourse, our elder had, insensibly to himself, advanced slowly up the aisle, keeping his eyes riveted on the speaker. The eager listeners behind had crowded close on his heels. Finally, Mr. Donnell, descending from the lofty pulpit, proposed that every one present, who felt bound for heaven, should meet him before the pulpit, and give him their hand. The good old elder could stand it no longer; he met the preacher half way up the steps, and exclaimed at the top of his voice, clasping the minister by the hand, and turning round, facing the audience, ' *Brethren,*' said he, ' *we are all wrong, and these people are right, for I feel the evidence in my breast to-day.*' That elder afterward left the old church, and with others, joined in heartily with the Cumberlands, and lived for many years a very worthy, energetic and devoted member and elder of the Cumberland Presbyterian church. His name is yet familiar to many Tennesseeans."

Mr. Donnell had, by his own labors, made full proof of the practical benefits of circuit preaching, and lived to see the unhappy effects of its discontinuance; and after duly weighing both sides of the question, in the light of long and close observation, he says: "Circuit preaching is a valuable auxiliary to the church, and should be revived and maintained in every Presbytery." Mr. Ewing also bore testimony, on his dying bed, to the importance of this method of preaching, and in his will left $1,000 to the church, the interest of which is to be applied to the support of circuit preaching. This bequest was made in full view of the footprints of Rev. R. D. Morrow, and others, as circuit riders in Missouri, through whose instrumentality many large and useful congregations had been collected and organized. **Mr. Morrow** was the pioneer of Cumberlandism in that State—supported for a time by an association of ladies of old Logan Presbytery.

It would be useless to attempt to prove, by abstract reasoning, the importance of circuit preaching. Facts are stronger than arguments. It is sometimes said, I know, that the itinerating system is only adapted to new countries and sparsely settled neighborhoods; this is a mistake. It is adapted to all countries, whether old or new, not yet occupied by congregations able to support settled pastors. There is not a country now in the valley of the Mississippi, where circuit preaching might not be successfully introduced. But the question is, how can it be revived and maintained? The difficulty is not owing to a want of preachers, or a disinclination on their part to ride and preach. Many are without any special charge, and would be glad to devote their whole time to a circuit. How to raise the means to support them, is the difficult question. Settle this *practically*, and every Presbytery will be supplied with circuit preaching.

CHAPTER XXI.

REMINISCENCES AND REFLECTIONS.—CONTINUED.

Laments the Instability of the Pastoral Relations—Origin of Camp-
meetings — Their Plainness when first Introduced—Regrets their
present want of original Simplicity—His Influence in the Judicatories of the Church.

MR. DONNELL was also a warm friend of a settled
ministry. In conversation, when on his death-bed,
with Mr. Calhoun, Jr., he lamented "that so few congregations were supplied with pastors, and that the
relation, when formed, was not more permanent." This
is certainly much to be desired; but the continuance of
the pastoral connection requires the convenience of
both preacher and people. Both must be pleased, each
with the other; and it depends greatly with the one,
what shall be the other's desires and feelings. Either
can show such a spirit, and exhibit such conduct, as
will produce a disruption; and either can do very much
toward rendering the union desirable and permanent.
But more of this hereafter. The evils of an unsettled
ministry first claim attention.

The expense of moving from place to place, by a
roving, unsettled ministry, is a matter of no small consequence. But a mere waste of dollars and cents, is a
minor consideration, when compared with other evils
involved in the temporary settlement of ministers.

Mutual confidence and affection between pastor and people, so indispensable to ministerial success, are not formed in a day, but result from a protracted acquaintance and kind feelings toward each other. A strange preacher may, and often does, succeed in attracting the attention of a community, and is the means of a powerful revival of religion; but he is not the man to develop the piety of a congregation in the practical duties of religion. This requires the permanent pastor, who knows the people and their circumstances, and shows himself ready and willing at all times to weep with them that weep, and to rejoice with them that rejoice. Scenes of affliction, above all other places, afford rich opportunities to a pastor for cultivating and gaining the affections and confidence of his people; and the longer these opportunities are enjoyed and rightly improved, the higher he rises in public estimation, and the more ample become his facilities for usefulness in the community.

A true history of the various causes that separate pastor and people, would doubtless tell a sad story of the frailty of human nature. The preacher himself is not always innocent. On first entering the pulpit, he attracts, it may be, much attention, and excites high expectations; but soon the old stock of sermons, already prepared, is exhausted, and he, through mental indolence, fails to make new ones. The people, discovering that they were deceived respecting the intellectual resources of their pastor, soon indicate dissatis-

30 —

faction, and thus a rupture commences. The preacher, seeing that he fails to meet public expectations, becomes dissatisfied with himself, and, of course, unhappy and restless; and a resignation is soon tendered and accepted. Indefatigable study on the part of the pastor, is the only remedy for this evil. No man can sustain himself in the pulpit, without hard study out of it. The advice of the late pious Christmas Evans, to a young preacher, will be in place here. He says:

"I am old, my dear boy, and you are just entering the ministry. Let me now and here tell you one thing, and commend it to your attention and memory. All the ministers that I have ever known, who have fallen into disgrace, or into uselessness, *have been idle men*. An idle man is in the way of every temptation. Temptation has not to seek him; he is at the corner of the street, ready and waiting for it. In the case of a minister of the Gospel, this peril is multiplied by his position; his neglected duties; the temptations peculiar to his condition and his superior susceptibility. *Remember this: stick to your book.* I am never much afraid of a young minister, when I know that he can, and does, fairly sit down to his book. There is Mr. ——, of such unhappy temper, and who has such a love to meddle with everything; he would long ago have been utterly wrecked, but his habits of industry saved him. Let no merchant in the town—no lawyer or physician of your acquaintance—no farmer of your parish, be more industrious than you in their calling. Give not a day of your life but for its work. Industry will keep you always busy, and always at leisure. It will give you time for everything, and enable you to do everything in its time, and to perfect everything you undertake. It will aid you in writing short sermons. It will bless you and your people, and the church, in a thousand ways. An example for your imitation, you will find in Luther, Calvin, Baxter, Wesley; in every man, in every department of life, who has risen to high position among his fellows. Shepherd, himself a great preacher, used to say, 'God will curse that man's labors who goes idly up and down all the week, and then goes into his study on Saturday.' "

But the blame is not all on one side for the frequent changes of the pastoral relation. The people are justly chargeable with a large share. It too often happens that, though their preacher studies day and night to render their pulpit attractive, and to present in his sermons "things both new and old," he fails to hold their attention. Many, so soon as the novelty of *the man* wears off, forsake his church, and either remain at home on the Sabbath, or become mere rovers, first to one house of worship, then to another, with itching ears, merely to compare the talents of ministers. When their pastor enters the pulpit, with a sermon arranged, perhaps with special reference to their spiritual necessities, he finds their seats unoccupied. Church members are also often very remiss in attending weekly prayer-meetings, and their absence contributes no little to the discouragement of the pastor. He is expected to be present, regardless of all obstacles; but a slight excuse will ease the conscience of the laity in remaining at home. How discouraging to lecture and pray, with little else than empty seats before him! Ministers of the Gospel, sustaining no special relation to the pulpit, but living in the congregation, often chill the heart of the pastor, by their non-attendance at prayer-meeting. Feeling no personal responsibility for the religious state of the congregation, they consult convenience and inclination on the subject of going; and if they have families, *they* fall under the influence of their example, and the infection spreads to other families in the immediate vicinity. No pastor can long bear up under the discouragement of seeing his congregation inattentive to the public means of grace, whether it be preaching on the Sabbath, or the weekly prayer-meeting. He invariably feels that his labors are not appreciated, and a change of location becomes a subject of thought.

Another cause of discontent to the pastor, is a failure on the part of the people to support him. No men, possessing the abilities of preachers, labor for less compensation, and still they often fail to realize the salary promised; and hence, necessity compels them to resign their charge.

It is conceded on all hands, that camp-meetings first occurred in Logan county, Kentucky, among the revival party in the Presbyterian church, that subsequently formed the Cumberland Presbyterian church. The late Hugh Stevenson, of Franklin, Ky., informed the writer many years ago, that *his* father was the first man that ever used boards at a camp-meeting, in preparing a shelter. I think it was at old Red river meeting-house, in Logan county.

Mr. Donnell, in conversation with Mr. Calhoun, in his last illness, stated that "the first shelters used at those meetings were covered wagons and cloth tents. Next, rail pens were built, and covered with boards. Then log and frame huts were provided, and even brick cabins were, in some instances, erected for convenience." In the early history of camp-meetings, he observed, simplicity was much studied by all concerned. The first day was uniformly observed as a season of prayer and fasting, and the plainest of diet provided throughout the occasion; while everything like ostentatious display was carefully avoided. Preaching on Friday was generally addressed to christians—often on the subject of prayer, and other duties connected with the meeting. On Saturday, ministers generally dwelt on human depravity; and on Sabbath, the principal topic of the pulpit was the plan of salvation. On Monday, appeals were made to sinners, and instructions given for the purpose of leading the penitent to believe on Christ. The meeting always closed on Tuesday morning, with an exhortation to those converted on the occasion, and young christians generally.

Mr. Donnell lamented that camp-meetings had greatly

"degenerated from their original simplicity, and consequently that their usefulness had much diminished; but thought they might still be rendered profitable in many places—particularly in a thinly settled country, where a preached Gospel was not regularly enjoyed."

The view of these meetings, as expressed by Mr. Donnell, is now the popular feeling of the church, and the tendency of public sentiment is to supercede them by protracted meetings, without camping on the ground. These meetings can only serve, however, as an imperfect substitute for camp-meetings; still, unless the latter can be reclaimed from the perversion and abuse that attend them, perhaps it would be better that they should give place altogether to protracted meetings—though the latter are not so well adapted to the laws of mind as the former, besides being attended with more labor and expense to the community.

The understanding too, that protracted meetings are to continue for a time *indefinite*, renders it more difficult to arouse christians to action, and to bring sinners to the point of submission to Christ. Sometimes, a week or more of hard preaching must be done, before any signs of a revival appear. Then, after preachers are exhausted, and duties elsewhere, perhaps, are demanding attention, the meeting must be continued a week or ten days longer. Camp-meetings, in their earlier history, were always confined to four days and nights, which prevented a postponement of effort; consequently, as much good was generally accomplished in four days and nights, as is now done at a protracted meeting in ten or fifteen.

President Anderson says : " I never knew Mr. Donnell's equal as a Presbyter. Though enjoying a degree of confidence among his brethren that might have placed him in a position to dictate to them, he had no ambition to be a leader, nor was he ever known to press the adoption of a measure by the weight of his personal influence. He never sought reputation, nor to render himself conspicuous ; never made what might be called a set speech ; was usually silent when matters of trivial consequence were under discussion."

The writer recollects that Mr. Donnell once remarked to him in an undertone, in the General Assembly, when speeches were made upon matters of no moment, that his custom was to guard and preserve the great principles of the church, and let the younger members dispute about little things. But President Anderson continues : " When he felt it to be his duty to speak, it was in a subdued, conversational tone, always avoiding everything like display, and never retorting upon an opponent. I never knew him excited in debate, or lose that calmness of feeling which results from conscious strength of argument.

" When party animosity or a spirit of rivalry seemed likely to arise in debate, he invariably interposed as mediator, pouring oil on the troubled waters, endeavoring to soothe the wounded feelings, and to restrain the belligerent ; and such was the general respect felt for his weight of character, that no one thought of assailing his feelings in discussion."

Mr. Donnell was, perhaps, in some instances, too conservative in the judicatories of the church; preferring to maintain an apparent neutral position, rather than take sides with either party in debate. The following incident will explain what I mean. In 1833, at the General Assembly in the city of Nashville, a very exciting debate arose, respecting old Cumberland college. As the discussion advanced, the excitement increased; but Mr. Donnell, rather to the annoyance of both parties, remained silent. One speaker after another addressed the Assembly, and at the close of each speech, a pause ensued, and all eyes turned to Mr. Donnell, as though he would certainly speak next. Still he remained on his seat. At length, Col. Smith, father of Mr. Donnell's first wife, made almost a direct appeal to him; fixing his eyes upon him, he said: "I want to hear from some of our more experienced members on this very difficult and perplexing question." When he sat down, after a moment's pause, and amid the almost breathless silence of the members, Mr. Donnell arose; but instead of speaking, called on the house to join him in prayer; and a more solemn and appropriate prayer I never heard from the lips of man. Disputants on both sides, arose from their knees with subdued feelings. A general calm pervaded the Assembly, and the question was soon disposed of.

In this particular case, perhaps the course pursued

by Mr. Donnell was judicious; still, it was believed that he occasionally erred by remaining silent in the midst of exciting debate, when he ought to have spoken. The probability, however, is, that more error is ordinarily committed in deliberative bodies by speaking too much than too little.

It is said that Dr. Witherspoon rarely spoke in the judicatories of the church, and his speeches, when made, were always short. He generally delayed his remarks till all the facts, on both sides of the question, were presented; when he would sum up the testimony and arguments on each side, and seldom failed to close the debate. Thus, like Mr. Donnell, he moved as a kind of "*balance-wheel*" in the judicatory.

CHAPTER XXII.

MR. DONNELL IN THE PULPIT.

First Sight of him in the Pulpit peculiarly Impressive—In the Pulpit at Russellville, Ky.—Reminiscence of him in the Pulpit by Rev. C. Haynes—By Rev. J. M. Penick—By Rev. Joel Knight—By Rev. M. Priest—By Rev. J. N. Edmonston—By Rev. Samuel McSpedden—By Rev. Isaac Shook—By Rev. James H. Shields—By Rev. W. Rolston —By Rev. J. C. Provine—By Col. J. S. Topp—By Rev. A. J. Steel—By James McCord, Esq.

I NEVER saw a man whose personal appearance was better adapted to fill the pulpit with dignity, than Mr. Donnell's. A stranger, seeing him for the first time in the sacred desk, never failed to be particularly struck with his appearance. The first time the writer ever saw him, was at a Synodical meeting in Russellville, Kentucky, before the Synod was divided, and the General Assembly formed. He was in the act of rising to preach the opening sermon when I entered the church. A solemn dignity, mingled with an expression of intelligence on his countenance, at once indicated that no ordinary man was before me. He was then in the full maturity of his intellectual powers, and high career of his popularity. The service was introduced by reading the well-known hymn of Dr. Watts, commencing, "Go preach my Gospel, saith the Lord." On reading the line, "On a bright cloud to heaven he rode," he turned his eyes upward, looking as though he actually saw the ascending Saviour. Singing being ended, prayer commenced, which seemed to be poured forth from a heart that was the very sanctuary of devotion. No redundant expression—no tedious repetition—every word appropriate, and uttered as if the preacher *felt* that he was talking with God. I thought it the most complete model of prayer I had ever heard—whether considered in reference to richness and appropriateness of matter, or power of utterance.

The text was, "We are laborers together with God." (*I. Cor. iii: 9.*) The hymn and prayer had so fixed the attention of the audience, that all eyes were directed to the pulpit when the text was read, and every countenance indicated high expectation. He was rather slow at the commencement of the discourse ; but as he proceeded, he increased in fervor, and his delivery became more rapid. A concise view was given of what God *had done,* and was *then doing,* to save sinners, and also what sinners themselves must do in order to be saved. I thought I had never before heard the line so clearly drawn between human and divine agency in man's salvation. The matter of the sermon was original, the manner bold and impressive, and the arguments irresistible—so plain that they could be understood by the most ignorant, and yet so rich and instructive as to be enjoyed by the most cultivated intellect ; perfectly systematic in arrangement of thought ; no confusion of ideas ; each part seemed to be a distinct step in the reasoning, and the main idea was felt at once to

be just so much of an advance of the one that preceded
it. In the application, an appeal was made to ministers, respecting their duty as laborers with God in the
conversion of sinners, that I have never heard excelled.
The effect was overwhelming. To use the language of
Gen. Jackson, in reference to a sermon preached by
Dr. Durbin, the whole discourse was the "logic of the
Gospel set on fire by the fervid zeal of devotion to
Christ. All were awed into silence and reverence, and
felt as though they stood before the awful majesty of
the eternal God." Never before did a preacher's abilities meet my expectations, when his fame had reached
me in advance of him. I had heard of Mr. Donnell,
and formed high expectations; but in his first sermon
they were more than realized.

He preached twice afterward, during the Synod, and
each discourse seemed to surpass the first. Perhaps
no minister ever visited Russellville, that attracted
more attention. One of his sermons was from Acts
xvi: 17—"These men are the servants of the most
high God, which show unto us the way of salvation."
A very eminent lawyer of the town observed, at the
close of the discourse, that "when it commenced, the
way of salvation appeared mysteriously dark; but at
the close, it seemed mysteriously plain."

It is said of Mr. Hooker, that " when he entered the
pulpit, he made all feel that they were in the house of
God, and at the same time looked as though he could
put a king in his pocket." No statement could be
more descriptive of Mr. Donnell in the pulpit.

While he was delivering a sermon in the city of Nashville, in the midst of the great revival, out of which the Cumberland Presbyterian church of that city grew, the audience became deeply affected. The late Judge Grundy, and the father of Hon. E. M. Foster were sitting near together, and were so overpowered with the discourse, that they caught each other by the hand, Judge Grundy audibly exclaiming, " That is the truth, Col. Foster, and it will stand in the day of judgment."

There was nothing in Mr. Donnell's style of preaching, of what might be called direct or personal address and appeal, until near the close of his discourse. A steady didactic chain of thought and argument was maintained, as though he was preparing a lever for some mighty work, and when he came to use it in a brief application, the effect was often irresistible. The whole weight of his accumulated reasoning was brought to bear upon the conscience and heart; and many a strong man felt his courage and insensibility give way under it, if he was an unbeliever; or his resolution for holy living and active zeal quickened. if he was already a disciple of Christ.

Several persons have kindly furnished reminiscences of their impressions, &c., the first time they ever saw Mr. Donnell in the pulpit, which cannot fail to be interesting, particularly to those who never saw him; and which will be better calculated to preserve some likeness of him when his cotemporaries and acquaintances shall all have passed away, than anything the writer could say.

Rev. Cyrus Haynes remarks: "My first recollection of Mr. Donnell was in 1810. I was then about five years old, but his dignified manner in the pulpit, and in his social intercourse, made an impression on my mind at that early period which I have not yet forgotten. He had studied in youth the rudiments of vocal music, and his voice was wonderfully adapted to singing. He never failed to interest an audience when engaged in that exercise. The hymn of Dr. Watts, commencing, 'My God, my life, my love,' was a great favorite with him; and I never see the hymn, or hear it sung, without thinking of Mr. Donnell.

"He began at a very early period of his ministry delivering a lecture on the distinctive doctrines of the Cumberland Presbyterian church. The first time I heard this lecture, was at Marshal's camp-ground, in 1820. He used as a motto, 'I speak as unto wise men, judge ye what I say.' He showed in a clear and most forcible manner wherein Cumberland Presbyterianism differed from Calvinism and Armenianism. A gentleman of much respectability for talents, as well as standing in the Presbyterian church, took exceptions to the lecture, so far as it referred to Calvinism, and spent nearly the whole night, after the discourse was delivered, in debate with Mr. Donnell, in a camp. A few persons sat up listening to them, and were of the opinion that Mr. Donnell was equally as conclusive in private debate as he had been in the pulpit.

"I will merely add, that I regarded Mr. Donnell as one of the most deeply pious and holy men I ever knew, and his usefulness as a preacher I think has rarely been excelled."

Rev. J. M. Penick: "The first time I ever heard Mr. Donnell preach, was at the General Assembly, at Elkton, Kentucky. His subject was the Holy Waters— Ezekiel xlvii. Several years afterward, a prominent lawyer asked me what had become of that old fisherman. Knowing to whom he alluded, I asked him if he had not forgotten that sermon yet? No, said he; and I shall not while I live. He was an irreligious man; but the reply indicated the deep impression made upon his mind by the discourse. He was not alone: the sermon made a lasting impression upon the audience. I heard Mr. Donnell preach but once afterward. His text was, 'Examine yourselves whether ye be in the faith; prove your own selves. Know ye not your own selves, how that Jesus Christ be in you, except ye be reprobates?' (*II. Cor. xiii: 5.*) I thought I had never before heard the Calvinistic views of the doctrine of eternal and unconditional election and reprobation so fully confuted."

Rev. Joel Knight: "The first time that I ever saw Mr. Donnell, was at the Synodical meeting at Princeton, Kentucky, in 1826. The Synod was then the highest judicatory of our church. He preached on Sunday, and I regarded the sermon, whether considered with respect to matter, manner or spirit, as one of the greatest discourses I had ever heard; and my opinion then formed has not yet changed."

Rev. M. Priest: "Mr. Donnell preached with the demonstration of the Spirit, and with power; and I regarded him as the greatest preacher of our church, if not the greatest of the age. He was not only great, but good. I fear his mantle has fallen on but few of his sons in the ministry. More than once I have known him close his sermon upon his knees, praying sinners to become reconciled to God. He lived for the benefit of mankind, and in his death the country has lost a benefactor. His works will follow him, and in heaven many redeemed spirits will hail him as their spiritual father."

Rev. J. N. Edmonston: "The first time I ever heard Mr. Donnell preach, was at a Synodical meeting, at Columbia, Tennessee. It was a doctrinal sermon, embodying the distinctive peculiarities of Cumberland Presbyterians. On the next day, he delivered a most impressive exhortation. He commenced by repeating, in his characteristic tone and emphasis, the text, 'Let us not be weary in well-doing, for in due season we shall reap if we faint not.' The church in town was small, and struggling for a position of usefulness. He dwelt with much earnestness and feeling upon the words, *in due season we shall reap*, &c. His words were as apples of gold in pictures of silver. The meeting continued several weeks after the close of Synod, and many were converted and added to the church."

Rev. Samuel McSpedden: "I heard Mr. Donnell preach Mr. McGee's funeral sermon, at the Beech, and at Smith's Fork. He used the same text, 'He being dead yet speaketh'—(*Heb. xi : 4,*)—at both places, and the sermons were substantially the same. At the close of each discourse, he called on all who believed they had been convicted and converted under Mr. McGee's preaching, to indicate it by a signal which he prescribed. Quite a number gave the sign. He then requested all who had enjoyed the comforts of religion, under the ministry of the deceased, to make it known. To that proposition, every christian in the congregation gave the signal, and a general burst of feeling prevailed all over the assembly. Mr. Donnell then showed, in his beautiful and masterly manner, how Mr. McGee was still speaking in that congregation, and would continue to speak in the lives of christians.

"In my estimation, there never has been a greater man in the Cumberland Presbyterian church than Mr. Donnell."

Rev. Isaac Shook : " Some twenty-five years ago, Mr. Donnell held a sacramental meeting in a very wealthy

32—

neighborhood of Limestone county, Alabama, where, unfortunately, most of the leading men were professed infidels. On Sabbath morning, he rode from home to the meeting, in company with one of his neighbors, who observed that he traveled most of the way with his head uncovered, apparently engaged in ejaculatory prayer. That day he preached a powerful and convincing sermon on the truth of the Scriptures. The result was, nearly all the infidels of the neighborhood were convinced of their error—soon made a profession of religion, and a very extensive revival followed."

Rev. James H. Shields, of the Presbyterian church: "It is perhaps about forty years since I first saw Mr. Donnell, and heard him preach. He was in company with Revs. Samuel King, J. B. Porter, Robert Bell, and Robert Guthrie—all, as I thought, powerful preachers. But Mr. Donnell, like Israel's first king, was head and shoulders above them all, both physically and intellectually. In person, he was large, portly, grave and dignified. His gestures in the pulpit were natural; voice commanding and strong, yet musical and well disciplined. His perception of truth was clear, and he possessed the happy art of delivering it so that others would understand it.

"The last time I ever saw him was in the fall of 1830. He attended a meeting, in company with the late Rev. John Morgan, in the town of Franklin, Tenn. After the latter had preached a most excellent sermon, Mr. Donnell delivered an exhortation, which I still recollect with much interest. Indeed, everything about that extraordinary man still has a hallowed place in my memory. But he has fallen; and who among his sons in the ministry will ever wear his mantle? Like him, may we all fall at our posts."

Rev. W. Rolston: "I became acquainted with Mr. Donnell in the fall of 1819, at a camp-meeting at the Beech meeting-house, Sumner county, Tenn. I was then a sinful youth, and had never before seen a camp-meeting. Mr. Donnell preached on Sabbath to a very large assembly of people, from the text, 'That as sin hath reigned unto death, even so might grace reign through righteousness unto eternal life, by Jesus Christ our Lord.' (*Rom. v: 21.*) I had heard Dr. Blackburn* preach in his most palmy days, but never before were such impressions made on my mind in reference to religion, as I received under that sermon. He called for mourners, and many appeared before the pulpit. I remember one remark he made in the invitation, with great emphasis, which was; 'Let the greatest sinner come first.' I did not present myself as a seeker of religion on that occasion, but ever afterward attended the ministration of truth by Cumberland Presbyterian ministers, believing that God was with them.

"After I made a profession of religion, and entered the ministry, I frequently attended camp-meetings with

---

* Dr. Blackburn was a celebrated preacher of the Presbyterian church, and one of the first orators of the country.

Mr. Donnell. In 1831, I aided him at one in Wilson county, Tenn., at which upward of one hundred persons professed religion. He preached on Sabbath, at 11 o'clock, with great effect, to a large audience. About an hour after closing his sermon, and while a powerful work was going on immediately before the pulpit, he took a position in the rear of the congregation, in the midst of a crowd of careless sinners, read and sung a hymn, prayed, announced a text, and then preached another most awakening sermon, and again called for mourners. Thus, the work spread throughout the vast assembly. He often pursued this course at camp-meetings, and with much success.

" He was never discouraged at small congregations, but preached as though he had a large audience before him. I recollect to have been present at one of his appointments, on a week-day, when, owing to its being quite a busy season of the year with farmers, but few came to hear him. He, however, preached as though the house had been crowded; and a great revival of religion commenced in the neighborhood. A young lady present was converted—introduced religion into a large and respectable family, and subsequently became the wife of a minister of the Gospel—and after a long life of usefulness in the church, left the world in the triumph of faith. The people of the vicinity had been in the habit, for many years, of celebrating the fourth of July in the woods, with what they called a bran-dance. Over the very spot that had been cleaned off for that purpose, a large arbor was erected, under which many sinners professed religion, from time to time, at camp-meetings—all growing out of the little unostentatious meeting already alluded to."

Rev. J. C. Provine: "Long will I remember a funeral sermon preached by Mr. Donnell, in reference to the death of my mother and uncle. It was delivered under the arbor of Big Spring camp-ground, to a large and attentive audience. The matter of the discourse was well adapted to the occasion, and the *manner* of the speaker was unusually solemn and impressive. Often have I heard aged persons allude to that sermon with great interest."

Col. John S. Topp: "When I first saw Mr. Donnell, and heard him preach, I was a youth of 16 or 17 years old. His personal appearance and bearing in the pulpit were commanding and dignified. His sermons were unusually attractive and edifying, and his earnest manner and power seldom failed to interest the large audiences that attended his ministrations of truth. His skill and prudence in calling out or developing impressions made under his sermons, were conceded by all; and his counsel at camp and protracted meetings was uniformly sought and appreciated.

"Under his preaching at Lebanon, Tennessee, I received my abiding convictions, which, as I trust, led me to submit as a guilty sinner to be saved by grace."

Rev. A. J. Steel: "The first time I ever saw Mr.

Donnell, or heard him preach, was in 1818. It was at Meridian church, Alabama. His text was, ' Who is on the Lord's side?' (*Exodus xxxii: 26.*) Great power attended the discourse, and myself, sister, and many others were deeply convicted. On the evening of the same day, he preached again, with great power, from 'Why stand ye here all the day idle?' (*Matt. xx: 6.*) I attended his ministry for several months that summer; witnessed frequent revivals under his preaching; professed religion myself, and soon afterward became a candidate for the ministry, in the Tennessee Presbytery, of which he was a member.

"It was my privilege to hear Mr. Donnell preach many years, and I do not recollect ever to have heard him deliver a sermon that did not produce a visible effect upon the audience. I have often heard wicked men say that it was impossible to listen to him in the pulpit without feeling the necessity of religion. His preaching seemed to have more weight, both with saint and sinner, than any man's I ever heard."

James McCord, Esq.: " The first time I ever saw Mr. Donnell, was in Franklin county, Tenn., in the neighborhood of the old Goshen church. He was then quite a young man, dressed in plain homespun; his coat after the fashion of the Methodists of 1800. He delivered his sermon, standing in the door of a cabin, a portion of his audience being in the house, and the rest in the yard, for want of room inside. The sermon produced a deep impression on his hearers—many of whom he doubtless found in heaven, on his arrival in that happy world.

"In describing Mr. Donnell's character in general terms, I would say, in the language of Scripture, 'He was a good man, and full of the Holy Ghost and of faith: and much people were added to the Lord.' He was the most industrious, untiring, zealous, faithful, humble and godly preacher I ever knew."

CHAPTER XXIII.

MR. DONNELL IN THE PULPIT.—CONTINUED.

Reminiscence by Rev. M. Bird, D.D.—By Rev. A. M. Bryan, D.D.—By Rev. S. Corley—By Rev. H. B. Warren, D.D.—By Rev. T. C. Anderson, D.D.—By Dr. J. S. Blair--By Rev. R. Burrow, D.D.—By Rev. R. Beard, D.D.

REV. M. BIRD, D.D.: "Mr. Donnell's manner in the pulpit was natural; his voice was singularly impressive and agreeable; his enunciation clear and distinct. In his attitude and gestures he was graceful and dignified; his action grave and appropriate, varied with the character of his subject. There was an unearthly unction in his delivery. The love of Christ in his heart showed itself in his countenance, in his eye, and in the tones of his voice. His eloquence was not artificial, manufactured by a mechanical observance of the rules found written in the books. These did not control him as did the *unwritten* rules of eloquence, which operate by a kind of instinct in the mind of the orator, and are those higher principles, which have ever guided the great masters of the art.

"Mr. Donnell was a working preacher, and in this respect stood in the front rank of his profession. In his day, no minister, in his own or any other denomination, excelled him in usefulness. He is still fondly remembered, and will be while his church lives."

Rev. A. M. Bryan, D.D.: "I first saw and heard Mr. Donnell preach about thirty-nine years ago. I thought him one of the finest looking and most dignified men I had ever seen in the pulpit. It was at a camp-meeting near Russellville, Ky.

"After preaching a most powerful and effective sermon, on the love of God in giving his Son to die for a lost and ruined world, he came out of the pulpit, as was common in that day with the preachers of our church, and passed through the congregation, singing and shaking hands with the people. I stood leaning against the pulpit, much affected with the sermon, as he came out, when he laid his hand gently on my head, saying, 'Oh, my son, you must have religion.' I then and there formed the purpose to become a disciple of Jesus Christ. Four years afterward, I was introduced into the ministry; and I still remember, with much tenderness, the name of Donnell, as the chief instrument, under God, of my conversion. I regarded him as one of the most forcible and powerful preachers I ever heard."

Rev. S. Corley: "The last time I heard Mr. Donnell preach, previous to his removal from Tennessee to Alabama, was at Big Spring camp-meeting, in Wilson county, Tenn. He had left his afflicted wife, by whose bed-side he had watched for many weeks, to visit a dying mother, in the vicinity of the camp-meeting. Having some distance to travel from his home in Jackson county, after hearing of his mother's approaching
33—

death, he did not reach her residence in time to receive her blessing, but in time to join the funeral procession, and witness the mournful service of committing her body to the grave. This being done, he set out for the camp-meeting alluded to. He arrived on Saturday morning, while the people were at breakfast. Mr. Calhoun had just risen from the table, and gone out to arrange preaching for the day; but was immediately called back, to see Mr. Donnell. I saw them meet. The greeting was, of course, most cordial; how could it be otherwise? Mr. Donnell wept; he had left a sick wife at home, and it was doubtful whether he would ever see her again; and on the previous day, had seen the grave closed upon the remains of a beloved mother. No wonder that he shed tears. But the good man, in whose camp he stood, wept too—for Calhoun had learned to weep with those that weep. For a moment there was silence. Mr. Calhoun spoke first, saying, 'How is your wife?' 'I left her quite feeble,' was the reply. 'How is your mother?' The weeping son replied, 'She is well now, for I trust she is in heaven.'

"At this moment, it was announced that breakfast was ready for Mr. Donnell; when Mr. Calhoun invited him to the table, saying, 'Excuse my absence; I was just arranging preaching for the day.' 'Have you directed any one to preach this morning?' said Mr. Donnell. 'Not yet,' was the reply. 'Then let me preach.' 'No,' said Mr. Calhoun; 'I want to reserve you for the service at 11 o'clock.' 'I want to preach this morning,' rejoined the other. 'Then,' said Mr. Calhoun, 'you shall preach;' and he *did preach*. God's people rejoiced, and sinners trembled under the sermon. My own fears were much awakened.

"At the hour of 11 o'clock, I saw Mr. Donnell again go into the pulpit, and take up the Bible. I knew what it meant. I was glad, and yet I was afraid. He sang, and God seemed to be in the hymn. His text was, 'Why will ye die?' (*Ezek. xxxiii : 11.*) I sat awhile, but so great were my convictions, that I fled to the woods. He preached again at night, with similar power and results. On Sabbath, he preached three sermons; and increased power attended each discourse. His text on Monday was, 'For tophet is ordained of old : yea, for the king it is prepared; he hath made it deep and large; the pile thereof is fire and much wood; the breath of the Lord, like a stream of brimstone, doth kindle it.' (*Isa. xxx : 33.*) He made a pile of wood, by supposing all the timber in Wilson county to be collected together; then all in the State of Tennessee; then all in the United States; then all in the world. After collecting the whole into one mighty mass, he set fire to it, and wrapped the sinner in the flames. The effect on the congregation was overwhelming. I again retreated to the woods; but the impression made by the sermon on my heart was abiding.

"Tuesday morning, he left to see, as he said to Mr. Calhoun, in a short time, the last of his beloved wife."

Rev. H. B. Warren, D.D.: "Mr. Donnell, in his personal appearance, was commanding, and his manner prepossessing. He was perhaps a little over six feet high; of stout, muscular frame, florid complexion, and aquiline nose. In gesticulation, he was forcible, not studied, but good—always indicating a heart deeply impressed with the importance and magnitude of his subject. Respecting his character as an orator, there would, perhaps, be some diversity of opinion. If true eloquence, however, consists in the speaker's feeling the importance of his subject, and making others see and feel it likewise, then was Mr. Donnell eloquent. He was a man of giant intellect, and, like the industrious bee, that gathers honey from every flower, he entered the vast laboratory spread out before him, and obtained knowledge, both from nature and revelation.

" He was my senior in the ministry, and from him I learned some of my first lessons in theology. I was often associated with him at meetings, and can say that there was a promptitude and energy in his discharge of ministerial duty, which I have seldom, if ever, seen in any other preacher of the Gospel."

President Anderson : " In my youthful and wild days, drawn by the prospect of agreeable company, I wandered off to a camp-meeting, at Big Spring. Very early on Sabbath morning, I was attracted to the stand by the soft tones of a mellow, plaintive voice, engaged in solemn and earnest prayer. After prayer, a very large, portly, and benevolent looking man, rose in the pulpit, sung a tender solo, and then said, 'His father required him, when a boy, to feed the sheep and calves before breakfast, and then do a full day's work besides ; and he supposed he ought to be willing to do as much for his Heavenly Father.' Struck with the appearance of the man, and delighted with the simplicity of his style, I inquired, ' *Who is he?*' The answer was, '*That is big Bob Donnell.*'

" Unacquainted as I was, at that time, with preachers beyond the limits of my own neighborhood, Mr. Donnell's fame had reached me ; and I determined to listen for the first time to the great Alabama preacher. For thirty minutes he talked to christians, particularly to the younger members of the church, in a style and manner that completely captivated me, sinner as I was; and from indications among the people, I concluded the sheep had indeed been well fed, and that they had truly relished the food.

" At 11 o'clock, he again occupied the stand, and delivered to about five thousand persons the most lucid, persuasive, and powerful sermon, I had ever heard. The whole assembly were spell-bound, and not a few melted into tears. Many of the ungodly said they had never heard such preaching before.

" He administered the sacrament of the Lord's Supper at 3 o'clock in the evening. His talk before the communion excelled anything I had ever heard on the subject. He first gathered christians around the cross, and held them there till they became melted with its sympathies ; then led them away, in imagination, to the sunny plains of paradise, and verdant banks of the river of life, till many seemed to fancy that they had already gained a sight of the promised land.

"I left the meeting with the conviction that I could not long stand such preaching, without becoming religious.

"In the fall of 1830, I saw Mr. Donnell again, in Synod, at Gallatin, Tennessee; and heard him deliver what he called his Theological System, with a perspicuity and conclusiveness, such as I have never heard from any other man. He then made an appeal to the unconverted, that brought scores of them to the altar of prayer—many of whom, in the morning of the resurrection, will appear as stars in his crown.*

"His exhortations were not less powerful than his sermons. I have yet to hear the man that could excel him in extemporaneous exhortations. When under excitement, his appeals were grand : rich in imagery, solemn as eternity, and subduing as the sympathies of the cross. In a word, he approached nearer my ideas of an inspired apostle, than any man I ever heard in the pulpit.

"If Timothy cherished for Paul more reverence than I did for Robert Donnell, his feelings were certainly chargeable with idolatry."

---

* The writer heard Mr. Donnell deliver the same lecture to which Dr. Anderson alludes, at old Mount Moriah, Logan county, Kentucky. I thought then, and still think, it was the most wonderful display of intellectual power and eloquence I had ever heard.

Dr. J. S. Blair, (of Athens, Alabama:) "At a camp-meeting, at Blue Spring, Madison county. Ala., held in the month of May, 1813. Mr. Donnell preached on the text, 'For there are three that bear record in heaven : the Father, the Word, and the Holy Ghost; and these three are one.' (*I. John v : 7.*) His object was to prove the divinity of Christ. In an adjoining neighborhood, there was a large and growing congregation of schismatics, or Stoneites, as they were then called, many of whom were present. The sermon was of thrilling interest, and so conclusive in argument that a prominent Stoneite rose to his feet, in the midst of the discourse, and walked to the pulpit, and taking the preacher by the hand, said: 'My conscience bears me testimony that you are preaching the truth.' That heretical congregation soon disappeared, while many Cumberland churches have been planted in that county, that will long cherish the memory of our beloved Donnell. I was present when the above incident occurred; and although a small boy, it is still fresh in my memory.

"From the first commencement of Mr. Donnell's labors in Alabama, they were attended with powerful revivals of religion; but many of the converts were drawn into other churches, under the influence of their time-honored creeds, numerical strength, &c. The impression had obtained, too, that Cumberland Presbyterian doctrine differed but little from other churches. To meet this difficulty, Mr. Donnell prepared an oral lecture, in which he drew the lines in a most clear and forcible manner, between the doctrines of *his* church, and the creeds of other denominations of the country. The lecture required nearly three hours in its delivery. It excelled anything I ever heard for its force of argument and clear analysis. It was called for on all popular occasions, and produced a great change in public sentiment.

"Not long before the death of Mr. Donnell, we passed by old Concord camp-ground, in Madison county, Ala., when he informed me that, at a camp-meeting at that place, he delivered, on Sabbath, his lecture for the first time; and then proceeded to give the details of its preparation. Among other things, he stated that he spent Saturday of the meeting, in the woods, except the time occupied in the pulpit, and slept none that night, until just before daylight, Sabbath morning. During the whole twenty-four hours, his mind was absorbed with the subject of his lecture."

Dr. Blair also furnishes the following incident, which illustrates, not only the deep piety of Mr. Donnell, but his extraordinary power in the pulpit:

"He appointed a sacramental meeting, at Fayetteville, Lincoln county, Tenn., to commence on the 4th of July, 1829. On his way to the meeting, he felt an unusual spirit of prayer, that God would be present on the occasion, to bless His truth, and save sinners. Uncommon access to a throne of grace, and a realizing faith in the promises of Divine truth, gave a comfortable assurance that a wonderful revival of religion was at hand.

" He arrived in town the evening before the meeting began; and the news was immediately circulated, that on the next day, he would preach a sermon, adapted to the anniversary of our National Independence. The church was crowded at an early hour, and high expectations were indicated by the countenances of the audience. The text is not recollected. The love of country, however, was the theme; and when the preacher saw that the spirit of patriotism was glowing in every bosom, he, with a skill peculiar to himself, changed the subject to a love of God, and His government. His arguments to prove a higher obligation to Jehovah, than to our country, were irresistible. Sinners saw and felt that they were rebels against Heaven; and at the close of the sermon, when the ambassador of Christ proposed terms of reconciliation, many acceded to the conditions offered, and became loyal subjects of the King of Kings.

" A revival of religion now commenced, that soon spread, not over Fayetteville alone, but over the surrounding country, embracing all classes of society. The following incident will show the extent of its influence. An old, hardened sinner, did everything in his power to arrest the progress of the work; but finding his efforts unavailing, assumed to act as the representative of his Satanic master, and wrote and put up a notice in several places, saying—

" 'I have opposed, with all the powers I possess, Jesus Christ, whom I hate, as I also do his followers, his worship, and ordinances. I have labored with ardor and

34—

perseverence to keep his religion away from Fayetteville; but all to no purpose. I now yield and give up the town, and five miles around, to that religion which I despise—reserving to myself the right still to oppose it *personally*. And I hereby give, grant, and bequeath my soul and body to the Devil, for whom I intend to live, and in whose service I intend to die;'—signing his name as the friend and agent of the Devil.

" But the revival spread in every direction, and Mr. Donnell followed it with his great and wonderful powers of mind, appealing to the irreligious, and arousing christians, and calling on them to come up to the help of the Lord against the mighty.

" I will barely add, that his power in the pulpit excelled any preacher I ever heard. At camp-meetings, I have seen him rise in the pulpit, after every other preacher had failed to reach the audience, and make appeals which it seemed impossible to resist."

Rev. R. Burrow, D.D: " When Mr. Donnell and I were in Pennsylvania, in 1831, we visited the town of Washington, in that State. On our arrival, the Methodist brethren expressed a desire to hear a sermon on the distinctive doctrines of our church; and tendered the use of their pulpit for that purpose—requesting, to use their own language, that the ship might be presented under full sail. Mr. Donnell accepted the invitation, and launched out in presence of a large congregation, making one of his most happy efforts. The sermon produced such an effect upon the audience, that it was thought best to close the door of the church against us afterward."

Rev. R. Beard, D. D.: "When I first saw Mr. Donnell, I was a little boy: I suppose, nine or ten years of age. I was living with my grandfather, and was absent one day on domestic business, during the forenoon. On my return, Mr. Donnell was there. He had called, in company with his mother, for dinner, and to rest an hour from a journey, which they were making. His name was familiar in my grandfather's family. I then thought preachers the greatest of men, as I now think they *ought to be;* and, of course, my childish attention was directed to him at once. Even then, his manly form and easy manner, made an impression upon my mind. I recollect one circumstance of the day, very distinctly. My grandfather had been a Presbyterian for many years, and had in his little library an old copy of the Confession of Faith. Mr. Donnell, in looking among the books, found it, and made some jocular remark about it. The old gentleman relished a joke, and retorted in a very pithy one. I shall never forget his words; but they were rather too antiquated for such a paper as this. The whole matter passed off very humorously and pleasantly.

"I saw him no more until the fall of 1817. He had then become one of the most popular preachers in the church. The occasion was a camp-meeting, at the Beech meeting-house. I had professed religion about six weeks previously. It was, of course, a great occasion with myself; and my recollections of it are very vivid. On the Sabbath of that meeting, Mr. Donnell delivered the sermon in relation to the death of Rev. William McGee. The circumstances were very impressive. Mr. McGee had formerly lived in that neighborhood, and, I believe, had been the pastor of that congregation. The same sermon was delivered elsewhere, and is no doubt recollected by many others. It was a powerful appeal to the feelings of those who had struggled through the difficulties attending the organization of the Cumberland Presbytery.

"In the fall of 1819, I saw and heard him again, at a camp-meeting, at Sugg's creek. My recollection is, that he did not then come up to my expectations. Perhaps the reason was, that the sermon was preceded by a very powerful one, by Mr. Ewing. He may have appeared to disadvantage on that account.

"In the fall of 1820, he attended a camp-meeting again, at the Beech meeting-house. The meeting succeeded the meeting of the Presbytery, at which I was licensed to preach. The weather was cold and uncomfortable. He preached on Sunday. The congregation were out of doors, without shelter, and the snow was falling during the most of the sermon; yet they heard, with fixed attention. The text was, 'That as sin hath reigned unto death, even so might grace reign through righteousness unto eternal life, by Jesus Christ our Lord.' I recollect distinctly, to this day, his manner of treating the subject. He explained how sin reigned, producing death intellectually, morally, physically; on the other hand, how grace reigned, counteracting the reign of sin. I received, that day, strange as it may now seem, my first ideas on the subject of mental philosophy. It was not what is called a metaphysical sermon; still, it was filled with *evangelical metaphysics*. It was the only sermon I ever heard, or read, that I attempted at any time to reproduce myself. For several years of my early ministry, however, I made a very free use of the materials of that sermon. I sometimes think now of that occasion, with astonishment. A man preaching in the open air, for two hours, in a cold, autumnal day, on a metaphysical subject; and a congregation listening with unflagging attention to the close—the snow falling all the while—would be a novelty in these days of fine churches, short sermons, and impatient congregations.

"The next particular occasion, which my memory calls up, was a camp-meeting, in the neighborhood of Russellville, Kentucky. The meeting immediately followed a meeting of the Cumberland Synod, in the town. Mr. Donnell preached on Saturday evening. His object was to set forth his theological landmarks. His text, 'I speak as unto wise men, judge ye what I say,' served merely as a starting-point. I recollect one principle which he presented, and illustrated with great clearness and force. The principle was, that regeneration is a *spiritual* or *moral change*, produced by the Spirit of God, operating by the use of moral means, in opposition to the theory that it is merely an *intellectual change*. I suppose the doctrine was not new to everybody, but it

was new to me. I had regarded regeneration, up to
that time, as a sort of physical change—of which, however, I had no definite idea. The next day, he delivered
a funeral sermon, in relation to the death of Judge
Ewing, a brother, I believe, of Rev. Finis Ewing. I
have seldom heard such a sermon; indeed, I do not
know that I ever heard such an one. The thoughts
were like masses of granite, piled upon one another.
Every word, too, seemed to be in its proper place and
time. The preacher was not inspired, of course, in the
ordinary sense of inspiration; still, the effort *seemed* to
have something of the supernatural in it. Great ideas
were invested in the most impressive language.

"These are some of my earlier recollections of Mr.
Donnell. I might multiply them almost indefinitely, by
following up my acquaintance with him, to the time of
his death. I need not multiply, however. The occasions of which I speak, were connected with the meridian of his life, and usefulness, and power. As his
sun went down, he lost some of his strength. This was
to be expected; still, he lost none of that dignity and
force of character, which always command respect.

"I may add, in a few words, my general impressions
of Mr. Donnell. It is proper to say here, that my acquaintance with him was rather a public, than a private
one. I was seldom in his society, except on public occasions. We met frequently in the judicatures of the
church; but for a long time he was so much my senior,
in age and relative position, that I could not become

very intimate with him. Later years, however, brought us nearer together. Still, even then my acquaintance was rather public than private. But no man could be with him without receiving impressions of his character; and,

"1. His *piety* was unquestionable. His sermons, his prayers, his conversation—as far as a judgment could be formed of them from a limited private intercourse—all indicated the same thing. I say it was *unquestionable.* It appeared in all his deportment; in whatever he did or said. His was a deep, as well as fervent, sanctifying piety. He *feared God*, and his aim was *to keep His commandments.*

"2. No one could hear him without feeling—I say *feeling*—that he had a spiritual call to the work of the ministry. There was an unction in the truths which he communicated, that even a superficial observer would detect; and his heart would attribute it to an unearthly source. He would feel that the preacher was a man divinely commissioned.

"3. His *kindness* and *gentleness* were remarkable. I have seen him in the midst of heated debate; surrounded by the most trying difficulties that the Cumberland Presbyterian church ever experienced; yet I never saw his temper ruffled, nor heard him use a sharp word. His counsels were always conciliatory; his words were words of peace. Particularly were his kindness and tenderness developed in his relations to young men. While some of his compeers in the ministry were by no means remarkable for these traits of character, in such relations, I never heard a complaint of him; never saw anything to which the most sensitive mind could object. The consequence was, that young men, brought into the ministry by his influence, loved him almost to idolatry. They still regard his memory with more than filial reverence.

"4. Mr. Donnell was a *great man*. I use this expression in no common-place sense. His physiognomy, his personal presence, his whole exterior, would have indicated to a stranger that he was no ordinary man. But the pulpit was his throne. Here he developed his strength, and I am very certain, that I have never heard the performances of his best days excelled by any pulpit orator. He was clear, self-possessed, dignified, often majestic; he never resorted to rhetorical arts, but always commanded attention. He secured more than attention; he was heard with respect. He had a constitution of great strength; his voice was like a trumpet. No man was ever better adapted to preaching to such crowds, as assembled at a South-western camp-meeting, than he. At the same time, he was equally at home in a city pulpit, as his labors in several of our South-western cities illustrate.

"5. I conclude this sketch, by remarking that, as it seems to me, it must be very difficult to overlook the providence of God, in raising up such men as Mr. Donnell, and his fellow laborers, in this country, at the time they were raised up. They were pre-eminently the men for the circumstances which surrounded them. Was all this the work of accident? Did the circumstances themselves form and develop the men? Believe it who can. I see in these things myself the operations of a wise mind, which is always looking to the exigencies of the church, and furnishing her with such agencies as those exigencies require. Whatever may be the future destiny of the Cumberland Presbyterian church—and I hope its destiny may be a realization of its early promise—a serious man, acquainted with its history, will find it difficult to deny that the hand of God was present in its organization, and in the struggles of its first years. Such men as Mr. Donnell, left their impressions upon society. The impression was deep. The results of their work are before the world. Many of those results are developing themselves in Heaven. Those of us who follow them, will take courage, and trust in the God of our fathers."

CHAPTER XXIV.

MR. DONNELL IN THE PULPIT.—CONTINUED.

Characteristics of Pulpit Eloquence—Skill in Adapting his Sermons to
Particular Occasions—Sermon in the Cabin of Mr. Gibson—Introductory Sermon of the First General Assembly—Often Consulted
Impressions in reference to some Special Duty—Delivers an Exhortation under Peculiar Impressions—Close of a Sermon at Mooresville, Ala.—Sermon to the Young Men of Mooresville—Leaves a Revival at Winchester, and Commences a Protracted Meeting at Fayetteville—Impressed that Dr. Burrow ought to Preach at a certain
Meeting.

FROM the reminiscences furnished by the numerous
friends of Mr. Donnell, it will be seen that he possessed,
in a very high degree, the elements of a *pulpit orator.*
This was conceded by all churches, and by those who
belonged to no church. His preaching was often pronounced, by men of good taste, the best specimen of
genuine eloquence they had ever heard. He certainly
came nearer answering the *Edinburgh Review's* description of an orator, than any preacher I ever knew. "If
we were compelled to give a brief description of eloquence," says that *Review,* "we should say it is practical
'reasoning,' animated with strong emotion." Dr. West
was once asked, if President Edwards was an eloquent
preacher? He replied: "If you mean by eloquence
what is usually intended by it in our cities, he had no
pretensions to it. He had no studied varieties of voice,
and no strong emphasis. He scarcely gestured, or even

moved; and he made no attempt, by the eloquence of his style, or the beauty of his pictures, to gratify the taste, and fascinate the imagination. But if you mean, by eloquence, the power of presenting an important truth before an audience, with overwhelming weight of argument, and with such intenseness of feeling, that the whole soul of the speaker is thrown into every part of the conception and delivery, so that the solemn attention of the whole audience is riveted from the beginning to the close, and impressions are left that cannot be effaced, Mr. Edwards was the most eloquent man I ever heard speak." Leave out the name Edwards, and insert Donnell, in the above extract, and you have a literal description of the "great Alabama preacher." If power to arrest and fix the attention of a large audience, in the open air—as Dr. Beard states Mr. Donnell did—amid falling snow, and to stir up the deep feelings of soul in the congregation, is proof of eloquence, then was he an eloquent preacher.

Mr. Donnell often attracted the attention of an audience by selecting a text adapted to the peculiar circumstances with which he was surrounded, and indulged in a little singularity in reading it. In the early part of his ministry, while riding the circuit in Tennessee, he was requested to visit and preach in the vicinity of Fayetteville. He sent an appointment to the cabin of Mr. Gibson, father of the late Rev. A. G. Gibson. On the day appointed, he made his way through the canebrake, to the cabin, where he found a large congregation assembled. Without speaking to any one, he took his position in the door—part of the audience being outside of the cabin—and said, without any preliminaries whatever, " I ask, therefore, for what intent ye have sent for me?" (*Acts x: 29.*) While gazing on the people for a moment, as though he was waiting for an answer, and breathless silence prevailed in the listening crowd, Mrs. Gibson sprang to her husband, saying, in an undertone, " *Why don't you get up and tell him ?*" In the meantime, Mr. Donnell removed the suspense, by proceeding to preach a most powerful sermon, from the text repeated; and a revival of religion commenced, out of which the present Cane Creek congregation grew, where hundreds of souls have been converted. This incident was received by the Rev. C. W. McBride, from Mrs. Gibson herself, at whose house the sermon was delivered.

Since writing the above, a letter has been received from Mrs. Sarah Erwin, at whose house Mr. Donnell lived at the time of preaching that sermon. She adds, that Mrs. Gibson, then a member of the Baptist church, became deeply impressed that there was something for her to do for the salvation of the multitude of sinners on Cane creek, and determined to send for Mr. Donnell to preach to them—her husband, and a large family of children, being without religion. Mr. Gibson, and all the children, were converted in the revival that followed; and many young men that became useful ministers of the Gospel—one of whom was her own son, the late A. G. Gibson.

Mr. Donnell was appointed to preach the introductory sermon at the constitution of the first Cumberland Presbyterian General Assembly. His text was, "I am but a little child; I know not how to go out or come in." (*1. Kings iii: 7.*) The sermon was very appropriate, and left an abiding impression on the minds of the members.

He once preached to a company of strangers, while traveling on a steamboat, from the text, "Whose art thou? and whither goest thou?" (*Genesis xxxii: 17.*) He excelled any preacher I ever knew in adapting his text to the character of his congregation, and the peculiar circumstances of the occasion.

He believed that impressions, relative to a special duty, are often made directly by the Holy Ghost upon the mind, and should be obeyed. At a camp-meeting, in Alabama, many years ago, one preacher after another preached, without any apparent success; christians remained cold, and sinners unfeeling. At length, Mr. Donnell was impressed to deliver a special exhortation. He arose in the pulpit, about the twilight of evening, and commenced, by stating in a way that no man could have done but himself, that he had a friend on the ground, who had been treated with entire neglect from the commencement of the meeting; that no one had invited him to enter a camp, nor given him the slightest indication of respect; that his friend was much grieved at the cold treatment he had received, and that he himself was greatly mortified, inasmuch as he had given his neglected friend a pressing invitation to attend the meeting. By this time, inquiry was passing from one to another, in an undertone, through the congregation, who it could be that had been thus neglected? One gentleman whispered to his neighbor, "If parson Donnell will tell me who he is, I will invite him to my camp." After thus exciting curiosity to the highest point, he began to describe his friend, saying that he wore a golden girdle, his feet were like fine brass, his eye as a flame of fire, his voice as the sound of many waters, and his countenance shining as the sun in his strength. (*Revelation i : 13–16.*) The writer was not present, but he has been told that the effect upon the audience was very powerful, and that the neglected friend soon found a place in the camps and hearts of the people, and that a mighty work of God ensued.

On another occasion, Mr. Donnell was preaching at Mooresville, Alabama, just after a very successful camp-meeting had closed in the vicinity. Several of the young converts were present, and were deeply affected with the sermon; but restrained outward expressions of joy, in view of the known opposition of many in the congregation to all religious excitement. The penetrating eye of the preacher soon discovered the state of feeling before him, and he determined to turn it to good account, by calling it forth. At the close of his sermon, he said, all that felt happy, might signify it by clapping their hands three times. Clapping instantly commenced, and shouting followed; but nobody pretended to count the number of times the hands were clapped. The revival that had commenced at the camp-meeting, was transferred to town, and many sinners were converted.

Mooresville, in its early history, was a very wicked place—infested with drunkards, gamblers, infidels, &c. Mr. Donnell sent an appointment to preach in the village, and endeavored to make such preparation as he supposed circumstances required; but when the day arrived, and he reached town, his mind was strongly directed to the following text: "Rejoice, O young man, in thy youth; and let thy heart cheer thee in the days of thy youth, and walk in the ways of thine heart, and in the sight of thine eyes; but know thou, that for all these things, God will bring thee into judgment." (*Eccl. xi: 9.*) With much trembling and hesitation, he changed his subject, but did not read the last clause of the text till he had dwelt at some length on the first part. For the first time in his life, he introduced wit and humor into the pulpit. He alluded, in rather a playful manner, to the fashionable vices and sinful amusements of the day; and ironically told the young people to indulge freely in them, and enjoy all the pleasures they afforded. The audience threw off restraint, and indulged even feelings of levity. At length the preacher paused for a moment, and then informed the congregation that he had not yet read the whole of his text, and repeated the last part of it. His feelings suddenly reacted, carrying the congregation with him. The realities of the awful day of judgment were depicted, and an appeal made that was irresistible.

The foregoing incident is stated on the authority of the Rev. B. C. Chapman, who also relates the following:

Mr. Donnell, in the midst of an interesting revival of religion, at Winchester, Tennessee, in 1829, was deeply impressed to leave the meeting in charge of other ministers, and go to Fayetteville, a distance of twenty miles, and commence a protracted meeting. He obeyed the impression, and forthwith a powerful work of God began at the latter town; and before it closed, about five hundred persons, in the village and surrounding country, professed religion.

When Mr. Donnell and Dr. Burrow traveled together as missionaries, in 1831, they agreed to preach turnabout, with the understanding that if either should feel unusually impressed with the duty of preaching, though it might not be his day, he should make it known, and the rule, by mutual consent, should be suspended. On a certain day, it was Mr. Donnell's time to preach; but after entering the pulpit, he discovered that Dr. Burrow was extremely restless, and that his countenance showed much anxiety of mind. On being asked by Mr. Donnell if he did not desire to preach, he answered he did. The books were immediately turned over to him, and the effort satisfied both parties that heaven approved the change. Dr. B. perhaps never before, nor since, preached with more power. This incident was received from the Rev. Isaac Shook.

While it is admitted, that impressions in reference to religious duty, should be consulted with great caution, and never reduced to practice without "trying the spirits whether they are of God"—(*I. John iv : 1*)—yet no one, who believes the Bible, can doubt the direct influence of the Holy Ghost upon the mind, urging the performance of some special duty. Without such belief prayer would be useless, and the doctrine of being "led by the Spirit of God," could have no meaning.

Dr. Payson rendered much attention to his "feelings," especially in connection with revivals of religion; and would sometimes tell his people that God was about to revive His work, when there were no signs of a revival visible.

CHAPTER XXV.

MR. DONNELL'S METHOD OF PREPARING FOR THE PULPIT, WITH REFLECTIONS.

Statement of his Wife—Had but little time to Write—Sketched " Miscellaneous Thoughts" while riding the Circuit—Extemporaneous Habits worthy of Imitation—Reading Sermons an unnatural way of Preaching—Unwise to form the habit of committing Sermons to Memory—Anecdote of a young Preacher in London—Mr. Donnell's Sermons embodied Doctrine, Experience and Practice — Let no young Man think lightly of a Systematic Education, because Mr. Donnell became great without it—Let no one despair of Usefulness in his Master's Vineyard, because he cannot preach like Mr. Donnell.

THE surviving wife of Mr. Donnell, says: "He read much, yet thought much more than he read." And here is the secret of the intellectual development of that great man—*he thought much.* Newton, on being asked by what means he worked out his extraordinary discoveries, replied: "By always thinking on them." In relating his method of studying to another friend, he said: "I keep the subject always before me."

Mrs. Donnell adds: "I have often known Mr. Donnell open a book, and read a few pages, then take a pallet on the floor, cover his face, and spend hours in thinking, and arranging a sermon. He would then lay the discourse away in his mind, till occasion called for it, when he would bring it forth as readily as if it had been before him in manuscript." Mrs. Donnell further states, that "he never, to her knowledge, used even brief notes in the pulpit; nor does she think he made much use of the pen in preparing his sermons." She regrets that he did not write more; but attributes the neglect to his itinerant habits in the ministry. He was literally an evangelist through life, being almost constantly from home, in the service of the church. He has been heard to say, that he prepared some of his best sermons when traveling alone, on horseback.

Although it is true, as Mrs. Donnell states, that her husband had but little time to write, yet specimens of composition are found among his papers, which warrant the belief, that practice would have placed in his hand the pen of a "ready writer." Children learn to walk by walking, and to run by running; and so a good writer, or able author, is the result of much writing. Dr. Dick says: "The habit of accurate composition, depends more on practice, and the study of good writers, than on a multitude of rules." The late Professor Edwards adds: "Habits of accurate composition are the slow growth of time—of long months' of hardy discipline—the result of many a painful process."

Mr. Donnell's "Miscellaneous Thoughts," as published in 1831, in pamphlet form, and subsequently in a bound volume, were mostly written, in brief notes, while riding the circuit. He carried his ink, as heretofore stated, in the head of his cane, and paper in his saddle-bags; and when a thought occurred, worthy of preservation, it was reduced to writing. Thoughts, thus preserved, were revised and enlarged, while waiting on his first wife, in her sickness at Medical Springs. When he could be spared from her room, there was a certain log, not far distant, under the shade of a tree, to which he resorted, to study and write. This he stated in his own last affliction.

Young preachers would do well to cultivate, at the threshold of their work, Mr. Donnell's extemporaneous habits in the pulpit. Reading sermons, is an unnatural way of preaching, and unadapted to the laws of the human mind. It was introduced in England, under circumstances that seemed to demand it at the time, but which have long since passed away; and the practice of *reading*, under the name of preaching, ought to have gone with them. It was interdicted by King Charles II, who pronounced it a "supine and slothful way of preaching." The custom was unknown in the Cumberland Presbyterian church, in her early history. Her first preachers were off-hand men, ready for all emergencies. Indeed, the practice would not have been tolerated in the days of Ewing and his contemporaries. I know, it may be said that ministers of other churches, who have left a broad and deep impression on the world, read their sermons. True, Dr. Chalmers read *his* sermons; *but he was a reader*, and his sermons were original —prepared with his audience before his imagination, and steeped in his own heart before he entered the pulpit. President Edwards also had the manuscript of his sermons before him in the pulpit; but he, too, was an original writer, and extraordinary reader. It should be remembered, however, that he did not usually confine himself to his manuscript; but if a new thought occurred, while preaching, he would present it: and it generally had a better effect on his hearers than what he read. It is a fact, too, that ought to be known, that President Edwards regretted, at an advanced period of his ministry, that he had accustomed himself to the use of notes at all, and recommended young preachers not to introduce them. It will be proper here to remark, however, that while Mr. Edwards advised to avoid one error, he recommended the adoption of another: which was, to write and commit sermons to memory. This would require more labor than any preacher can bear, even in the vigor of manhood; and in old age, should he live to that period, it would oblige him to give up preaching altogether. Besides, no man's memory, even in youth, can be depended on for every word and syllable in a written sermon; and the slightest mistake would always produce embarrassment, both with the speaker and hearer.

A young preacher once visited London, with a letter of introduction to the Rev. Matthew Wilkes. On reading the letter, Mr. Wilkes said to the bearer: "Well, young man, I suppose you want to preach in London?" He replied: "I am going to spend a few days here, sir, and should like to give your people a sermon." "Well, meet me next Wednesday morning, at the church, and you can lecture in my place." The young man promptly attended, and darted along the aisle, into the pulpit, as though he was entering a ball-room. The pastor took his seat in the congregation. The introductory services were performed with much apparent confidence, and the young man then read his text; but alas! his manuscript was not before him, and memory proved treacherous. Even the first sentence of the sermon could not be recalled. He hesitated, and hemmed, then forced a stout cough—coughed again and again—but memory could not be awakened by a cough. He shut his Bible, and left the pulpit in quite a different state of mind from that in which he entered it. The pastor met him, saying, "Well, young man, you have preached in the city of London, and I have heard you—heard every word you said."

Let young preachers, if they have time, write out every important sermon they deliver; but never adopt the method of either reading or committing, but by prayerful meditation, make themselves familiar with the leading ideas and arguments, and when they enter the pulpit, depend on the spur of the moment for suitable language. *Never commit phraseology.*

The *matter* of Mr. Donnell's sermons generally embodied doctrine, experience, and practice. They were neither *highly doctrinal*, nor *dryly practical;* but blended the doctrine and practice of the Gospel with the affections and feelings of the heart. As he advanced in life, having indoctrinated the churches planted by his ministry, he became more and more practical and experimental in the pulpit. The following thoughts on the importance of experimental and practical preaching, are from his own pen:

"The most successful preaching, is experimental and practical preaching. Men who preach experimentally, preach to the heart, and commend themselves to every man's conscience, in the sight of God. To tell what we have felt, will have, more influence on others, than to tell what we know. A simple narrative of a sinner's conversion, may be found in the unvarnished story of the man born blind. 'A man that is called Jesus, made clay, and anointed my eyes, and said to me, Go wash in the pool of Silome. I went, and washed, and I received sight.' Our most successful ministers, and useful church members, are those who tell what the Lord has done for them. Many preachers, who have but little doctrinal skill, have been most successful in bringing sinners to Christ. An infidel, who was warmly, and, as he thought, strongly opposing an humble christian, met with this resistance from the good man: 'If that is all you have to say'—placing his hand upon his heart—'I have felt more here than all you have said.' The reply proved the conversion of the infidel. May ministers all practice what they preach, preach what they feel, feel what they believe, and believe the truth."

Mr. Donnell did not regard the Gospel as a code of ethical precepts, or a system of abstract truths addressed merely to the intellect. He believed that religion appeals as really and earnestly to *all* that *feels* in man, as it does to all that *thinks.* He also insisted that true religion was pre-eminently a system of action, as well as doctrine and feeling: that it is one thing to *speculate* and *talk* as a christian, and another to *feel* and *live* as a christian.

It has already been stated, that Mr. Donnell was not a classical scholar; but let no young man, having the Gospel ministry in view, think lightly of a systematic education, because men, like Mr. Donnell, have become distinguished without it. Thus far, the Cumberland Presbyterian church has known but one Robert Donnell. By *self-directed* mental efforts, he arose to a degree of eminence in his profession, that few preachers reach, however great may have been their early opportunities for literary improvement. It is more than probable, that the best scholars of his day, on hearing him preach, felt as did Dr. Owen, when he heard Bunyan for the first time, namely, that he would freely exchange all his literary advantages for Bunyan's power in the pulpit to move an audience.

But let no young man despair of becoming useful in his Master's vineyard, because he cannot wear Mr. Donnell's mantle. Luther said: " Our common Father has need of all sorts of servants in His great family." All work done for God is honorable. " The highest angel has no prouder charge than that of the true disciples sent to unloose the colt for Jesus to ride on." Let every young preacher, however, aim high, and he will be more likely to hit an elevated mark, than if he were to aim at a low one. But let none decline to labor in God's vineyard, because they do not possess the abilities to work with which others have been blessed.

CHAPTER XXVI.

LAST SICKNESS AND DEATH OF MR. DONNELL.

Extraordinary Effort at Bethlehem Camp-meeting—His last Sermon, November, 1853 — " Valedictory to the World "—His Letter to the General Assembly at Lebanon—The Assembly's Reply—Interesting Incidents in his last Illness—Administration of the Lord's Supper at his Residence—His Prospects on the morning before his Death— Passes away in a Tranquil Slumber—Funeral Services—Erection of a Monument to his Memory.

THE last sickness of Mr. Donnell, was occasioned, it is believed, by an extraordinary effort he made in the pulpit, at a camp-meeting at Bethlehem, Madison county, Ala., on the fourth Sabbath of September, 1853. His text was I. John v: 7, 8—" For there are three that bear record in heaven, the Father, the Word, and the Holy Ghost; and these three are one; and there are three that bear witness in earth, the spirit, and the water, and the blood; and these three agree in one."

After reading the text, he said, that at the first camp-meeting held at that place, many years ago, he had, on Sabbath morning, preached from the same text; that at the close of that sermon, about fifty persons appeared before the pulpit, upon their knees, as seekers of religion; and he hoped that similar success would attend the effort then about to be made.

The prime object of the discourse, was to prove that,

in Christ Jesus, there is eternal life for every sinner that will accept of it. In sustaining this proposition, he adduced the testimony of the three that bear record in heaven: the Father, the Word, and Holy Ghost; and also from the three that bear witness in earth: the spirit, and the water, and the blood, which agree in one. He argued that, if there be life in Christ for one sinner, there must be for every sinner. For,

1st. If God loved any fallen sinner, the cause of such love existed in Himself; and that the same cause that induced him to love one sinner, would induce him to love every sinner, as all sustained the same relation to him in their fallen federal head.

2. He also showed that the design of Christ's death was to legalize the bestowment of life to every believing sinner.

3. That every sinner, under the influence of the Holy Ghost, has access to this life.

In the delivery of this sermon, Mr. Donnell's physical labor was very great. He preached in the open air, with a brisk wind blowing in his face all the time; besides, in consequence of a rain that had fallen the night before, the atmosphere was damp, and hard to penetrate so as to reach the large audience, without great exertion of voice. The friends saw the difficulties under which the speaker labored, and endeavored to protect him from the wind, by hanging bed-clothes around the pulpit—which, however, only afforded partial relief. He closed the discourse with an appeal which produced a happy effect upon the congregation; but he was so much exhausted, that it was deemed best for him to return home the next morning. On his way, he was exposed to a heavy shower of rain; which, in connection with his previous day's labor, he regarded as fixing the commencement of his last sickness. He informed the Rev. M. H. Bone—to whom I am indebted for the foregoing items—that he never felt well afterward.

That camp-meeting, I believe, was the last he ever attended; and, owing to the state of his health, he preached but seldom on ordinary occasions after that meeting. On the second Sabbath of the following October, he preached twice, feeble as he was, in Athens. The following was his text in the morning: "Yea, I think it meet, as long as I am in this tabernacle, to stir you up by putting you in remembrance; knowing that shortly I must put off this my tabernacle, even as our Lord Jesus Christ hath showed me; moreover, I will endeavor that ye may be able, after my decease, to have these things always in remembrance." (*II. Peter i: 13–15.*)

This sermon was called, by those who heard it, his funeral discourse. On the first Sabbath of the next November, he preached the dedication sermon of his own church, at Athens; and on the third Sabbath of the same month, he preached his last sermon. It was at McCombs Cross Roads, five miles south of Athens, and on the occasion of the funeral of three very aged christians; the text being, "These all died in faith."

The following thoughts are supposed to be the last he ever put on paper, without the aid of an amanuensis:

"VALEDICTORY TO THE WORLD.

" Being about to leave thee, my mother earth, I think it meet and becoming, as one of thy sons, not to depart without bidding thee farewell. You have opened your bosom to nourish and afford me many blessings during the last three-score and ten years. From you, I have learned many lessons, that I trust will be of service to me, in that far-off land, to which I am going. You have delighted my eyes with your beautiful scenery, and gratified my taste with your generous fruits. You once furnished a beautiful garden, in which were placed my eldest brother and sister; and in your bosom lie many of my dearest personal friends.

" I remember, with pleasure, the many blessings you have bestowed so bountifully upon your children; and also that, on your bosom, many tears of bitter anguish have fallen, and many sad changes have marred your beauty. You are now getting old, like myself, and must one day disappear.

" Soon you must furnish me a resting-place in one of your valleys. Your flowers will bloom around me, but I shall see them not. Your streams, as they pass, may offer a lullaby, but I shall hear them not. Your sun, moon, and stars, will all continue to shine upon your hills and valleys, but I shall heed them not.

" And now, my mother earth, before parting with you, I would ask that you be kind to my younger brethren, as you have been to me. They will also soon leave you, as I shall shortly do; but when the mighty trumpet shall sound, and the last fires are kindled to burn thee up, we shall all return, to witness thy last day. Till then, farewell!

"R. DONNELL."

During the long affliction of Mr. Donnell, religion, and the interests and prosperity of the church, were the absorbing topics of his conversation; and, with the aid of an amanuensis, he occasionally reduced thoughts to writing, that he supposed might be of use to his brethren. The following was addressed to the General Assembly, in session at Lebanon, Tennessee, but a short time before his death:

" ATHENS, ALA., May 8, 1855.

"To the Moderator of the General Assembly of the Cumberland Presbyterian church, to meet at Lebanon, Tenn., Tuesday, the 15th day of May, 1855:

"DEAR BROTHER:—Permit me to address you, perhaps for the last time, and through you, the body over which you preside. I feel like I have served my day and generation, and will likely soon fall asleep, and close my thoughts and efforts for the church, that has so long employed my mind.

"Although of no distinction in the world, I have, perhaps, been raised up to aid in the commencement and advancement of a conservative church, which seems to have taken root downward, and is bearing fruit upward. I lived before her separate organization, and was with her all through her subsequent trials, and am now about to leave her, as I hope, in a prosperous state. Her moral, literary and theological character, seems now to be established. I long had my fears that she would fail to carry out fully the designs of Heaven in raising her up; but now, when about to take my leave of her, my confidence is greatly strengthened. I am gratified to learn, that her ministers and members are determined to advance her interests; and that, at the present time, many promising young men are turning away from other callings, and consecrating themselves to the vocation of the holy ministry. Truly, the church is on the verge of an important crisis.

"The General Assembly will encourage, I hope, the compilation and publication of a full history of the origin, progress and doctrines of the Cumberland Presbyterian church.

"Our Confession of Faith, though not as perfect in phraseology as it might be, yet has system and perfection enough to make us all think alike. This unity is in accordance with the nature and tendencies of experimental religion; for our very system is founded upon experimental religion. And while we maintain true experimental religion, we will have a united church; but if we suffer her to cry 'peace, peace, when there is no peace,' and to 'daub with untempered mortar,' we may expect to have division in our ranks.

"I would write more, but am too much enfeebled. I can only say, in conclusion, dear brethren, 'I die, and

God will surely visit you,' and help you to carry out the great designs for which He has raised you up.

"By the grace of God, I feel like 'I have fought a good fight; I have finished my course ; I have kept the faith ; henceforth there is laid up for me a crown of righteousness, which the Lord, the righteous judge, shall give me at that day, and not to me only, but unto all them also that love his appearing.'

" ROBERT DONNELL."

This letter was referred to a committee, and their answer is here subjoined :

" LEBANON, TENN., May 19, 1855.

"EVER DEAR AND VENERABLE BROTHER :—The General Assembly of the Cumberland Presbyterian church, in session at Lebanon, Tennessee, having received your highly esteemed favor, and appointed the undersigned to report, we now enter on the interesting duty.

"Your letter was read and re-read, in a full house, and called forth from your brethren and sons in the Gospel, many expressions of tender regard and heart-felt sympathy. With sorrow, we had all heard of your affliction; and with mingled emotions of regret and solicitude, we had anticipated the loss of your valuable counsels on this important occasion. Many prayers have been offered, that, if consistent with the Divine will, your useful life might be prolonged, and your labors still enjoyed by the church you loved so well. But God, whose we are, and whom we serve, is just, as well as good. He has a right to call his favored and faithful ones, who are wearied and worn with incessant toils, to serve Him day and night in His temple above; and since our anticipated loss is your eternal gain—since faith assures us that a short separation here, will be succeeded by an eternal re-union hereafter—we bow in humble acquiescence.

"Language fails in the expression of our grateful acknowledgments, for this evidence of your kind regard, under existing circumstances. In pain and affliction, you have remembered us. In your sick room, your thoughts have been centered upon us. Your bodily sufferings could not restrain your prayers for Divine wisdom to guide us. And from a bed of languishment, when about to end life's toilsome journey, and enter on a heavenly home, you send us affectionate greetings, and afford us sympathy, counsel and encouragement. It is like you. It is consistent with your benevolent character—ever forgetful of yourself, but always mindful of your brethren and the church. It is in harmony with the general tenor of your whole life—first, to consider the glory of Christ; next, the best interests of his people; and lastly, your own ease and comfort. We hope never to be unmindful of this instance of your brotherly kindness, nor forgetful of those numerous evidences of your ardent anxiety for our usefulness and happiness, manifested on former occasions. The grace of God assisting us, we mean to be true to the interests of the church, for which you have lived, labored and

38—

prayed; for which, in times past, you, and others who have gone to their reward before you, have sacrificed and suffered; and in the growth, and prosperity, and usefulness of which, we are all permitted this day to rejoice.

" Many bright spirits, now rejoicing before the throne of God, have passed lives of labor in promoting that purity of doctrine and experimental religion, of which you speak. While you expect soon to go to join their exalted ranks, and share their glorious reward, we are, entered into their labors. And when the mournful period shall arrive, when death shall part us asunder, and you go up to Heaven, may we, ready to take up the falling mantle, cry in the spirit of Elisha, ' My father, my father, the chariots of Israel, and horsemen thereof !'

" With christian affection, we have the honor to subscribe ourselves, your brethren and sons in the Gospel of Christ,

" F. R. Cossitt,
" R. Burrow,
" D. Lowry."

This, no doubt, was the last communication Mr. Donnell ever dictated, to be reduced to writing; as he died on the 24th of the same month in which the letter is dated.

But before we enter the chamber of death, to witness the last moments of this extraordinary man upon earth, it may be edifying and encouraging, particularly to the christian reader, to be made acquainted with some facts which transpired at different times during the earlier part of his protracted illness, evincing the power of the christian religion. The following incident is from the pen of Rev. John H. Erwin:

"The last Presbytery Mr. Donnell ever attended, was held at Athens, Alabama, embracing the first Sabbath in October, 1853. He sat in the pulpit during the delivery of the opening sermon, by the Rev. F. Johnson, D.D. He was unable to be present again during the meeting. At his request, the Lord's Supper was administered, on Sabbath night, at his residence. Several ministers, and a few lay members, joined him in celebrating the ordinance—among whom were the family of brother B. Deckerd, then on their way to Texas. While singing the closing hymn, every one present went to Mr. Donnell, and gave him their hand. As they approached him, he embraced them in his arms, and after the patriarchical manner, invoked a blessing in their behalf. The words of each petition were in an undertone, so that I heard none except the one offered for myself. When I threw my arms around his neck, he said, 'Lord, make this dear son a Timothy.' Sister Deckerd became so happy that she praised God aloud; and all felt that it was better to go to the house of mourning, than to the house of feasting."

The Rev. N. A. Davis, of Texas, says:

"My last interview with Mr. Donnell, I never can forget. It was during his last illness. When I bid him farewell, he pressed me to his bosom, saying, 'Lord, as I am no longer able to carry the standard of the cross, may many sons of the church be raised up to do it when I am gone.' "

The Rev. George N. Mitchell, the writer of Mr. Donnell's obituary, says, some months previous to his death, he had a " severe hemorrhage, and was for some minutes in a state of suspended animation." When he recovered, he said: "I was perfectly conscious of all that was going on. I could see my lifeless body lying there, while my soul seemed like a bird let loose from its cage, instead of at once flying away, was circling round and round its former nest, and I thought if this be death, O, how pleasant it is to die !"

On the morning before his death, he was asked by a brother, what were his prospects now, when so near the end of his course ? To which he replied : " That business has long since been settled with me. It is too late now to call it in question. I can now say whether I live, I live unto the Lord ; and whether I die, I die unto the Lord. Whether I live, therefore, or die, I am the Lord's."

The day before his death, he sank into a profound, sweet sleep, from which he awoke only when aroused by some one. In the latter part of the night, his wife awoke him, and offered him some medicine, to whom he replied, in a soft, beseeching tone : " Please don't make me take it ; don't trouble me now, for I never felt better in my life;" and immediately fell asleep, and spoke no more, neither awoke again, until he awoke to the glorious realities of heaven.

The following is an account of the funeral services observed in reference to the death of Mr. Donnell; and it shows the high estimation in which he was held, not only by his own church, but other churches, and likewise by the community at large. It was written by the Rev. J. R. Finley, of the Presbyterian church, and published in the *"Banner of Peace,"* from which it is now copied:

"FUNERAL SERVICES OF REV. R. DONNELL.

"*Mr. Editor :*—Having been privileged to be present, when the funeral sermon of Rev. Robert Donnell, late of this place, was preached in the Cumberland Presbyterian church, and presuming that a brief notice of the interesting services on that occasion, will not be unacceptable to your readers, while it may be gratifying to his numerous friends, who were not in attendance, I take the liberty, at the suggestion of one of our most worthy citizens, of forwarding to you such a notice for publication in your columns.

" The morning was one of those whose calm loveliness affords a beautiful type of that eternal Sabbath, upon whose services and ecstatic joys, in the upper sanctuary, our beloved Father Donnell had already entered;—a fitting day for a tribute of respect to the memory of that great and good man. On arriving at the church— a neat edifice, located in a convenient part of the town —I found already congregated a very large audience, made up of persons of all the religious denominations in Athens; every other house of worship being closed,

out of respect to one whom all revered, and delighted
to honor. The pulpit, with the Holy Volume resting
upon it, the front of the gallery, and various other portions of the house, were tastefully draped in mourning;
the tribute, as I am informed, of friends, who thus ap-
propriately expressed their respect for the dead, and
their sympathy with the bereaved. In the pulpit were
seated the venerable Dr. Lindley, for so many years
the distinguished President of Ohio University; the
Rev. William Sellars, the worthy pastor of the Baptist
church in Athens; Rev. J. W. Allen, so long known as
an eminent minister of the Methodist Episcopal church,
South; and Rev. J. G. Wilson, of Limestone county,
who enjoys so well-earned a reputation, both as a christian minister, and instructor of youth; while in the
seats, from front to rear, and in chairs, which filled up
the entire space around the altar, as well as standing at
the door, unable to procure seats within, was assembled
a crowd of hearers—not a few of whom were from the
country — whose sad countenances indicated that a
great grief had fallen upon the community, and upon
the church at large.

" At the appointed hour, the services were commenced
by singing that beautiful hymn of Muhlenberg's—

" 'I would not live alway: I ask not to stay,
When storm after storm rises dark o'er the way ;
The few lurid mornings that dawn on us here,
Are enough for life's woes, full enough for its cheer.' ,

" The excellent pastor of the church then read, as the

Scripture lesson for the day, the 2d chapter of I. Thessalonians; and as its appropriate and beautiful language fell upon my ear, it seemed to me as the utterance of the sainted dead, speaking back to the living from the spirit land, in intonations of encouragement to the followers of Jesus, whom he had left on earth to complete their pilgrimage; and as the exultation of a father in Israel, who had gone up from the watch-towers of Zion, to his reward in the skies, there to be greeted by the hundreds and thousands in whose salvation he had been instrumental;—while looking upon these, his rapt soul exclaimed, in the language of the Apostle, ' Ye are our glory and our joy!'

" This was followed by a fervent address to the throne of grace, by the pastor; whose heart seemed to teem with ' emotions too big for utterance,' as he devoutly acknowledged the Divine sovereignty in the affairs of earth, and poured out earnest petitions for Divine grace to sanctify this afflictive dispensation to the public good, and that of the church; and to sustain and comfort the weeping relatives and friends. The services were continued by singing—

> " 'How blest the righteous when he dies,
>   When sinks a weary soul to rest;
>   How mildly beam the closing eyes,
>   How gently heaves the expiring breast!'

"Then followed the sermon, from Romans xiv: 8— the text being suggested, as we were informed in the opening of the discourse, by a conversation which

Father Donnell had, a little while before he closed his
eyes in death, with a brother beloved of his church;
and in which he gave, as the last expression of his feelings, in view of his approaching dissolution—a response
to a question asked of him, in the words of the Apostle,
slightly altered from their common reading, but fully
expressive of his readiness to die: 'For whether we
live, we live unto the Lord; and whether we die, we
die unto the Lord: whether we live, therefore, or die,
we are the Lord's.'

"The sermon was appropriate, full of deep religious
feeling and sentiment, pathetic and eloquent, and every
way worthy of the reputation of Rev. G. W. Mitchell,
the pastor, who delivered it, and of the occasion on
which it was preached. It would afford me pleasure to
give you a sketch of the discourse, for the satisfaction
of your readers; but as it is hoped it will be published,
and as I have already, perhaps, occupied too large a
space in your columns, I forbear.

"The writer, by courteous invitation, then gave out
Charles Wesley's hymn—

> "'And let this feeble body fail,
> And let it faint or die;
> My soul shall quit this mournful vale,
> And soar to worlds on high.'

And offered the concluding prayer; when, the doxology
having been sung, and benediction pronounced by Rev.
Dr. Lindley, the large congregation retired to their respective homes—many no doubt feeling that, though

sad the occasion which had called them together, the place where they had assembled was ' none other but the house of God, and the gate of heaven.' Long may the savor of that morning rest upon the people; and may the gracious truths to which they listened abundantly, console the bereaved widow and the afflicted son, whom the sainted dead has left on earth to mourn his departure.

"My object in this notice, has not been to eulogize the departed—he needs no such empty tribute from my pen—but to show how generally and how highly he was esteemed in that community, in whose midst his sun has set with such mellow radiance—there and elsewhere throughout the wide scope of territory in which he traveled, and preached, and labored for the salvation of souls, and the glory of God."

But Mr. Donnell's Presbytery determined to erect a more lasting monument over his remains, than mere funeral solemnities. The following is an account of its action on that subject, which was also written by a Presbyterian clergyman, and published in the "*Banner*" shortly after the service was performed:

" ERECTION OF THE MONUMENT TO THE MEMORY OF REV. ROBERT DONNELL.

" ATHENS, ALA., November 9, 1858.

" BRO. WARD :—It was my privilege, yesterday, to attend the imposing ceremonies of erecting a monument to Rev. Robert Donnell, at this place. The Presbytery

39 —

of which he was a member, has seen proper thus to honor and perpetuate the memory of one who was not only dear to them, but to thousands of others who knew him, and to the whole church of which he is one of the fathers.

"A large procession, composed of the citizens, members of the Presbytery, and relatives, formed at the Cumberland Presbyterian church, marched out to the cemetery, where we found the monument partly erected, waiting for the closing exercises.

"The monument consisted of a square base, some five feet square. Three pedements, of less dimensions than the base, forming steps on which was a square hollow shaft, six feet high, and about two feet in diameter. In this was deposited books, manuscripts, pamphlets, and tokens of affection, by different members of the Presbytery, and friends of the deceased—making a monument in the monument, crowned with a boquet of flowers, as a token of affection by a lady. As these articles will be described by some member of the Presbytery, I will not anticipate.

"After these deposits, with appropriate and touching remarks by the donors, the cap was put on. Rising, upon this ornamental cap, was a shaft, conical, but square, some ten feet, making a column of near fifteen or eighteen feet high; the whole cut from a marble limestone, and forming as substantial a memento to departed worth, as it is honorable to the heads and hearts of those who erected it.

"All this was followed by an address from Dr. Baird, of Winchester, appropriate and touching, full of pathos and heartfelt eloquence. Rev. M. H. Bone, Rev. W. D. Chadick, and others, spoke as those only could, who had seen as they had seen, felt and loved as they had the brother departed.

"The scene was one full of instruction. The parting hymn and closing prayer, touched and melted the hearts of the audience. What a stimulant to imitate his virtues, and follow his example! His praise is in all the churches; and I will only add, I was glad to be there to do him reverence, and honor his memory as a Vice President of the American Tract Society—the oldest, at the time of his death, in our country. He was also a warm personal friend. His words have cheered me, and his co-operation has greatly advanced the interest of the Tract cause, as it did every good object, while he remained among us. To have such a fragrant memory, we must live his useful, self-denying, and holy life.   Yours,

"SHEPARD WELLS."

The secular press was also lavish in giving expression to the public appreciation of Mr. Donnell's character, both as a citizen and minister of the Gospel. After noticing the constitution of the Presbytery, &c., the editor of the *"Athens Herald"* says:

"The Presbytery proceeded, on Monday, the 8th, to the business for which it had expressly met, viz: the erection of the monument to the memory of Rev. R.

Donnell, one of the fathers of the Cumberland Presbyterian church, whose remains have recently been removed to the cemetery of this place.

"A large concourse of citizens, and friends of the deceased, from a distance, formed a procession, in front of the Cumberland Presbyterian church, followed by the family and relatives of the deceased, and in the rear came the Presbytery, and visiting ministers; in which order they proceeded to the cemetery, under the direction of General James Lane, marshal. When the procession entered the grave-yard, the citizens opened its files, the Presbytery marched to the front, followed by the family and relatives, and thus surrounded the monument.

"Rev. G. W. Mitchell, the Moderator, stepped forward and deposited a book and some written memoranda in the vault of the monument; and then in turn, as their names were called, the members of the Presbytery came forward and did likewise, each having borne something in the procession for that purpose. The deposits consisted of a large copy of the Holy Bible, books published by the church, newspapers, likenesses of the deceased, &c. After this was done, Miss Eliza Brickell handed to the Moderator a beautiful boquet of sweet flowers, which he held to the audience, remarking, 'It speaks to the eye and the heart,' when there was an involuntary burst of tears from nearly or quite every eye in the large assembly. So soon as the vault was closed, the crowd repaired again to the church, where they were enraptured, moved and melted under the address delivered by Rev. A. J. Baird, followed by short, touching, and impressive remarks, by Rev. Messrs. Bone, Chadick, and Dr. J. S. Blair.

"The Moderator gave out and sung, the congregation all joining, that beautiful and appropriate hymn of Montgomery's. After which, an appropriate prayer was offered by Rev. Mr. Chadick. The congregation was dismissed with a doxology and benediction by the pastor. We are not prepared to give even a sketch of the remarks made by the eloquent speakers on the occasion. But, in conclusion, we would say, never was a man more worthy such testimonial of high regard; and the tribute bestowed, reflects credit on the Presbytery, and all who participated in the bestowment."

Thus closed the services of erecting a monument over the remains of our beloved Donnell. Long will that consecrated spot be remembered and visited. Many eyes will yet weep and tears fall around that monument, while the image of that great and good man, when in the pulpit, is recalled. But his appearance in the sacred desk, accents of his voice, &c., will not only be remembered, but his great moral excellence will be often thought of; and lessons imparted by his pious example, will rise up before the mind, to strengthen its purpose to walk in the footsteps of him whose "hoary head wears a crown of glory, because it was found in the way of righteousness."

But he is gone, to join that great cloud of witnesses, who are above us and around us. He has seen Jesus Christ, whom not having seen, he loved. He has seen the multitude, which no man can number, out of every nation, and kindred, and tongue, and people. · He has been welcomed to glory by his cotemporaries in the ministry, who reached Heaven before him, and hailed by thousands, who recognized him as the instrument of their salvation.

With him, all is now *rest*, and *peace*, and *reward*.

A Brief Sketch of the Life of the Late

HUGH BONE, ESQ.

HUGH BONE.

HUGH BONE was born in the State of Pennsylvania, on the 19th of October, 1764, and was the second son of Thomas Bone. His parentage, on both sides, was of Scotch-Irish Presbyterian descent, and united in his great grandfather, John McWilliams, of Scotland, who was remarkable in his day and country, for his intelligence and piety. He emigrated to America in quite an early day, and settled in Pennsylvania Colony.

Hugh Bone was removed, while yet a boy, by his parents, to North Carolina, county of Iredell; and there raised and trained to manhood, under the ministry of James Hall, D.D., of the Presbyterian church. His opportunities for early religious education, were not surpassed, perhaps, by any of his age and country. His parents were eminently pious and intelligent, and well qualified to afford such instruction, both by precept and example, to the juvenile mind, as to fix those deep and lasting impressions in favor of the religion of Christ, that will, by Divine influence, lead to an experimental knowledge of the truth, give cast and character to a life of piety, and make it conformable, under all circumstances, to the precepts of the Bible; and more espe-

40—

cially when assisted by the constant, vigilant, and pious pastoral labors of such an enlightened and devoted man as was Dr. Hall.

It was the lot of Hugh Bone, to grow up during the time of the Revolutionary struggles of the country, which were so well calculated to imbue the youthful mind with the spirit of patriotism, and with that indomitable energy and perseverance in a cause, believed to be right, which knows of no discouragements or failure. But such was the disorganized state of society in the struggling Colonies, that the cause of education was mainly suspended, especially in its more systematic and advantageous form. From these facts, and also that his father and elder brother were, for much of the time, called into the service of their country, leaving the care and support of the family at home upon him, he was deprived of the advantages of a liberal education, which he always most deeply regretted. This, however, he endeavored to supply, as far as practicable, by application to such books as were approved and within his reach. Being possessed of more than ordinary strength and powers of natural intellect, with most acute observation of men and things, he succeeded in the liberal development of his mind, and in furnishing it with a rich and varied store of most useful knowledge. He lived in a practical age; and his mind was trained to the investigation of truth more from motives of practical utility than mere show. He was peculiar in his method of thought. When he took up any subject for investigation, it constituted the theme of thought and study with him day and night, until he became satisfied that he had mastered it. Then he laid it up for practical use, as occasion might require, and never forgot it.

When quite a youth, he passed the session of Concord congregation, in which he was raised, upon an examination of his knowledge of experimental religion; and in a short time afterward, by a unanimous vote of the congregation, and ordination by the pastor, he was added to the same corps of eldership. But it was not until he had removed to the West, and was surrounded with the light, life, and power of religion, as it was taught and enjoyed in the revival of 1800, that he became fully satisfied in his own mind as to his personal acceptance with God in Christ Jesus. Though from the time of his admission to the communion of the church, he had been most exemplary in his religious morality, and exercised his talents in a public way, by exhortation and expounding the Word of God, and in the official and energetic exercise of the office of ruling elder.

In the 27th year of his age, he was united in marriage to Mary Hill; who was, while she lived, a true help-mate to him, in all the vicissitudes of life. He knew how to appreciate the worth of an intelligent and confiding woman, who had given him, in this holy relation, her hand, and heart, and life. While their family was small, he removed to Madison county, Kentucky, where he served, as ruling elder, for seven or eight years, under the pastoral charge of Rev. Matthew Housten—whom he ardently loved, and whose brilliant talents he admired, but in whom he was wofully disappointed on his joining the *Shaking Quakers.* Shortly after Mr. Bone had removed to Tennessee, Housten visited him—in company with his compeers, Dunlavy, Ranken and Young—with the most sanguine expectation of making him a proselyte to the new light of mother Ann. Father Bone met him in "stern and awful combat." Calmly, courteously, but firmly, and with the tried sword of the Spirit, which had long been his study, and with which but few were more familiar, he soon vanquished and put to flight his quadruple foe. They had each alternately fired their artillery of sophistry at his rampart of truth, but without success. They retreated, "shaking" indeed, but not so much to "subdue the flesh," as from the effects of mortified pride and ambition of spirit. They never came back. He often said, that that victory, over such odds of numbers, learning and tact, in polemics with all the subtlety and cunning mischief of Satan himself, gave him more confidence in the power of *truth,* than anything he had ever before experienced.

He witnessed something of the great revival of 1800, before he removed from Kentucky, to Wilson county, Tennessee ; but it was among those who soon afterward abused it, by running into the fanaticism of *Arians* and *Shakers.* At that time, his mind was not satisfied that the revival was of God. In the fall of 1802, he removed to Smith's Fork, Wilson county, Tenn., where he found the revival spirit pervading the entire population of the county. He carefully examined it; weighed it in the scale of a sound and unbiased judgment; watched and marked all its fruits and effects, and judged of them in the light of the Word of God. Then, in much prayer and fasting, came to the conclusion that it was of God's own spirit and power, and he fell in with the tide of holy and divine influence, then sweeping like a flood all over the land. His own soul became filled with light and love, never before to him revealed. The revival spirit, now heartily received, joined to his tenacity correct discipline, and good order in all things, especially in things appertaining to the church, together with his knowledge of theology, and love of sound doctrine, rendered him an efficient member, both in respect to christian example, counsel, and public teaching and exhortation.

He was often in the councils of the revival party of Cumberland Presbytery, while they were under orders of silence by the Commission of Kentucky Synod; and was regarded as a conservative and safe counselor— though firm against all ecclesiastical aggressions and unconstitutional oppressions, with which that evangelical party was in those days afflicted, in their efforts to promote spiritual piety. He acted a full share in those measures, which led to the new and independent organization of Cumberland Presbytery, out of which grew the Cumberland Presbyterian church. And, therefore, the name of Hugh Bone is eminently entitled to be enrolled among the names of those who are to be remembered and honored as the fathers of the church.

He, with the entire congregation of Smith's Fork, received and adopted the revised Confession of Faith and constitution of the church, as soon as it was published. This was done in the house of Mrs. Bumpass, which house still stands in the village of Statesville, Tennessee, and is held by the members of that congregation as in some sort sacred to the memory of that event.

There is still a large and flourishing congregation at that place. Rev. Mr. Ivy has been, and is yet, its devoted and beloved pastor. For many years, this congregation regarded Mr. Bone as its shepherd; and though they had stated preaching by Calhoun, King, McSpedden, and Dillard, yet the burden of the care of the church devolved on him. Every Sabbath day, when they had no other preaching, he would meet them, and explain and enforce the Gospel of Christ unto them. Crowds attended his appointments, pleased and delighted to hear him; while many, very many, were led by him to the cross of Christ.

Rev. F. R. Cossitt, D.D., who was an intimate acquaintance of Mr. Bone, said of him, in the "*Banner of Peace*," soon after his death: "Father Bone was a remarkable man, indeed; and no mere newspaper article can ever do him justice. With a native intellect of the first order, an energy of character equaled by few, a zeal which knew of no abatement, and a benevolence as unbounded as disinterested he stood in the church of God as a tower of strength ; and his whole life was an epistle of Christ, 'written not with ink, but with the spirit of the living God.' Many can testify to the excellency of his example—many have experienced to advantage of his counsel—and many will cherish his memory with fondest recollections. He had made his mind a store-house of scriptural knowledge, his heart a reservoir of christian experience, and like pure streams from a perennial fountain, truth flowed from his lips in rich aphorisms."

The character of God, his laws, Christ as the God-man mediator, and the wisdom, grandeur, and adaptedness of the plan of salvation, were his favorite topics of theology. His thoughts on those, and other subjects, were clear, strong almost to overwhelming. His manner of expressing his thoughts was peculiar, and without any ornament of language, except the sublime adorning of truth, told without any trappings of human embellishment.

As an illustration of what is above said, as to his manner of expressing his big thoughts in divinity, he was once exhorting, in the presence of the members of the General Assembly of the Cumberland Presbyterian church; the divinity of Christ was the subject of the discourse, and speaking of his death, he said : " 'Twas not the Jews that killed him ; all the Jews in Palestine couldn't do that. It wasn't the Romans, neither, that killed Jesus; all the Romans of the seven-hill'd city couldn't kill him. Nor," said he, " all the devils in hell couldn't kill him." Then, with a calm tone, he added: " Some one may think, perhaps, 'Old man, are you going to say that *God* could not kill Jesus?' Well," he responded, " that might seem to be rather strong terms. But this I will say, that GOD HAS AS MUCH POWER TO LIVE AS TO KILL."

The Bible was his great text-book, the Holy Scriptures he made his principal commentary on Holy Writ, comparing Scripture with Scripture. His observations upon the administrations of Divine Providence, were most acute, and afforded to him a delightful and constant field of contemplation. He *saw* God in all His works of creation and providence, as well as in His revealed word.

His family government was taken from the Bible; and was administered with tender affection, but with most *absolute positiveness* and precision, making the holy prophets his exemplars. His confidence was firmly established in the stipulations of God's covenant with *believers* and their *children*. And as God promised to be the God of Abraham, so did the promise embrace, in covenant relation, Abraham's *seed* with him. But he believed that covenant blessings, bequeathed by promise to the children of believing parents, would only be realized in proper moral training in the family nursery, according to the declaration of the wise man, viz: "*Train* up a child in the way he should go, and when he is old

he will not depart from it." Then the covenant promise
is *sure.* Thus he taught, and upon these principles he
proceeded most strictly in the government of his own
family. And during the minority of his children,
rigidly enforced upon them the constant practice of
moral precepts. As an example, in this respect, it was
his custom, and that of his very estimable wife, to call
their smaller children, each night, before retiring, for
prayer, which they superintended, at their knees. This
was especially attended to on each Sabbath night. His
son, Matthew Housten, was about four years old when
called up to say his prayer before his father. At the
close of the exercise, the father said to him: "Housten,
you are old enough to pray by yourself." The boy was
old enough to think himself too young. The following
morning, before breakfast, the father said to him, "Well,
my son, have you prayed this morning?" "No, sir,"
was the reply of the boy. "Well," said the father, "go
away by yourself, somewhere, and get on your knees,
and pray to the Lord." "I am too little," was the boy's
reply. "*Go this minute,* and do as I tell you, or I will
whip you," was the positive command. The boy knew
then, that compliance must be had, in some sort. He
retired in the back yard, got behind the smoke-house,
leaned for a moment against the wall, and thus solilo-
quized: "Well, pa has sent me here to pray. *I don't
want to do it ;* but if I go back, without trying, and tell
him so, I know he will whip me, for he always does as
he says he will do. If I say I tried, when I did not, it

41 —

will be a lie, and then God will be angry with me, and that will be worse." So he came to the conclusion that there was no other way, then, between God and his father, but to try to pray. He crept down on his knees, and as best he could, tried to pray; arose, and with a light heart, bounded away to his father, and threw his little arms about his neck. "Have you prayed?" said the father. "Yes, sir," said the happy boy. "Then," said the father, "*see that you do that every day while you live.*" The boy felt the force of the injunction, and right then resolved to comply. He in some sort carried out the injunction, until, in his seventeenth year, God converted his soul; and he has still tried to pray, every day, up to the present time.

This narrative will serve as an example of the manner in which Hugh Bone trained his family. The result was, that, in early years, each of his seven children embraced, by faith, the promises of a covenant-keeping God. Two of his sons, viz: Thomas, now in the vicinity of Memphis, Tenn., and Matthew Housten, of Winchester, Tenn., are both devoted ministers of the Gospel, and have been for the last thirty years. The other three sons were ruling elders in the church, and regarded standards of piety. James lives in Arkansas; Andrew, the eldest, died in Kentucky, 1858; and Abner, the youngest son, died at the same place the year before —both greatly lamented by the church. His daughter, Elizabeth, died in the triumphs of faith, in Kentucky, 1824. Jane still survives, a devoted christian, living with her brother. The grand-children are mostly pious members of the church.

In the spring of 1819, Hugh Bone removed, and settled in Hopkins county, Kentucky, which was then quite a newly settled country, and almost entirely destitute of the means of grace. Soon he assembled, on each Sabbath, his neighbors, at some private house, to whom he would read and explain the Bible, and exhort them to reform, and seek the salvation of their souls. They attended, with growing interest. Soon he procured preaching from the church, which he had assisted, in some good degree, to organize; a congregation was formed of Cumberland Presbyterians; a camp-meeting was held; multitudes from the adjoining settlements and counties attended; God poured out abundantly of His spirit; many were converted, and carried home the holy influence; others were induced to seek, and hundreds found the same blessing.

Churches were organized out of these converts, all over the Green river country, which have done much for the general cause of God, and for the Cumberland Presbyterian church in that section of the country; while others have removed to other countries, and become the nucleus of other congregations. Many useful and effective preachers were the fruits of that first revival at Rose creek, Hopkins county, where Hugh Bone lived and prayed, and labored publicly and privately, for twenty-seven years, and where he closed his earthly career, in peace with God and all mankind.

In 1826, he followed the remains of his beloved wife, Mary, to their resting place. No man was ever more devoted to the wife of his bosom, than was he to his; yet he meekly bowed to the Providence which deprived him of her society for the remainder of his days; often saying, in the language of Job, "The Lord gave, and the Lord hath taken away," &c.

It was his custom, from the first night that he lodged under his own roof, to hold worship in his family twice every day, unless absent or prevented by sickness; and then, his true helpmate filled his place at the family altar, and kept the holy fire still burning. Every man who lodged with him, was first invited to officiate in family prayers, and "say grace" at the table, if he ate in his house. He never was in the company of any man, even a stranger, one half hour, without introducing the subject of religion. Everything about him rested on the Sabbath day, which was with him, and all his, a holy day unto the Lord. No conversation of a worldly character was permitted on this day, in his house, or in his presence.

His influence was felt among his family relations. Besides his two sons, he has had eight nephews in the ministry of the Cumberland Presbyterian church—two of whom have gone to their reward. It is a matter of history, that Hugh Bone's great grand-father, John McWilliams, was a man of extraordinary prayer; that he never prayed without praying for his posterity, unto the last generation; and that neither of them have ever died without leaving evidences of having made peace with God. Generally, they professed faith in Christ before they reached the age of twenty-one years.

Hugh Bone was uncommonly interesting and instructive in social conversation. In this he was indeed impressive. Many persons have traced their first religious impressions to conversations had with him. He was affable and courteous in his manners; dignified in all his bearings; and of noble and commanding appearance. He was beloved by all who knew him; and if he ever had an enemy, at any time, he was not able long to remain such, before he was converted into a most devoted and enduring friend.

He departed this life, June 6th, 1846, full of years— being in his 82d; but retained, in a remarkable degree, the vigor of his powerful natural intellect, to the last moment of his existence. He died full of the hope of a glorious immortality.

His sun went down without a cloud.

ERRATA.

Page 17, in tenth line from top, read *division* instead of decision.

Page 28, in fourteenth line, *Burnett* instead of Barrett. In second line, page 29, same correction.

Page 95, in second line from bottom, *Arminian* instead of Armenian. This word occurring elsewhere in the book, same correction.

Page 121, in line above signature, *your* instead of you.

Page 194, in third line, *unconditional* instead of unconditioned.

Page 232, in eighth line, *concurrence* instead of convenience.

www.ingramcontent.com/pod-product-compliance
Lightning Source LLC
Chambersburg PA
CBHW060515030726
47498CB00004B/960